THE LETTER OF THE LAW . . .

I expressed my thanks for the lunch on the way to the front door. Where we met an unusual sight. Sunni Smargon, chief of our five-person police force, in her muted blue-gray uniform, stood leaning against her patrol car, its blue and red lights winking in the cool air. Sunni's arms were folded across her chest, a serious expression on her face. Before we reached the bottom step, Ross Little, one of Sunni's officers, exited the car, and he and Sunni came forward, in step, each with a hand resting on a holster. I could have sworn I heard dramatic music from an old Western in the background.

"Scott James." Sunni, a small woman with red highlights in hair that was barely contained under her hat, announced his name with an air of authority and a touch of threat. "We need you to come to the station and answer some questions."

"What's this about?" Scott asked. His voice was soft and shaky, with no conviction, as if he knew the answer . . .

JEAN
FLOWERS

DEATH TAKES
PRIORITY

BERKLEY PRIME CRIME, NEW YORK

BERKLEY
PRIME
CRIME

An imprint of Penguin Random House LLC
375 Hudson Street, New York, New York 10014

DEATH TAKES PRIORITY

A Berkley Prime Crime Book / published by arrangement with the author

ISBN: 978-0-425-27910-6

PUBLISHING HISTORY
Berkley Prime Crime mass-market edition / November 2015

PRINTED IN THE UNITED STATES OF AMERICA

10 9 8 7 6 5 4 3 2 1

Cover illustration by Teresa Fasolino.
Cover design by George Long.
Interior text design by Kelly Lipovich.
Interior map by Richard P. Rufer.

Penguin
Random
House

ACKNOWLEDGMENTS

Thanks as always to my critique partners: Nannette Rundle Carroll, Margaret Hamilton, Jonnie Jacobs, Rita Lakin, Margaret Lucke, and Sue Stephenson. They are ideally knowledgeable, thorough, and supportive.

Special thanks to Linda Plyler, retired postmaster with a thirty-year career in the postal service, for her generous assistance. I received the full benefit of her professional experience as a training and development specialist in a large city and a postmaster in a one-woman office in a small town. Linda is also an award-winning quilter, whose "zip code quilt" received national recognition and media coverage.

Thanks also to the extraordinary inspector Chris Lux for continued advice on police procedure, and to the many other writers and friends who offered critique, information, brainstorming, and inspiration; in particular: Gail and David Abbate, Sara Bly, James Boudinot, Mary Donovan, Karin Hart, Mary McConnell, Don Nimura, Diana Orgain, Ann

Parker, Jean Stokowski, Karen and Mark Streich, Daniel Uemura, and Ellyn Wheeler.

My deepest gratitude goes to my husband, Dick Rufer. I can't imagine working without his support. He's my dedicated Webmaster (minichino.com), layout specialist, and on-call IT department.

Thanks to the copyeditor, the artists, Bethany Blair, and the whole staff at Berkley Prime Crime for all their work on my behalf.

If it seems like a whole village wrote this book, it's because it's true.

Finally, my gratitude to my primary care editor, Michelle Vega, who put it all together. Michelle is a bright light in my life, personally supportive as well as superb at seeing the whole picture without missing the tiniest detail. Thanks, Michelle!

NORTH ASHCOT POST OFFICE

MAIN STREET

DELIVERY ROOM

COMMUNITY ROOM

Window

Window

Door

Door

Door

RETAIL SUPPLY SHELVES

Door

RETAIL COUNTER

Window

POSTMASTER'S DESK

Door

Window

UTILITY & STORAGE

Door

MAIL SORTING AREA

Door

Window

REST ROOM

Door

Side Door

P. O. Boxes

LOBBY

Window

Front Doors

TABLE

Forms

FLAG POLE

1

On most days, I love my job. Who else gets to start the day by raising the American flag outside her office? Military personnel, I suppose, and maybe law enforcement officers. But they have to suit up with a belt full of tools and weapons, while I just shrug into a comfortable blue shirt and a striped scarf with its special, ready-made, sewn-in knot that sits low and soft on my neck. Not exactly clubbing clothes, but then there aren't any clubs in North Ashcot, Massachusetts, and, anyway, it's Monday and I'm here to work.

"Postmaster Cassie Miller reporting for duty," I mumbled this morning, resisting the temptation to salute the flag. Instead I smiled and waved at a group of seniors trotting along the sidewalk as fast as they could, their version of jogging. Thanks to their easy pace, they didn't have to slow down to exchange cheery "good morning" greetings with me.

I was grateful for their attention. Each day, it seemed, I got a slightly friendlier vibe than the day before. The town's warming up to me, I thought, a glass-half-full moment.

Today I got a tip of the headband and a "Looking good, Miss Miller" from "Call-me-Moses" Crawford, said to be the town's oldest citizen and a "Hey, sweetie" from Harvey Stone, probably the second oldest. Only one frown, from Harvey's wife, in bright pink sweats and matching sneakers. I figured I was slightly ahead of the game.

I crossed the lawn, kicking a few late fall leaves from the path, and reentered my beautiful building through the side door. The old, one-story, redbrick Colonial Revival, trimmed in newly refreshed white and gold paint, looked good for its age. Over one hundred years old. The building was a popular backdrop for tourists' photos, which delighted me, as long as I was not included in the picture.

The mid-November air was crisp and dry, which didn't rule out a rainstorm, or even an early snow, later today. We were past the peak of foliage and thus also past the height of the tourist season in western Massachusetts, but I believed what the locals claimed about New England weather— expect anything, anytime. Or, as my dad used to say: "If you don't like it, wait a minute; it'll change."

I used to be a local, until I graduated from high school and left for college and a career in the postal service. Here I was trying to reclaim my native status, if that was possible. I'd been back in my hometown of North Ashcot only a little more than three months. Many pluses and minuses so far, but I never regretted coming back to help my aunt Tess through her last days. Time would tell whether there was enough to keep me here now that she was gone.

For now, I removed my outer layers of clothing and focused on sorting last night's mail delivery and setting up for retail hours, which would begin in forty-five minutes. Pretty soon the early birds would arrive. The waiting time in the lobby, before I unlocked the glass doors, was as much a coffee klatch as part of an errand run or a business chore for townspeople. Customers stood with their morning drinks and shared their latest news, covering topics from birthday parties to arthritic joints; from home remodels to money struggles; to the state of downtown shopping. No one objected when I began a new custom—donuts from Hole in the Wall, our local bakery, every Friday, courtesy of me, as long as they lasted. Nothing wrong with a little pandering.

I walked past the business side of the post office boxes, the open slots where I'd stuff each customer's mail; past the worktables and chairs, the nested piles of white plastic tubs, and the various generations of machines, some depending on electricity, others manual contraptions from long ago, but operational in a power outage.

As I reached my desk, behind the retail counter, I had the sense that something was off—the corner by the delivery room, where the truckers dropped the mail, looked cleaner than usual. Strange. Had a housekeeping fairy stopped by with a mop and broom? I chalked the feeling up to my Monday morning re-entry sluggishness. Not that my weekends were that exciting. I assured myself they'd pick up as I made new friends. Another moment of positive thinking.

I prepared the cash drawer and straightened a framed thank-you note from Mrs. Baldwin and her second-grade class, who'd come for a tour of my building last week. It had been a struggle to get my mentor, outgoing-PM Ben Gentry, to agree to the children's visit.

Ben—formally Benham, after one of the first settlers in Massachusetts—sometimes acted as if he himself had been on the *Mary and John,* the pilgrim ship that landed north of Plymouth Rock in 1630. One of his prized possessions was a limited edition print of the vessel, which to me looked like all the other ships of that era. I wasn't sorry when he packed it up and took it home recently. Given a chance, Ben would remind his customers that he was also the namesake of Benjamin Franklin, the country's first postmaster general. Ben had at his fingertips more facts than you'd ever want to know about the U.S. Postal Service.

When I'd proposed the field trip for the schoolchildren, he'd grimaced, pulled himself to his full height, near six feet, and said, "This is a government office."

"Not anymore," I'd replied, as if Ben needed reminding that the postal service had been an independent agency of the government, run by its own board of governors, for more than forty years.

"A technicality," he'd answered. "It's still not a playground. Not yet."

The energy of fifteen seven-year-olds eventually overwhelmed Ben, however, in a good way, and at the end of the day I could have sworn I heard him say, "Maybe we should do this again next year." Curmudgeon or not, Ben had come to my aid more than a few times since my arrival and I was glad he was only semi-retired.

On quiet mornings like this, with things running smoothly, I was happy with my decision to give North Ash-

cot another try at feeling like home. Other mornings, I wondered how I got here. Had I been too quick to bail when
Adam Robinson, my fiancé back in Boston, walked out on
me? Was it as dumb as some claimed that I'd quit my job at
the main post office in Boston for this sleepy town in the
Berkshires where I was born?

Things seemed to have happened too fast. The news of
Aunt Tess's terminal illness, coming on the heels of Adam's
departure, had sent me running from my big-city apartment
to Aunt Tess's bedside. She'd taken me in after my parents'
death during my junior year in high school, and I had to be
here for her.

I was lucky that my years of experience at so many levels of postal work in a major zip code, and my professional
connections, coincided with Ben's wish to ease into retirement. I'd taken this job on a temporary basis, but now Aunt
Tess had been gone a month and here I was. Her home had
become mine, legally at least, and I was sole proprietor of
my hometown post office. A smart move? A hasty decision?

Useless musings.

I turned from the counter and walked toward the delivery
room. For a moment I expected to trip, as I'd done last Friday, because—I looked at the floor—there had been piles
of telephone directories in the way. There had been one for
each of the more than two hundred households that had a
post office box, stacked in the corner where the interior wall
of the delivery room met the wall of the adjoining community room. I'd shoved them there on Friday morning,
some still in the cartons, some wrapped in slippery green
plastic, others separated from the pack, ready for handing

out to customers. Now they were gone. The polished wood floors were clear, not a trace of the phone books. No wonder I'd suspected a housekeeping fairy.

The post office interior was simple, no nooks or crannies that might be hiding such a large amount of paper. Where were the books?

The truckers who dropped off our mail had a key that fit only the lock on the outside door to the delivery room. No one except Ben and me had a key to the postal area itself. The North Ashcot PO had no carriers, no records keeper, no mail handler in the back room, and no window clerk other than yours truly and Ben when he was needed. My one luxury was a part-time cleaning service, in the person of the widow Brenda, who claimed to enjoy working a few hours every two weeks. She had no key and worked only while I was present.

I'd left the side door unlocked as usual this morning while I hoisted the flag, but that was only for a few minutes. No one would have had time to remove all those books. A fleeting thought was that Ben might have figured out another way to distribute them. But he was very careful to respect my position and wouldn't have done that without telling me.

I was faced with the possibility of a theft, though I couldn't think of a single reason why anyone would steal a load of phone books. Who even used them anymore? News streams and blogs predicted the imminent death of the paper directory, but the phone company still paid us to distribute them to our customers free of charge. I guessed that anyone mid-thirties like me, or younger, used the Internet for phone numbers and addresses, both personal and business.

So, where were the books? I nearly screamed out loud, but took a breath instead. Too much stress. Where was that easy, friendly Monday morning?

Should I report this theft to the inspectors, the law enforcement arm of the postal service? A few days ago, I read about a press conference with our inspectors and at least six other federal agencies, after they'd arrested more than fifty people involved in large-scale heroin trafficking into New England. What kind of attention could I expect for stolen telephone directories, each about one-inch thick and filled with ads for goods and services in North Ashcot, Massachusetts, population three thousand, give or take?

I could alert the local police. I could call Wendell Graham, the local phone company rep. *Uh-uh*. Not him. I'd rather talk to a cop than to an old high-school boyfriend. Or I could wait it out, hoping this was a simple mix-up that would magically resolve itself.

As with any crisis, big or small, I called Linda Daniels, my best friend in Boston. I didn't have a best friend in North Ashcot yet, but dwelling on that thought would take me to more useless musings. Other than a serious polarity in musical taste, from Ricky Skaggs (me) to the Smashing Pumpkins (her), Linda and I were of one mind about most of the usual BFF topics, including books, purses, and office politics. Linda was still climbing the career ladder in the capital city's main post office. If it had been up to her, I'd be on the ladder with her.

I poured out my tale of grand theft phone book to Linda, then added, "I think I should at least inform the police department."

Linda laughed. "Such as it is. You're not in Boston anymore, sweetie. There's no BPD there with two thousand cops and a special robbery division."

"What I mean is, I should tell Sunni Smargon."

"Your friend, the police chief. Why do I always smile when I say that?"

I resisted the temptation to lay into Linda for her condescending attitude. As if Sunni weren't a real, sworn officer of the law, in charge of four other officers and responsible for protecting and serving our three thousand citizens. "What if there's something else missing that I haven't noticed yet? What if this is the start of some kind of crime wave that Sunni should watch out for?"

From two hundred miles away, Linda tried to put things in perspective for me.

"Are you saying you think there's a serial phone book thief loose out in the boonies?" she asked.

"It's not the boonies," I said, finally ready to defend my old-new home. "It's a tourist attraction, a charming town with one of the lowest crime rates in the state."

"The rate's gone up," she said. "I believe a crime was just reported to me?"

"Good point." One that got us laughing.

I pictured Linda behind her desk in Human Resources at the main plant in Boston, looking out her window at the large fleet of vehicles bearing the post office eagle. We always joked that we were meant to be friends since we were the two tallest women in the building, both five-nine and relatively fit, but easily distinguished by our hairstyles—hers short, blond, and neat; mine long, dark, and too curly to ever be neat.

For all her uppity tone, which I knew stemmed from her desire to have me back, I missed Linda. I hated to admit it, but I missed Adam. I missed ubiquitous great pizza and bad-for-me donuts on every street corner. I missed drivers who thought nothing of passing on the right even if it meant pulling up onto the sidewalk.

"Is that old cheerleader still hassling you?" Linda asked. "Bunny something? Maybe she committed local larceny in retaliation for when you went to the prom with what's-his-name."

"High school grudges die hard, but I can't see *Bonnie* orchestrating this kind of payback. Besides, I think she went to college in California and never came back. And I don't even remember what's-his-name's name." I heard Linda clear her throat, waiting. "Oh, okay," I admitted. "What's-his-name was the once-very-hot big man on campus, Wendell Graham."

"And where does he work now?" she asked, adding a "Hmm," in a tone that suggested I should do the math: missing phone books, plus ex-boyfriend who works for the phone company, equals: blame Wendell for the theft of the directories.

I'd forgotten that I'd shared with Linda how strangely Wendell had behaved when he stopped in at my post office a month ago. He'd introduced himself formally as a stranger might, as a field supervisor from the local central office of the telephone company. No "Good to see you after all these years." No handshake paired with "Let's get together and catch up." Barely a "Good morning, Cassie," and he was down to business. This certainly was not the personality that got him a large retinue of buddies in his adolescence.

I'd tried to remember if there'd been even a whiff of animosity in our last meeting before I left town those many years ago. Had I broken a date with him? Forgotten his old Mustang's birthday? Had too long a conversation with another guy? My memory failed to call up anything antagonistic. Or anything we'd said, in fact. On the other hand, I wished I could suppress as well the image of that horrid green prom dress I'd worn, with the asymmetric balloon hem. And the matching shoes, which were flats because I was two inches taller than Wendell.

Other than Wendell being height-challenged for a male, I couldn't help but notice that the former quarterback hadn't lost his physical appeal. Light brown hair with a hint of red, combed back from a high forehead and full eyebrows and lashes that many women envied. A square jaw and muscular physique. Not that I remembered very well.

"Phone books come yet?" Wendell had asked during that one awkward business visit. I doubted his mind was on our crepe-papered gym-turned-ballroom.

I'd barely gotten out a "Not yet" before he broke in.

"I'll check with the main office. You should have them before the end of the month," he'd muttered, and plodded out.

Linda's voice interrupted my thoughts of Wendell Graham, the old and the new. "Anyway, it's worth considering that the whole stealing-the-directories thing was a prank by Wendell, who's still hung up on how you ditched him."

"I didn't ditch him."

"Did he stay in your hometown after you left for college?"

"So what?"

"That's a 'yes.' Did you keep in touch?"

"He had a lot of friends who stayed in town, and—"

"That's a 'no.' You ditched him."

"If this was a prank, a better theory would be that it's harassment from some grown-ups here who think I should have stayed in Boston."

"Like me," Linda said. *Uh-oh*. Since I'd started the thread, I let her go on for a while. "You didn't hear it from me, but your so-called replacement is a ditz," she continued, a rant I'd heard before. "The files you so carefully organized are already a mess. Everyone misses you. I miss you. Steve goes around as if he's lost his best friend. Speaking of which—"

"I'd better go," I said. I didn't want to hear about Steve or any other of my former employees and coworkers. I was afraid I'd agree with Linda and beat it back to Boston. I could be there in time for a late dinner on the wharf. Fresh grilled food, the lights across the water . . . But I needed to make my own decisions about this new venture, without the aid of a sentimental pull or well-meaning but strong-minded friends like Linda. "I have to unlock the front doors and start the retail day," I said.

"Oh, the throngs," Linda said, chuckling.

When we hung up, I was no smarter about the missing phone books, and no less homesick for my old city life. But neither was I ready to declare my North Ashcot experiment a failure.

2

I'd sifted out the usual amount of problem mail—forwards, postage due, and pieces marked "not at this address," among other items needing special handling. I wondered how long it would be before I'd stop looking for a certain letter addressed to me. I pictured it. To: Cassie Miller. From: Adam Robinson.

I imagined a note of apology, admitting to his stupidity in letting me get away. In my fantasy, Adam would have seen the light, wanting us to be partners, a working couple with a family, as I thought we'd agreed on. In real life, he'd been diverted by a career path that meant whirlwind international travel as a corporate attorney for him and a clear role for me: hanging on his arm, hosting important parties.

It was about time I marked that fantasy letter "return to sender." Besides, Adam had dumped me not with an eloquent "Dear John" letter, but by way of four text messages, beginning with:

I'm sure u agree. Time 2 call it.

Coward, I labeled him now. *Immature.* And once again resolved not to think about him.

I threw back my sagging shoulders, cleared my dreamy mind, and gave my attention to the counter, where customers had lined up. I was ready for whoever might need stamps, shipping service, prepaid envelopes, or change of address cards. My morning began as usual, except for the fact that at least a dozen people asked when the phone books would be available. It was all I could do not to glance over my shoulder at the empty spot where they should be. Eventually, I'd have to call Ben for advice on the protocol for missing directories, but it would have to wait until I closed shop for lunch. The long line of customers came first.

I peered across my counter and surveyed the Monday crowd, noticing many regulars I looked forward to seeing. Carolyn and George Raley, both with fluffy gray hair, both retired from the school district, sat on the lobby bench, waiting for a break in the line. Each held a small animal, wrapped in a knit blanket. Last summer, before I returned to North Ashcot, I wouldn't have been able to identify the tiny catlike African genet on Carolyn's lap, or the larger, white-nosed coatimundi, a member of the raccoon family, nestled against George's chest. I felt smart, zoologically speaking. I'd have to tell Linda: North Ashcot had broadened me in some ways.

The Raleys were volunteer trainers of exotic animals that would eventually reside in a zoo or become teaching animals in a program for schools or public educators. Their job was to raise the newborns and socialize them, getting them used to riding in cars and being handled by humans before they'd be exposed to children and the general public. I admired the people who did this, and I was happy to offer the use of the largest scale in town, but I didn't want to know the details of potty training a coatimundi.

Carolyn and George had been turned away by my predecessor, citing postal regulations that prohibited all except service animals from entering the building. When they approached me soon after my arrival, carrying a sweet little African fawn, I couldn't resist.

"Would you say this is a service animal?" I asked.

George started to shake his head no, but Carolyn nudged him. "Of course she is," Carolyn said. "Bella and all our animals *serve* children in classrooms and park programs across the country."

"Good enough for me," I said, as the three of us smiled.

That led to the weigh-in today and nearly every Monday.

"Here you go, Snappy, onto the most accurate scale the U.S. Congress can approve," gray-haired George said to the pointy-snouted animal. "Stay still for Cassie while she weighs you."

The coatimundi and I were used to each other by now, so I no longer cringed and worried about Snappy snapping. For the minute that it took me to arrange his long striped tail properly and give Carolyn the scale reading for her notebook, Snappy was well behaved.

"Two pounds, one ounce," I declared, and repeated the

process with the small spotted genet. "One pound, four ounces for little Ama," I said.

George and Carolyn put on gloomy faces. "Only a few more ounces and it will be time to turn them both over," Carolyn said, her voice sad. "So, if you want to feed them and say good-bye before we take them to the Center, you'd better come by the house this week."

I promised I would, and looked forward to the next set of four-legged post office customers.

The second Monday ritual, one I was not happy about, involved Sally Aldritch. Here she was carrying a large package she'd labeled "media mail." No surprise, the box, recycled from an online shopping site, was addressed to her son in Montana. It had taken me a while to figure out what just about everyone in town knew, that Sally sent her boy, a bachelor in his thirties, staples every week—cereal, snacks, toothpaste, underwear. Everything but books, CDs, or anything else that could be legitimately classified as eligible for media mail.

I thought I'd give her another chance to obey the law. "Is there anything in here besides printed or recorded material, Sally?"

She shook her head soundlessly. As if by not saying the word *no* out loud, she was not technically lying.

"Shake it," said a voice from behind Sally.

"Smell it," said another, laughing.

"Drill a hole in it," said still another, laughing harder.

My post office was a fun spot today.

But mail fraud was serious business, and I'd obviously failed to convince Sally and the rest of my customers of the fact. I ignored all their hands-on amateur investigative advice, but resolved that the next time this happened I'd give Sally a gentle reminder that media mail was subject to inspection, that I could open the box at will in front of all of her gawking neighbors. If she called my bluff, her spoiled offspring would receive the package via priority mail, with postage due, and maybe be shamed into persuading his mother to follow the rules.

For now, I stamped the box—I wasn't one hundred percent sure that it contained more than media mail, after all—and let it go, mostly because I saw Monday ritual number three in the background. Scott James, arguably the most eligible bachelor in North Ashcot, and certainly the best looking—in a shuffling, Jimmy Stewart kind of way, Aunt Tess would have said—stood at the back of the line.

The assistant manager of a small antiques store in town, Scott came by regularly with his assortment of flyers, invoices, and other routine mailing. I noticed how he made himself useful while he waited, straightening the various forms in my racks. He'd lined up the edges of customs, special delivery, vacation hold, and registered mail slips; retrieved pens from the floor; and neatened the Land of the Free Boxes display, a fond reference to the slots containing flat-rate envelopes and boxes. A neat freak. I liked that in a guy.

Scott was becoming a friend, probably because we hadn't gone to high school together. He'd had no opportunity to develop a long-standing grudge against me. I didn't know much about him, except that he seemed trustworthy. I'd trusted him with Aunt Tess's old furniture and silk hankies, hadn't I? He was relatively new in town, having arrived little more than a year ago. So what if he wasn't very forth-coming about his former life. Neither was I. In any case, I liked Scott, and on days when I was in a hoping mood, I hoped to get to know him better. Linda's special therapy, which she named "Recovering from Ex-ism," and delivered direct from Boston, seemed to be working as images of Adam faded in the presence of Scott James.

Scott approached the counter, his turn at last. He set his small tub of mail close to the scale, then removed an enve-lope from his jacket pocket. I liked his casual, fleece-lined look, the polar opposite of Adam's sharp, custom-made Ital-ian suits.

"Hey," Scott said, waving the envelope in front of me. "Okay to do a little personal negotiation during your work hours?"

I pointed to the large clock on the wall, its second hand chugging toward twelve. "It's almost noon," I said, smiling, and plucked the envelope from his hand. "A check, I presume?"

He nodded. "We sold both of your aunt's dressers."

"Wow. Good news. Bought by someone on the tour bus that came through from Albany on Saturday?"

Another nod. "One of the last buses of the season, but they spent a lot, all starry-eyed over genuine forties and fifties furniture."

I'd given Scott two of Aunt Tess's dressers on consign-ment. They were beautiful, solid oak period pieces, but much too bulky for my taste. And one of them was built for someone about a foot shorter than I was, making the draw-ers too low while the mirror cut me off at the neck. Aunt

Tess had also been a tall woman, leaving me to wonder which short member of our family, most likely on my mother's side, had bought the piece in the first place.

I tucked the envelope in the pocket of my regulation blue sweater, and gave it a pat. "Thanks," I said, moving along to take care of Scott's mailings. He paid me with cash and took a turn checking out the clock on the wall, almost an antique itself. I followed his gaze. Five minutes after noon.

"Hungry?" Scott asked.

The missing phone books floated through my mind. "Sort of, but I have a little problem to take care of during lunch."

"Can it wait? I was hoping you might join me for a bite."

My heart gave an unfamiliar, ever so slight lurch. The phone books weren't going anywhere, I reasoned. Not that I could be sure of that, since they'd already migrated from my back room to parts unknown. I weighed my options. Lunch with Scott, which might even count as my first North Ashcot date, or a conversation with ornery old Ben to confess that I'd lost control of inventory and needed his help.

"You have to eat something. Somewhere," Scott said.

"Can you give me a minute to lock up?"

There weren't too many lunch options in North Ashcot. Townsfolk joked that there were two: Betty's diner and the diner run by Betty. Which was why I always kept a fallback peanut butter sandwich in the little fridge in my building. And why I was surprised when Scott drove his shiny, silver four-wheel drive past Betty's to the edge of town.

"Do we really want all our customers to see us having lunch together at Betty's?" he asked, his eyebrows raised.

"Only if it wins a big headline in *The Weekly Register* and a feature on the local news."

"I can see the article now. Right under the one about the male peacock found in the Monroes' yard." He put his fist to his mouth, microphone style. "Anyone lose a peacock?"

Scott pulled his new-looking Red Sox cap down even farther until it reached the top of his sunglasses. I liked his playfulness and saw it in his face, but was there a touch of furtiveness also? Was it really that awful to be seen with me? Maybe this wasn't a date, but a business meeting after all. I imagined Scott's boss dispatching him to soften me up with a BLT, then having him make a special request like home pickup or delivery, or a further discount on postage. I'd been worried that I was presenting a big-city image, but maybe instead I came across as an easy mark.

"It can be hard to maintain privacy in a town the size of ours," I said, keeping us on the personal track.

"I'm beginning to realize that," he said, still serious.

We drove along quiet roads surrounded by maples and birches in the last vestiges of their red, orange, and yellow dress, across a small bridge, and eventually across abandoned rail tracks into a crowded parking lot. I guessed we were about ten miles from the center of North Ashcot, still in beautiful Berkshire County. We stopped and parked at the end of a gravel road, where an old cottage stood, now a combination tea shop, antiques emporium, and vintage clothing store. The venue was fitting for an antiques dealer, if not for the tall, muscular man Scott also happened to be.

"Charming," I said, reaching to unhook my seatbelt.

The usual press-and-yank movement to unbuckle myself didn't work, so I twisted in my seat to check the mechanism.

Something was caught in the metal, something that presented no problem going in, but was offering resistance now as I tried to take the buckle out of its slot. I gave it another tug and it came loose.

A piece of plastic. I looked closer. Ugly green plastic. My breath caught. The same kind that the phonebooks had been wrapped in? How could that be? Scott . . . ? No, surely the phone company couldn't be the only one that used this product for shipping. I wouldn't be surprised if Scott had his own bulk rolls of the stuff.

I pulled the plastic fragment free and undid my buckle as Scott came around to the passenger side.

"Problem?" he asked.

For reasons unknown to me, I curled my fingers around the plastic scrap and stuck it in my jacket pocket. "Everything's fine," I said.

Our waitress could have been from another era, posing for an ad for a turn-of-the-(last)-century tea shop. Tammy, the young woman who welcomed us to our table, seemed lost in a heavy black dress that was much too big for her slim body. Her thin neck moved chickenlike within the circle of a white Peter Pan collar. But it was the deckle-edged headdress that made the outfit. A stiff black-and-white fabric crown rested low on her freckled forehead, just above her eyebrows. I tried to avert my eyes, which had focused on the ruffled trim on the crown, but I was too late to prevent stifled laughs from both Tammy and me. I guessed I wasn't the first customer to react to the uniform, and Tammy seemed pleased to join in the fun.

She set down a lovely china three-tiered serving piece with delicate blue and yellow flowers around the edges. Neat arrangements filled the tiers: creamy scones; crustless bread spread with mixtures of olives, cucumbers, and cream cheese; small fruit tarts; and chocolate nibbles. My first lunch date in North Ashcot was going well, except for the baffling scrap of green plastic in my pocket.

"This place reminds me of a shop in Harvard Square," I said. I sniffed the slightly musty smell of clean but old clothes and dusty knickknacks.

"Same uniform?" Scott asked, tilting his head toward our waitress. Apparently he hadn't been oblivious to the non-verbal wardrobe communication between Tammy and me.

"Everything except the uniform," I said. I swiveled to take in the inventory of vintage dresses and hats, cases of old jewelry, and small furniture pieces that surrounded the area set aside for lunch tables. I'd been looking for a newspaper and magazine holder and thought I spied the perfect candidate in a dark corner.

"Not to be pushy, but I have a couple of magazine racks at the shop that you might want to take a look at," Scott said.

I felt my face redden, as if Scott were my boyfriend and I'd been caught cheating on him. As potential BFs went, Scott ranked high in the observant and sensitive-to-needs category. And with good business sense, too, if he was able to get rid of two aging dressers so quickly.

After I'd promised to stop by his shop soon to check out the racks, we took off on the usual banter runway for a first meal together. Scott was skillful in directing questions at me rather than telling long stories about himself. Thoughtful? Or a man with something to hide? I smiled to myself.

Green plastic aside, it was hard to imagine any wrongdoing from this man who shuffled back and forth from homespun talk about his vegetable garden to erudite questions involving nature versus nurture arguments in his college philosophy course. Not that he said which college.

I heard that he'd arrived in North Ashcot from "out West," not quite a year before I did, but no info was forthcoming on his family, or why he moved, unless "needed a change" counted. I heard about his summers in construction work and his junior year abroad, with no clue about his professional life before becoming an antiques dealer. We compared big-city adventures, mostly mine in Boston, and the only specific geographical fact I pulled from him was that he'd ridden the Loop in Chicago.

The answer to my question, "How did you get into antiques?" was brief, and quickly followed by another question, from him. "What made you sign up with the postal service?"

I was only too happy to recount my initial love affair with the USPS, starting with a temporary job over a Christmas vacation. A small town post office north of Boston, one that offered home delivery, hired college students during the heavy rush of holiday mail—girls in the sorting room, boys out in the snow stuffing mailboxes.

"It was boring at first," I told Scott, "until one day a couple of boys were no-shows, and they needed volunteers from the girls to brave the elements."

"'Neither snow nor rain . . .' Isn't that your motto?" Scott asked.

"Nor heat nor gloom of night stays these couriers from the swift completion of their appointed rounds," I added. "Actually, the postal service has no official motto. That

22

phrase is the inscription on the main post office building in New York City. The building is a historical landmark, and so is the phrase, I guess."

"It's a cool phrase, anyway," he said, and I agreed.

"You wouldn't believe what a rush it was, delivering mail." My story was unstoppable now. "I felt so important—unlike when I was cleaning motel rooms all through the summer before. Here I was taking a greeting card that some-one wrote out in Colorado or even Germany, and delivering it in person to her friend in Massachusetts. Eventually, I realized that every job in the postal system was just as im-portant in connecting people to each other, but there was nothing like that hand-to-hand delivery."

Scott did his best to humor me with appreciative nods and exclamations as I rambled on like a true believer. Lucky for him, an alarm went off in my head as I remembered that I was on my lunch hour. Hour and a half, to be exact, but closing in on the end. "I almost forgot," I said. "I need to be back at one-thirty."

"No problem. I ought to get back, too. We're expecting a nineteen-forties estate delivery today. Five rooms of fur-niture and all the odds and ends you could hope for."

"Save me a pink princess telephone if you see one," I said.

"That would be the sixties," he said.

"Oops."

"Let's do this again," he said, with a wide grin.

While I suppressed a too-girlish, "Okay," Scott sum-moned Tammy, whose starched crown had fallen toward her left ear. She repositioned it with practiced grace, then, with an air of experience in diplomacy, she placed the check on the table halfway between us. Even Tammy was unsure of the exact nature of this lunch. "My treat," Scott said, slipping a few bills on the table.

He looked at me with what I felt was disappointment that our lunch was over. "Soon?" he asked, without further elaboration.

"I'd like that."

I expressed my thanks for the lunch on the way to the front door, where we met an unusual sight. Sunni Smargon, chief of our five-person police force, in her muted blue-gray uniform, stood leaning against her patrol car, its blue and red lights winking in the cool air. Sunni's arms were folded across her chest, a serious expression on her face. Before we reached the bottom step, Ross Little, one of Sunni's officers, exited the car and he and Sunni came forward, in step, each with a hand resting on a holster. I could have sworn I heard dramatic music from an old Western in the background.

"Scott James." Sunni, a small woman with red highlights in hair that was barely contained under her hat, announced his name with an air of authority. "We need you come to the station and answer some questions."

"What's this about?" Scott asked. His voice was soft and shaky, with no conviction, as if he knew the answer.

Ross, a large man, despite his surname, opened the back door of the cruiser. Scott stepped back and the two officers took another step forward. I couldn't keep myself from entering the well-choreographed scene.

"What's wrong?" I asked, moving in front of Scott. It occurred to me that I was acting like his lawyer or his mother rather than the person who handled his mail service needs.

Sunni gestured toward the patrol car, directing Scott to enter. Without further argument, Scott slipped into the backseat of Sunni's cruiser. Ross positioned himself in the driver's seat of Scott's silver Jeep as my mind raced to keep track of the movements and understand what was happening.

Could this be connected to the tiny scrap of green plastic in my pocket? Had Sunni found out about the phone books? Did stealing free telephone directories count as a prosecutable offense? I saw myself turning the scrap in as evidence and hearing Sunni tell me I was too late, possibly charging me as an accomplice. I felt as though the green plastic was itching to jump out of my pocket.

Sunni walked toward me. "Deputy Little will be taking Mr. James's car in, Cassie." *Mr. James*? *Deputy Little*? Something was way off. At least she hadn't called me *Postmaster Miller*. "Do you think you can get a ride back to town?" I must have looked forlorn, because Sunni immediately offered an alternative. "I'll call for another deputy to come get you, but it might be a while before I can free up someone. Are you okay waiting here? You know I'd take you—"

"No, no," I said, interrupting. I knew the rules, small town or not. "I'll be fine." I smiled as best I could, given the condition of my nervous system. "I'll get Ben to cover the office for me," I said. Ben lived for moments like this. Not Scott's predicament, but the chance to take over his old post.

Scott caught my eye. He squeezed his lips together as if holding back what he would have said to me if he were free to do so. An explanation? An apology? I felt the connection, though all I could do was press my lips together, too.

The cars drove away, leaving me as confused as if the

postmaster general had announced an unlimited budget for widespread construction of new postal facilities in every town in the state. I climbed the steps to the tea shop and noticed that several patrons had moved to the window to witness the police action outside. I imagined the news of Sunni's official visit and Scott's ceremonious exit traveling from the young receptionist, back to the floor employees, on to the curious diners, and out to the nearest cell towers and to everyone in town. I took a seat on a bench in the entryway, hoping new patrons would think I was waiting for a late lunch companion and not a police escort.

My sense of duty to my post in town kicked in and I dug out my phone. Ben picked up on the first ring. "Heard everything on the scanner," he said. "Don't worry. I'll be ready to open up in ten minutes."

There might as well have been drones flying over North Ashcot, for all the privacy its citizens had.

3

At a time like this, stranded miles from town, a circle of friends would have come in handy. But I was still a virtual stranger in North Ashcot. Maybe worse—a native who'd taken off for a big-city college nearly twenty years ago and, except for infrequent, hurried visits to my aunt, never looked back. When I first returned three months ago, I had made a few attempts to contact friends from high school, but most of them had not only a new life, but a whole new generation to deal with. It was hard for them to find time for me between family dinners and carpools, sports tournaments and music performances. Or maybe they didn't want to try.

Opt-outs I heard were often of the form, "I'd love to visit, but Lily's recital is tonight," or "You know, Jake has so much homework," or "We have tickets to the (fill-in-the-blanks) game." No one suggested I might enjoy the recital, or be able to help with homework. No one offered to pick up an extra ticket for the game.

For a brief moment, I thought of calling Wendell Graham. After all, we did share a lot of movies and popcorn, and one special photo op, standing next to each other, arms at our sides, in stiff, formal outfits. It would be a way to reestablish at least an amicable relationship, and for me to mention the strange fate of the phone books he'd arranged for. As businesspeople in a small town, we had more in common now than we did in high school.

Bad idea, I decided. If Wendell took offense and heard my report as a complaint, an insinuation that he wasn't doing his job right, the distance between us would increase. Better not to contact him until the directories issue was resolved, and the best person to hear about that, I decided, was Chief Sunni Smargon.

But first, I had to get home. I could think of only two women who'd seemed open to a reunion and who might be able to pick me up in the middle of the day. Beth Keller was my old chem lab partner, never married, and now a grade-school teacher who might be on her lunch hour. Sue Olson, a homeroom pal, had stopped to chat for a while when I ran into her at the market. A significant welcome, relatively speaking.

I started my search for a ride by calling Beth. I'd hardly begun to describe my plight, stranded outside town, when she interrupted.

"Whoa, did you say you were having lunch with Scott James? Does that mean you were with that guy when he was arrested?" she asked, excited, as if I might give her a scoop.

I suppressed my astonishment at how far and quickly the news of Scott's predicament had spread, and at the same time it dawned on me that I hadn't heard the word "arrest" as Sunni and Ross carted Scott off. She'd simply mentioned "questions." She might even have said, "Please," but that was too much to ask.

"He's not under arrest," I told Beth with as much assurance as I could muster. "They just want to talk to him."

"Sure, sure. About the body, right?"

This time my surprise made its way out of my mouth. "What body? You mean a dead body?"

"Ohmygosh," Beth said, as one word. "You're kidding me. You were there when they came for Scott and you don't know? Really?" I heard deflation in her voice. Good-bye scoop.

"I guess not," I said, in an only slightly annoyed tone. I did, after all, need pick-up service.

"I don't know all the details, but they found a body over past the reservoir by the old factory." A pause, possibly brought on by her realization that I knew less than she did and, therefore, was of no further use. "Listen, Cassie, I'm getting another call and have to take it. It's crazy here. I have parent conferences all afternoon or I'd love to pick you up. Another time?"

"Yeah, thanks," I said, now fully annoyed. *We can chat the next time I'm stranded and desperately need a ride.*

The other possibility for a lift to town didn't pan out either. Sue Olson was a full-time caregiver for her dad and had no one to take over for her. But she did have a few minutes and some sketchy details about the dead body that was weighing on my mind. The victim was a North Ashcot native, male, shot in the chest, name still being withheld.

"Rumor has it that the guy worked for an Internet company," Sue said.

My mind did a crazy spin as I imagined the Internet guy stealing my phone books to boost his online business, then getting shot with his own gun while Scott, my hero, tried to get the books back for me, leaving a small piece of green plastic behind in his car. Right, a very plausible scenario. In a movie, maybe.

Sue continued. "I also heard—this came from one of Dad's therapists who doesn't even live in town—I heard that he might have been a trucker, just stopping at Betty's for breakfast." She paused. "Or was it closer to lunch?"

There was no way I could fit Scott into the trucker theory, and I gave up, even though Sue seemed proud to have more than one theory to offer. I signed off with her, promising to stop by for lunch with her and her dad sometime. No more candidates for a ride came to mind. I hoped the North Ashton police force, with its fleet of three patrol cars, hadn't forgotten about me. Maybe Tammy, the crowned tea shop waitress, would drive me back to town. We seemed to have gotten along pretty well.

I tried to keep busy for what was turning into a long wait for a ride. I moved from the cold, metal outside bench to the warmer, faux-leather inside bench and back again. I took short walks around the parking lot, checking my webmail on my smartphone. I played two games of solitaire (lost both) and made calls to vendors to order supplies and forms.

I called Ben, ostensibly to remind him that we needed to assemble the special box for Mrs. Hagan's parrot. She'd be bringing the bird in this afternoon for shipment to the Midwest. But my call was really to sniff out what Ben knew about Scott and/or the dead man and/or the missing phone books. He saw through me and offered, "There are as many stories about the murder as we have customers. Hurry on back and you'll hear them all." If only. At least, it seemed, he hadn't noticed that the directories were not around. Maybe he had confidence in my efficiency and thought I'd already handed them out.

"Cassie Miller? I heard you were back." I looked up from the mail inbox on my phone, which I'd checked only seconds ago, and noticed a familiar man standing over me. A boy, the last time I saw him.

"Derek Hathaway?"

"Still with that runway model figure," he said, his eyes giving me a once-over that caused me to squirm.

I took the remark not as a compliment but as an assessment. I stopped myself before I brought up how much he'd changed, from geek to financial rock star. I settled for, "I've read great things about you."

"Such as?" Derek took a seat beside me on the bench and turned toward me. He straightened his shoulders and raised his chin.

"Do you really want me to list all your creds as reported in business magazines and who's who listings?"

"Why not? I'm listening." He sat back and cupped his ear with his hand.

A little pompous, but I decided to oblige him. I used my

right arm to cut a horizontal swath in the air and looked up, as if I were reading a headline in skywriting. "'Small-town boy builds multimillion-dollar empire.'" Derek's grin reeked of satisfaction and the revenge of success. I felt sorry for anyone who'd bullied him in high school. "In real estate, right?" I added.

"Close enough."

As if I wouldn't understand the details. He was probably right, but still, his laugh did nothing to smooth over his boastful attitude. Though it took me by surprise, I couldn't blame Derek for his confident, *I made it big* air. He'd survived an adolescence of thick spectacles and skinny legs at a school where the jocks were kings. He'd been a failure at every sport, and dateless every weekend. He was a geek before there were geeks. I was sure everyone on the yearbook staff of Ashcot High now felt foolish for not having appreciated his academic achievements and foreseen his great success.

"Don't let me keep you," I said, gesturing toward the front door of the tea shop.

"Are you waiting for a ride?" he asked.

Strangely correct guess. "Yes, I'm expecting a ride back to work."

"Hey, I can drive you. No prob. We can catch up."

"Didn't you come to eat?"

He shrugged. "I was just going to have a snack between meetings."

"I thought you lived in Albany now."

"I do, but my ex and kid live here."

In the nick of time, a police cruiser pulled up, with Officer Ross Little driving. "My ride. I might as well take it," I said. "He came especially to get me."

Derek raised his eyebrows. "A police car, no less. I guess we really do need to catch up."

"Right," I said. Meaning "Wrong."

Before I knew what was happening, he tucked a card in the pocket of my jacket. Not an endearing move.

"Call me," he said.

"Yes," I said. Meaning "No."

It was two forty-five when I rode off with Ross. I was full of questions, and a lot of guesses.

"Is Scott still being questioned?" I asked. Ross busied himself looking into the rearview mirror, adjusting his sunglasses. I tried a more general query. "Being questioned is not the same as being arrested, right?"

"Did you say home or office, Cassie?" he asked. Well trained, in spite of his boyish look.

I blew out a breath and a sort of groan, hoping he'd hear my exasperation and take pity on me, but there was no change in Ross's expression and no tidbit of news forthcoming.

"Is there something wrong in town? Was Scott's house vandalized or something? A break-in at the shop?" I imagined teenage thugs carrying off Aunt Tess's floor lamp and area rugs that I'd taken in last week. I thought about the discovery of a dead body that Beth and Sue had been so fascinated with, and Beth's assumption that Scott's summons to the police station had something to do with it. I quickly dismissed the two events. Coincidences happened all the time, and this timing of events was just that. Until I heard otherwise, that explanation worked for me.

"No need to worry. I can take you right to your door if you like," he said, as if he'd misunderstood my question.

I sat back, resigned to my state of ignorance. "Drop me at the post office, please." I relaxed a bit. Soon I'd be at the heart of the rumor mill.

"So, I've always wondered. What's it like, running the post office all by yourself?" Ross asked. "Is it interesting?"

"Yes."

"I'll bet you see a lot. Like who's writing to who and how often. Or maybe who's stopped writing to who," he added with a chuckle.

"Yes," I said, this time closing my eyes and pretending to nap. A dose of his own clamming-up medicine. Information had to work two ways. If my lack of response discouraged a young man who was looking into a career change, so be it.

My resolve lasted about ten minutes. Then I opened my eyes, not wanting to miss the midafternoon sun on the last of the orange and gold birch leaves. We passed the occasional large white farmhouse, dots of gray barns, fields of lush, aromatic green grass, mellow horses next to weathered fences. The sounds of rustling weeds and little else. There might as well have been a sign reading "Small Town, Next 50 Miles."

Did I miss the imposing skyline of Boston? The gold-domed capitol building and the endless brick plaza at Government Center? The mix of historic sites, shopping, and the nightlife of Downtown Crossing? The sailboats and the regatta on the Charles? Yes and no. I wondered how long it would take me to be sure I'd made the right choice. I hoped the feeling of being home again would make up for what I was missing.

No one could remember the last time North Ashcot had been the scene of a murder. No wonder my post office looked like someone had called a town meeting and we were the hosts. To accommodate the overflow, Ben had opened the inside door off the lobby to the community room. It would have been much better for our business if the crowd were here to spread their gossip by using USPS products. Our little post office would have been overflowing with letters, postcards, overnights, and every other kind of special delivery available. But today's crowd consisted mostly of people who'd dropped in to chat about what they knew and what was showing on their smart devices. And once word got out that there were leftover snacks from the weekend crafts fair in the community room, there was no holding anyone back.

I spotted our Board of Selectmen, four men and one woman, wandering through the crowd. They didn't appear to be doing anything to manage the impromptu citizens' assembly, but were rather using the opportunity for informal campaigning.

Gertrude Corbin, the lone female board member, saw me and made her way through the pack. She was a tall, rather heavy woman with past-blond, shoulder-length hair and a loud voice that I figured she'd cultivated in order to be heard at meetings.

"Cassie Miller, isn't it?" she asked me, shaking my hand, an earnest look in her eyes.

"That's me," I said, thinking of the small blue pot holder in my kitchen with her name on it.

"Gert Corbin," she said, still grasping my hand. "I've been meaning to stop in and welcome you back to town. I'm sorry I had to miss the memorial for your aunt Tess." She shook her head and tsk-tsked. "Tess and Uncle Mike, rest in peace, were big supporters of mine."

Thus the pot holder in my kitchen. Today Gert, in her mid-fifties at least, I guessed, wore a full-length navy blue coat with a blue-and-red paisley scarf. Under it were traces of a light denim-colored dress. She carried a navy leather business tote and looked as patriotic as my post office décor, and ready for a campaign speech.

"Thanks," I said. "For the welcome," I added, lest she'd read my mind and thought I was thanking her for the pot holder.

"We should chat sometime." Gert rolled her head to take in the crowd. "When it's a little less hectic." Her voice turned somber. "Terrible thing, isn't it? A murder in our town?"

"Terrible," I said, and stepped aside as another voter, a man about her age, maneuvered his way in to address Gert.

"I hope you're pushing to get that new betting club for us," he said to her. "It's the best idea to hit North Ashcot in a long time. We need something else to attract visitors besides a few colored leaves in the fall. These parlors are cropping up everywhere and it's about time we caught up."

"Now, Coach," Gert said, a little patronizing to my ear, "is that really the way you want to spend your hard-earned money? Gambling it away on some dumb race horses?"

"Now that should be my choice, shouldn't it, Madame Selectwoman?"

Coach—a name? a title? I couldn't tell—used Gert's designation in a decidedly sarcastic way. I had the feeling this wasn't their first encounter. Then he seemed to notice that I was standing there, too and decided to recruit me.

"What do you think?" he asked, and, without waiting for an answer, began his pitch. "My brother told me about this club out near San Francisco. Three hundred screens. You can watch and bet on horse racing anywhere in the world." He handed me a color brochure with "all the facts you need before you vote."

What fun, I thought. It was a good thing he didn't need a response from me.

"Tell you what," Gert replied, at the same time taking her own flyer from her tote and handing one to Coach. "Read this and then tell me if you want to attract the kind of people who patronize these clubs. I know you better than that, Coach."

I knew the voting wouldn't take place until early in the new year—a special referendum off-season, but for politicians it was never off-season for pushing an agenda.

I was impressed at how Gert could disagree with Coach and still maintain a smiling countenance and an air of caring about him and how he spent his money. But the last thing I was interested in was a place to gamble my own hard-earned money—or debating the issue—so I accepted the flyer she held out to me and excused myself. The two, still intensely engaged, hardly noticed as I moved on.

I scanned the crowd again and noted that Derek Hathaway seemed to have beat the cruiser here. Or maybe his driver did. As short as he was, Derek was conspicuous for his well-cut suit, one that would have done my ex-fiancé proud at a party in Boston. He caught me looking at him and winked. Too bad he'd moved to Albany; we could be friends. Not. There was something off about a guy who drove to a tea shop for a snack and then didn't go in, but instead rushed back to town to gossip about a murder.

I heard conflicting comments being passed off as fact. The only claim that was verifiable: Early this morning the body of a North Ashcot man had been found in the woods near an abandoned glass factory on the outskirts of the town. He'd been shot; his name wouldn't be released until his family could be contacted. The other confirmed truth: Scott James, beloved antiques dealer, was now in the custody of the North Ashcot Police Department.

As for other details, there were more rumors than holiday cards in December. The victim was either early forties or a senior citizen. A longtime resident or a newcomer. Bald or wearing a cap over a mop of hair. Shot with a small-caliber handgun or a sawed-off rifle. Dressed in a suit or a jogging outfit. It was anyone's guess what was what. And concerning the prime suspect, not that anyone had heard that term from an official, I thought I heard volunteers agreeing to sit on his jury.

Even Mrs. Hagan's parrot, Blackbeard, seemed to have an opinion, though we had to take his owner's word for it that he was screeching "Danger! Danger!" The bird and his owner hadn't been expected to arrive until just before closing time, when the pickup truck would be here, precisely to avoid subjecting everyone to chirping that was unintelligible to most human ears. But who could blame Mrs. Hagan for wanting to be in on the excitement downtown? I was grateful that this bird was not as loud as others, like the squawking pheasants that often passed through the post office on the way to a new home.

The gossip continued, easily drowning out the wildlife. I had the bright idea that all we had to do was take attendance right now, figure out who was not present, and that would be our victim. Or maybe our killer. I stepped back into a corner and surveyed the crowd, keeping out of the way in case the opposite were true of the killer.

"Muffin?" An attractive young redhead in an olive green parka seemed to have followed me to the corner. She held out a paper plate with two small blueberry muffins.

I smiled and shook my head. "Two days old, I presume?"

"You're right, they're left over from the crafts fair," she said, and tossed everything into a wastebasket under the table with the postal forms Scott had so carefully rearranged only a few hours ago. "What was it like having your lunch interrupted by the police?"

My smile collapsed. "Excuse me," I said, moving away from her and into the crowd. "I have some business to take care of."

"I'd just like to talk to you for a minute or two and get your impressions of what happened today."

"Sorry," I said, as I kept inching away from her, toward the counter.

She held out a card. "I'm Wanda Cox. Will you call me?"

Too bad I could barely hear her as I was swallowed up by the people who were not reporters. Also, too bad my hands were in my pockets and not free to accept her card.

When our chief of police entered the lobby, the noise level began to die down, ending with an offering by old Harvey Stone. "I heard the dead guy's fingers were on the other side of the border, all the way into South Ashcot," he said.

"I wish I could say the case was South Ashcot's responsibility, but it's ours." The voice of our police chief finally brought the chatter of man and beast to a halt. Sunni used her thumb and fingers to show us just how close the call was.

It was up for grabs whether the townsfolk were enjoying their own stories too much to be constrained by facts as presented by their chief of police.

Most of the border between North and South Ashcot was in the form of a small stream, but a patch of woods at one end, where the body was found, was the subject of many measurements over the years. Especially when it came to zoning issues, it was the North versus the South, all over again.

Responses to the South Ashcot rumor ranged from several who yelled, "Dang," to others who muttered, "Thank goodness."

"Everybody back to business," Sunni said. "Let me and my squad do our jobs and pretty soon you'll have all the facts you need to twist into a good story." She winked at the crowd in general, then approached me. While the townsfolk resumed conversation, undeterred by the word of the law, Sunni addressed me in a near whisper. "Can you come down to the station, Cassie? A few questions, if you don't mind. We can wait till you close up."

My throat clutched, as if I weren't just another member of the uninformed, but a person of interest. I tried to focus on Sunni's tone. A request, not a command. Almost giving me a choice—*if you don't mind*—unlike her approach to Scott.

I'd known Sunni only for the three months I'd been home; she'd arrived in North Ashcot about four years ago, long after I'd left for Boston. I'd had to deal with various official protocols regarding my aunt's death, and Sunni either took care of things or directed me toward those who could help. We'd developed a friendship of sorts. Now and then she'd bring her lunch to the post office and we'd rap about politics and world affairs, or our preference in hairstyles. One time we'd met at the farmers' market and gone for coffee together afterward.

I had a feeling that our upcoming conversation would be more of the cop-to-citizen variety than the girlfriend-to-girlfriend variety.

I looked over the heads of the slowly dissipating crowd to catch Ben's eye. In one corner, Selectwoman Gert Corbin was in a huddle with Derek Hathaway. I would have assumed that Derek had little business here, now that he was a star in the New York State capital. It was hard to tell who was pitching to whom when the high and mighty gathered. Was Gert preaching about a gambling-free North Ashcot, or was Derek negotiating a land deal that would bring him more money?

Although he was stuck behind the counter, Ben, my loyal back-up, hadn't missed a beat. He gave me a nod that I took to mean I could leave with Sunni now; he had it covered. I guessed that no matter how sweetly a member of law enforcement asked you to report to her office, it was best to respond immediately.

I gave Sunni a neutral smile. "I'm ready to go if you are," I said.

"No one's going to miss me here," she said.

"That makes two of us."

4

The North Ashcot police station was across the street and down three blocks from the post office. In the first block, well-kept lawns were spread in front of mostly white or pastel-colored clapboard houses. Various combinations of tricycles, leather-seated swing sets, and the beginnings of what would be Christmas scenes were visible on porches and on the pathways.

I had a flashback to neighborhood tours with my parents when I was a kid, when families competed with each other for the most elaborate decorations in town. Santa and his reindeer on the roof? Easy. Elves in the garden, making motion-activated robotlike gestures? So last year. Metal sleighs, candy canes, giant plastic snowmen, oversized candles, scary-tall wooden soldiers? The bigger, the better.

I'd heard that the custom did not survive the years. Neither had my parents, who'd died in a car crash, their vehicle loaded with Christmas presents a few months before my sixteenth birthday. It had taken a few years, but, with Aunt Tess's help in the beginning, I finally learned to dwell on the best memories, and how lucky I'd been to have them through my childhood. Still, I hadn't looked forward to Christmas the same way since. Nor my birthday either, in fact.

The conversation, or lack of, between Sunni and me today required little attention, which was handy for my reverie. We walked abreast whenever the broken sidewalk permitted, and chatted about the lovely fall weather, the new shoe shop in town, and the burning question of whether the introduction of off-track betting would be good or bad for us. No hint of the fact that I'd been on an almost-date with someone she brought in for questioning, presumably in a murder investigation; no hint of what were her questions for me that had prompted this walk in the first place.

The second block was perfect for more small talk. Shops and service offices lined both sides of the street. We passed a bank, a salon, a hardware store, a title company, in quick succession on one side, while across the street was my favorite coffee shop, which just so happened to be the only one in town. Café Mahican's owners made no apology for its mixed ancestry name or its spelling, claiming authentic familial links among Native Americans who settled around Albany in the early sixteen hundreds. The décor was part European, part American Indian.

We had no trouble complaining about banking rules and bemoaning the lack of time we had for a mani-pedi or a leisurely cappuccino. Enticing, noteworthy aromas came from the Swiss bakery, but we settled for olfactory satisfaction only. Instead of indulging in cupcakes, we stopped for a moment to look in the window of a fabric shop next to the bakery. Sunni pointed out a particular bolt of red cloth that was close, but not perfect for her current project: sewing a quilt with each patch celebrating the history and culture of North Ashcot. She was awaiting the arrival of the special shade of red cotton that she'd ordered.

"One of the patches will represent our spring kite festival," she said. "It's a great event. Lots of them are handmade. You should participate next year."

I wasn't sure whether she meant I should quilt or fly kites, but it was good to know that she expected me to be free then and not watching the festivities through heavy metal bars. "I don't sew at all. I'd need to take some classes first," I admitted, feeling as though I'd betrayed my small-town roots.

"I can help. We have a great group of quilters in town. The schedule will be different with the holidays coming up. I'll let you know."

Uh-oh. I wasn't sure I wanted to be part of a quilting bee, if they still called them that. I smiled and thanked Sunni anyway. I told myself that once the day was over, she'd forget she'd mentioned it to me. Or she'd remember and be as sorry as I was that she did.

As hard as I tried, I couldn't give my mind over completely to this delightful girl talk. I was on my way to be questioned about a murder I knew almost nothing about and, probably, a handsome lunch date I knew equally little about.

We crossed in front of the elementary school, just short of an abandoned church that was now home to its remodeler, Tim Cousins. Seeing it reminded me that Tim, who'd been friendly to me, might have agreed to come to my rescue and provided a ride this afternoon. I made a note to make contact with him as soon as things were back to normal. Maybe he'd teach me to scrape paint, which sounded a little more interesting than learning to sew. There was only so much I was willing to do for a little companionship.

Sounds of ten-year-olds at music practice poured out from the schoolhouse and brought shaking heads and chuckles from the chief and me. I hoped I'd be chuckling on my way home.

The journey to the police department building, which seemed to have sapped more energy than an entire day's work, had taken only about ten minutes of real time. I entered the redbrick building behind its chief officer, still with only random notions as to why I was there.

The police force, five officers in all to serve a town of thirty square miles, about one third the size of Boston proper, was housed in a two-story brick Colonial-style structure, not too different from my post office, but much shabbier inside. Except for the state-of-the-art coffeemaker, which stood on its own heavy oak table next to the floor-mounted American flag.

"Surprised?" Sunni had asked the first time she caught me staring at the sleek black appliance. "My little indulgence, paid for it myself, of course. It's fully programmable." She'd run her finger along the steam pipe. "Espresso drinks, three cup sizes, timer, temperature control. The Cadillac of coffeemakers."

"Dishwasher safe?" I'd asked.

46

She'd smiled and told me she was saving up for the newest model in red.

"Cappuccino?" she asked now.

I accepted Sunni's offer and took a seat as she'd indicated. Soon, I was propped in a battered but comfortable chair across from her large oak desk, which bore stains and scratches from unnamed incidents over the years. Old wooden file cabinets, similarly scarred, and a bulky castiron radiator completed the look. Altogether, the furniture in Sunni's office was of the kind our local antiques dealer would immediately put through the wringer of restoration. I wondered where said dealer was at that moment. Not downstairs in the two-cell jail, I hoped.

I sipped rich, strong coffee through whole milk foam and waited patiently while Sunni dealt with the crises of the day: a male officer with a flag patch on his sleeve, like his boss's, gave a verbal report on a rabid skunk that was terrorizing Mr. Jayne's backyard; and a female officer told another tale about a vandalized restroom at the high school shared by North and South Ashcot. Sunni checked off a sheaf of paper forms for each officer. Another time, I would have been curious to know what the paperwork was all about.

No one yet had mentioned the murdered man found in our woods. At least, not in front of me. The officers gone and her own steaming cappuccino ready, Sunni took her official seat and readied a pen and notebook. Her look was all business.

"How long have you known Scott James, Cassie?"

And we were off. I was grateful to still be "Cassie" to the woman in uniform. I cleared my throat. "Just since I've been back, about three months. I met him around the same time that I met you."

"What do you know about him?"

I swallowed. "Not much. Not as much as you do, I'm sure. I don't know what he did before he came to North Ashcot. I don't even know where he's from. Do you?" *Ramble on, Cassie.*

"You were at lunch with him today?"

"Yes, but just lunch. I mean it wasn't really a date." I hoped I wasn't blushing. Dark hair notwithstanding, I'd been blessed with fair skin that reddened easily, whether I was embarrassed or just thought I might be embarrassed in the future.

"What did you talk about?"

"General stuff. A lot about me. How I came to be a postal employee. A little about his garden. He mentioned Chicago, but I don't think that's where he's from. He said 'out West' but that could be anywhere. And I have no idea if he was in the antiques business there, or . . ." I shrugged and finally fell silent.

Like all good cops on television, Sunni nodded, wrote a few words on her notepad, and waited me out. She raised her eyebrows slightly, as if to ask, "Anything else?" At first no words came out, but like all good interviewees on television, guilty or not, I couldn't stand the silence. "Can I ask, does this have something to do with the murdered man in the woods? Is Scott under suspicion?"

"Do you have reason to think he should be?"

I threw up a mug-free hand and let it fall onto my lap. "No, no. I'm clueless here."

Sunni sat back. "Do you have any idea why there would

be a stack of telephone directories in his apartment, a couple hundred of them, addressed to the Postmaster, North Ashcot, Massachusetts?" She paused. "That's you, right?"

My phone books? I gulped. Loudly, I thought. This time there was no doubt that my face was red. I set my mug on a napkin on the corner of Sunni's desk. "I should explain."

"Uh-huh."

I told Sunni as much as I knew—emphasizing that it was just this morning that I'd noticed the phone books were missing. I infused my narrative with numerous excuses as to why I hadn't notified her office immediately about the theft: I'd thought maybe Ben had moved them; I wasn't sure I hadn't simply misplaced about two hundred pounds of paper; I'd had a flood of Monday morning customers; I didn't want to bother her with something so trivial; I was going to do it right after lunch, but then . . . blah, blah, blah.

Sunni let me go on. When I was out of excuses and nearly out of breath, convinced that the theft was connected to the murder in the woods, I pulled the scrap of green plastic from my pocket. I placed it on her desk, smoothing it out while I explained how I came to have it.

"I should have known when I found this in Scott's car," I said, rubbing my wrists in anticipation of the handcuffs I was sure were coming. I needed to tell Ben I might never be back. I gave Sunni an apologetic look. "I'm sorry. I should have—"

"Okay." Sunni took pity and stopped me, holding up her hand. She ignored the slippery green evidence. "Scott, or Quinn Martindale, as he's also known, would like to talk to you."

My eyes widened. A different name. Who uses an alias?

A fugitive? Or just someone needing a change? Maybe I should have done that last spring. What would I have chosen?

I snapped to the present. "Scott has another identity? Is he in Witness Protection?"

"No, not WitSec, but we're still checking out other possibilities."

"Is he in jail?"

She shook her head. "We're just holding him for now. The victim had Scott's names and address on him."

"A business card for his store or a memo to stop in?" I asked, as if five trained police officers wouldn't have thought of that.

"Not a card, not business. A piece of paper with the names Scott James and Quinn Martindale, and Scott's home address. We ran the names and that's how we found they're the same guy. Then we found the phone books in his home."

"Addressed to me." I inadvertently let out a loud sigh.

I thought back. It was more than a little likely that while Scott and I were eating delicate sandwiches and lifting our teacups, Sunni and her officers were going through his house. And probably his shop. I'd been to each location only once, while negotiating about pieces from Aunt Tess's estate. Now I pictured the small blue cottage he called home, and its detached garage, being invaded by uniforms. I imagined the neat shop where he worked, with people carrying radios and clubs and guns marching down its narrow aisles.

"You didn't know him by any other name?" Sunni asked.

"No, I swear."

"Well, a flag has been raised. We're checking to see if there's maybe a warrant for him under either name in another state."

I couldn't help thinking how quickly the Boston PD would have had more information on the man I broke bread with. Sunni's office seemed to shrink while I sat there, reminding me how small her operation was. No wonder I'd had to wait so long for transportation home.

Sunni sat back and looked at the cracked ceiling before addressing me again. "He's declined a lawyer, but he's asked to talk to you."

I'd almost forgotten that part of Sunni's revelation. "I can't imagine why," I said. Unless he wanted to apologize for taking the phone books.

"Are you willing to see him? There'll be an officer in the room with you."

"Of course," I said, though I thought Scott/Quinn would be better off with an attorney. And maybe I would, too. "By the way, am I . . . uh . . . on the hook for not letting you know right away about the directories?"

"Don't worry about it," Sunni said. "Technically, you had twenty-four hours to track them down yourself. But next time . . ."

"You'll be the first to know." I mentally wiped my brow, the expression *dodging a bullet* coming to mind.

Officer Ross Little opened the door to a small room in the opposite corner of the building from Sunni's office. Scott/Quinn was staring at the mirrored wall we all knew was also a window, his posture more relaxed than I expected, given that he was here involuntarily. Unless he *had* expected this interruption of his life. I had so many questions. I wondered just what right I had to answers, given that he'd asked to talk to me. But for all I knew he'd sent for me to ask me for a favor. Not that I could think of a single thing I could do for him, other than forgive him for taking my property, which I wasn't ready to do until I had it back.

He stood and offered me his hand. Ross stepped in to discourage me from taking it, and then retreated to his corner spot once Scott and I sat down. I wondered at the strange circumstances. Scott wasn't cuffed or restrained in any way, yet we couldn't shake hands? Obviously, he hadn't been charged with anything, or he'd have been downstairs, in jail. As it was, he had a plastic cup of coffee in front of him. Across the table, I could see that it was weak. I doubted it had been brewed in the fancy pot I'd been served from.

"Thanks for seeing me," Scott said. Looking more closely, I saw that his face was gray and drawn, his eyes glazed. Not the funny, pleasant lunch companion of a few hours ago. Just being in a police station interview room could have that effect. It did on me.

"Do you know what all this is about?" I asked, turning my head from one corner of the room to another, my eyes meeting no obstruction other than Officer Ross Little.

"I have an idea why they brought me here. But first I want to apologize for, you know, the phone book thing."

The phone book thing. I couldn't wait to hear the *why* of the unlikely theft, but Scott started with the *how*. I sat back as much as possible in the very straight-backed chair.

"Remember that function in the community room on Saturday?" he asked.

There weren't so many events in North Ashcot on any given weekend that I wouldn't remember. "The Seniors Club crafts sale," I said, and thought of the stale muffin offered to me by a nosy young woman named Wanda.

"It was a nice time."

I agreed, recalling a special purchase I made from a local photographer, Siena Roberts. A set of lovely color prints of small-town Massachusetts and New Hampshire in all four seasons. I almost fell for Scott's diversion by commenting on them. Instead, I said simply, "Yes."

"You volunteered, which you do a lot, I notice, when there's a cause you can help with."

I blushed at the secret truth that my motives for volunteering didn't always stem from altruism, but often from the need to connect with people and show support for the town I hoped to call home again. "So do you," I said. "Didn't you provide extra tables for the special exhibits? And weren't you part of the cleanup committee for the weekend?" Not that I'd been paying attention.

"Yes, but I had an ulterior motive."

"You, too?"

"Huh?"

"Nothing." I looked over at Ross, who was shifting his weight from one foot to the other. I expected him to call a halt to the so-called visit any minute. "What about all that?" I asked in a hurried tone. "Why is the crafts event so important?"

"It got me a key to the community room for the weekend. And there was so much buying and selling and eating going on, it wasn't hard to rig the door between the room and the post office so I could get back in on Sunday."

"And on a Sunday, you'd have all the time you needed to haul away those phone books while my office was closed."

"That's right." His look was just sheepish enough to take away my desire to slap him.

"I don't understand why you took the directories in the first place. And what do the books have to do with the dead man and why you're in the police station now? And are you really Scott James or Quinn Martindale?" I thought I'd asked enough questions. It was time for some answers.

Scott leaned on his elbows and put his head in his hands. When he came up for air, he said, "I don't know where to begin."

"Yes, you do."

A wry grin. "With my mother, I guess."

I gave him an annoyed look. We didn't need flipness. "I'm serious, Scott."

"So am I. Really, it begins with my mother."

"What about her?"

"She's been charged with murder."

I was glad I hadn't brought my coffee into the room. It would have been dripping down the table leg, and mine, by now. "What? You mean . . ." I stuttered. "She's connected to the man they found in the woods today?"

Scott smiled. I don't know how he did it, but he almost laughed. "No, no. Not our murder. She's back home."

"Chicago?"

"San Francisco."

"Of course." I was on the edge of many emotions. Sympathy. Anger. Resentment. Fear.

"I'd like to explain."

"I'd like to hear it."

But I wasn't destined to hear any more today, it seemed. A knock on the door interrupted us. A signal to Ross apparently, since he approached us without directly acknowledging the *tap, tap*. "Time's up," Ross said, not harshly, but with no room for negotiation, either.

Scott and I both stood. "Will you come back?" he asked me. His slumped posture and shaky voice were enough to evoke my sympathy, even if I didn't already feel sorry for him.

"If they let me," I promised.

I had a couple of reasons to keep the promise. Though I now knew how he'd gotten into my inner sanctum, I was still curious about his motive for wanting the phone books in the first place. And even more curious about why he'd asked to see me. Surely not simply to apologize for his crime, which was small in comparison to a possible murder charge. Which, apparently, his mother was facing. I felt a shiver at the thought. If he and his mother were killers, maybe I shouldn't keep that promise after all.

5

Sunni had left the building. I left, too, doubting that I'd get any information from Ross, who'd shown his mettle for maintaining secrecy when he picked me up at the tea shop; or from the other remaining officer, a stone-faced woman who muttered good-bye to me without making eye contact. I felt a wave of pity for Scott, left for the night with this crew. But, for all I knew, he deserved whatever they'd mete out.

The sun had set, lowering the temperature enough to make my light jacket inadequate for a leisurely walk. I retraced our steps back to the post office at a quick pace, only now and then slowing down to admire dried yellow leaves along the sidewalk. I loved hearing the crunch when I stepped on the leaves, and inhaling the scent of autumn. I was also glad I wasn't responsible for raking them.

I regretted that I wasn't much smarter than I'd been on

the reverse journey, from the post office, with Sunni. Near the front of my building, I stopped at the row of dented newspaper vending machines, half expecting to see headlines about Scott/Quinn, but, of course, there'd be no new local paper until Friday and until then we'd be getting all our news from a not-very-local television station and the ever-accurate word of mouth.

My building was dark except for the lobby and the nightlights in the sorting area. Ben had kindly taken down the flag and closed shop. I picked up a few candy wrappers and empty chip bags from the parking area, stuffed them into the trash container at the edge of the lot, and walked around to the side door. I let myself in, my gaze reaching to the far corner, where the phone books had rested what seemed like ages ago. I smiled at the ridiculous idea that somehow the directories might be back, perhaps delivered by the police. I had a moment of satisfaction that I hadn't filed a theft report with the postal inspectors. Though I'd always found them very helpful and dedicated, I was glad not to have taken attention away from more serious cases like identity theft and hazardous mail. There was hardly a crime they didn't deal with, if it in any way involved misuse of mail service.

I'd forgotten to ask Sunni about the disposition of the books, and wondered if they were now considered evidence in a murder investigation. Who would break the news to Wendell, who'd facilitated the delivery, to the merchants who'd bought ads, and to those residents who may be counting on the updated books? New questions and problems were sprouting as if it were springtime and the trees were sending forth blossoms, instead of becoming more dry and barren every day.

I made myself some coffee, inferior to the police department's, and decided to put in a couple hours of work to make up for my absence this afternoon. I needed the satisfaction of completing chores that could be checked off and put behind me. Ben had, unwittingly, I guessed, obliged by leaving me a list of things to be done in the next day or so. He often set aside a pile of special pieces of mail, labeling them with notes that said FUNNY, or STRANGE, or simply adding a large question mark.

I sat on my stool and surveyed the envelopes on the counter. One of today's notes from Ben read DUMB. Under the note, I found what looked like a bill addressed to *Masinmary Olly Pendergast.* Our school principal Molly Pendergast, who lived a couple of streets over, had apparently failed in her efforts to spell out her first name. It was hard to figure who in Ben's mind deserved the "dumb" label, Molly or a faraway clerk who took her literally. *M as in Mary* . . .

Under the FUNNY label was a news magazine with a cover article, "The State of the Service Industry." The magazine's front cover and first few pages had been nearly torn to shreds by the originating post office. "Mangled in Delivery" was the official designation, and OOPS might have been a better tag from Ben.

One more piece set aside by Ben was labeled DLO? for DEAD LETTER OFFICE. He'd written the letters with a red marker, which he used when there was an official issue in play. Like many older workers, Ben had yet to adopt the newer, more uplifting and hopeful designation of "MAIL RECOVERY CENTER," or MRC. I could hear Linda in my head, ranting about how much money had been spent on the committee meetings involved in coming up with the new name.

I picked up the first-class DLO/MRC letter to a person in Ashcot, Massachusetts. No street address. No clue about the sender through a return address label or a return zip code. Also, there was no such town as Ashcot. The letter had been delivered first to South Ashcot, whose postmaster forwarded it to us. In itself, not an unusual occurrence. At least a couple of times a month, mail was addressed either to North Ashcot when South Ashcot was intended, or vice versa. The two offices cooperated fully, not designating a letter officially "dead" until both facilities had signed off on it, in which case, the letter would be forwarded to our recovery center in Atlanta.

This letter had an added complication, however: The name of the person to whom it was addressed was QUINN MARTINDALE.

The name Sunni referenced as Scott James's real name.

I nearly fell off my stool. My amateur handwriting analysis led me to believe the envelope had been addressed by a woman. The modest flourish, especially in the upper case letters, and the tiny circles used to dot the i's gave the words a distinctive feminine flair. Finally, a dead giveaway to me was the peacock blue ink the sender used.

The day just got better and better. I stuffed the letter in my desk drawer and locked it. Later I'd decide what the official disposition should be.

A banging on the front door further startled me. I peered across the retail counter and was relieved to see, not a burglar, but Tim Cousins, the architect who had bought the abandoned old church down the street. Not that I knew Tim very well, but at least he wasn't a stranger on a killing spree through our town, which was one of my first thoughts. A murder at my doorstep had affected me on many levels. It didn't help that Tim was a tall man, all in black this evening.

I figured Tim saw the light over my desk and thought I was open for after-hours business. I waved to him, shook my head and mouthed what I hoped was a clear, "Sorry. Closed."

Tim waved back but kept pointing at me and then the door, signaling that he wanted to talk to me. I had no interest in establishing a precedent that said any time a customer saw me in the office, I was fair game for service. On the other hand, could I really afford to leave a bad taste in the mouth of any potential friend? If I could be nice to Tim, my friendship score for today would balance out. One friend lost to the police, one gained if I gave Tim a little leeway.

Continuing our nonverbal conversation, I motioned Tim to go to the side door, where I'd meet him.

"Hey, Cassie," he said, seeming delighted to have a chance to talk to me. "I heard about all the excitement today. Sounds like you were in the thick of it."

Tim had a boyish look about him and the physique of a desk-bound architect rather than a carpenter, though I knew he was doing most of the rebuilding of the church himself and I'd even seen him in action on its roof. I guessed he was probably at least five years younger than me. He'd made an effort to enter my building as soon as I opened the door, but I discouraged him by standing firm in the doorway.

"It's been a long day, as you can imagine, Tim, and I'm just about to pack up. Was there something you needed?"

"No, no. I'm just curious, you know. It's not every day something like this happens in North Ashcot."

"It's very sad for the family of whoever the victim is."

"Oh, yeah, of course. They're all sayin' he's a local, huh?"

In spite of his charming Southern accent, he was starting to annoy me. I was eager for him to be gone.

"I don't know any more than you do, Tim, and I really would like to finish up here." I smiled through my tense jaw. "I'll be back in the morning, same as always."

I made a move to close the door again, with me on one side and Tim on the other. I had a creepy feeling, which subsided when he didn't resist. It was hard to account for my reaction. Tim hadn't been intimidating in any way, and it was early, after all, not even five-thirty in the evening. But it was already dark and there was no one else around. I chalked my reaction up to exactly what Tim had observed: It wasn't every day that someone was killed in North Ashcot.

In any case, Tim backed off. We agreed we should have lunch sometime, and said good night.

I watched his car drive off, then rushed out to my car and headed home.

I knew that the house I'd inherited from Aunt Tess didn't need to reflect her taste any longer. The trouble was I couldn't decide what my taste was. Aunt Tess's furniture was heavy, characterized by dark wood trim even on the living room chairs. Too old and serious for me, but neither did I want light and pretty cottage chic. I couldn't see myself curling up with my laptop or e-reader on a white wicker chair with floral cushions.

My one-bedroom apartment in Boston's West Fenway neighborhood had been small enough to remain undefined as far as style. A simple beige couch, vertical blinds instead of curtains, an eclectic mix of concerts and plays represented in posters—the Boston Symphony Orchestra on one wall, a revival of *Blithe Spirit* on another, along with an oversized movie still from *Casablanca*. And to keep in touch with my hometown roots, some C&W tunes from Reba McEntire or Tim McGraw on my computer.

Linda, whose apartment had a definite modern twist, mostly black and chrome with touches of red, claimed I hadn't moved on from the college dorm motif. Whereas, if she changed one item in a room, the rest of the furniture had to go as well. I had to admit I preferred to surround myself with images that meant something to me personally, rather than worry about whether the pillows and bedspread provided the proper color accents for the drapes in the bedroom.

Adam, who agreed with Linda, had tried to reshape my environment and bought me furnishings and accessories more suited to his executive suite. Geometric, abstract wall art in primary colors; a kitchen chair that looked like a giant suction cup on a pedestal; a lamp with a cylindrical chrome shade and a base that resembled a triad of alienlike legs. As far as I knew, they were now all part of the flea market scene or the landfill around Boston.

Right now, I was glad I'd had my faded blue glide rocker and ottoman shipped here last summer. I'd kept Aunt Tess's grouping of two stuffed easy chairs on either side of a coffee table, but added my glider to the arrangement.

Sobered by the thought that I could no longer call downstairs and order-in from several different ethnic eating establishments, I'd fallen back on my second favorite meal plan: When in desperate need of food, sprinkle bits of cheese over whatever's left in the fridge, nuke the mound of food, add bread, and eat. I plopped onto the rocker and dug into a hot, cheesy faux-casserole of broccoli, carrots, mushrooms, tomatoes, and zucchini.

Something seemed off about the angle of my rocker this evening, as if someone had moved it. Impossible. Nevertheless, I put my plate on the coffee table, stood back, and surveyed the configuration. It wasn't my rocker, but one of the easy chairs that was off. Probably nudged the last time I vacuumed. No more vacuuming, I vowed, as I fixed the setup and smiled at my own joke. I couldn't help thinking that Adam would have been proud of me, fussing about a couple of inches left or right. I was tempted to shove everything around to annoy him in absentia, but decided he wasn't worth the effort.

Back on my rocker, I bit into a stale-but-warmed buttermilk biscuit and pondered the current events of my life. Starting with the most recent, I mentally listed pressing concerns.

Priority one: I needed to decide how to handle the first-class letter to Scott/Quinn that I figured was burning a hole in my desk drawer at the office. At least I hadn't already broken the rules by taking it home with me. By now I'd convinced myself that an old girlfriend had written to beg him to come back—wherever that was. I warned myself that I was on the edge of investing in a friendship that was doomed. But I wasn't exactly famous for heeding my own advice.

There were a number of reasons for a piece of mail to be designated UAA—Undeliverable As Addressed, formerly called "dead letter," as Ben had labeled the one now on my mind. In my career, I'd seen standard anomalies like incomplete addresses, deceased addressees, damaged packaging, and failure to comply with a business code. More heartrending were letters to Santa and the Easter Bunny that would never find a home.

An ordinary piece of UAA would be opened at the center and checked for enclosures or clues as to the identity of the correspondent on either end. Valuables like jewelry, coins, or electronics would be removed. If there was no way to determine who had sent the letter or who was to receive it, the rest of the contents would be destroyed to protect the privacy of both parties, whoever they were. Appropriate items would be sold at auction. Case closed.

In this situation, I first had to answer Ben's written question. Was this a dead letter? He couldn't have known at the time that there was indeed a Quinn Martindale in town. To the best of my knowledge, Chief Smargon had told me, but not the general public, about Scott James's earlier identity. Ben must have passed the letter on to me in case I knew someone that he didn't, someone new in town named Quinn. He'd been half right.

On the surface, the letter was UAA, undeliverable. It was lacking the necessary information for delivery by a postmaster. On the other hand, it *was* deliverable by this postmaster, me, since I knew the addressee and where he lived. In fact, I knew where he was at that exact moment. I could simply drive a couple of miles to the police station and deliver the letter. Case closed.

But not so fast. To further complicate things, I knew that Quinn Martindale was also Scott James only through a confidential discussion with the chief of police about a pending investigation. Unless she was wrong about that. I hadn't actually heard Scott James admit to being Quinn Martindale. Case wide open.

It seemed fruitless to keep debating myself, taking both sides over a single thin envelope. And how ironic that one of the most complex post office issues I'd ever had to deal with had arisen in North Ashcot, and not in Boston, where we handled a huge amount of mail daily and where you could stop at the post office to buy a greeting card, have a passport photo taken, or pick up a burial flag for a vet.

North Ashcot offered phone books; that was it. And not always.

I was dismayed by the lack of local response when I had needed a ride from the tea room earlier today, but I couldn't bring myself to call Linda in Boston for advice. The last thing I wanted was for her to think I couldn't handle my new job. She'd have my employee forms back in the HR active file in minutes. My own training and experience had to be enough to solve this problem. I hadn't had to review decisions regarding privacy rights in a while, but I recalled a few cases and even some of the history as it pertained to the postal service.

I corroborated my memory with an Internet search and found that, indeed, fourth-amendment rights had been extended to mail during litigation in the nineteenth century. Unlike the decision for a person's trash can, for example, the ruling for mail was in favor of privacy. Drop your trash into a container and push it onto the sidewalk, and the contents were fair game, all privacy bets off. The box from your last Thai takeout was now anyone's bounty. But once a person glued an envelope shut and dropped it into an official mail repository, he was judged as having the expectation of privacy, even though he might have mailed the letter on the same sidewalk, a few yards from his trash can, or in front of a long line of people in the post office.

For a "dead letter," however, there was a kind of dispensation for postal personnel at the recovery center to open the letter, to search for clues as to the letter's origin or destination. We often referred to them as the detectives of the postal service.

My cell phone rang. Linda Daniels, with perfect timing. In spite of my attempt at bravado, I wanted nothing more than to discuss the letter to Scott/Quinn with her.

We set up a Skype call and after a bit of juggling, we were face-to-face, or computer-camera-to-computer-camera.

"I'm working late, subbing out here in South Station and I need a break," she explained.

I surveyed the scene behind Linda on my laptop screen. Her back was to her window, overlooking a T station, part of the oldest mass transit system in the country, and a convenience I'd taken for granted nearly every day I'd lived in Boston.

"Anything new in North Ashes?"

I ignored the timely slur and told her about my disastrous lunch and the subsequent discovery of a murder victim at the edge of town. I heard and saw her gasp and immediately clarified that it wasn't I who'd found the body.

Linda gasped again anyway. "Still, that's a lot more than petty theft. Or even grand theft. How are you holding up? You should have called right away." Linda's words came out in a rush, her face moving closer and closer to her camera. I could feel her concern and was sorry I hadn't called the one person I knew would always be there for me.

I took a breath and told her the rest of the Scott James/ Quinn Martindale story. "So now I have this letter. Well, it's in my desk at work."

"And it's calling to you. You have to make a decision, Cassie, and get it off your mind. Not that I think there's an easy answer. But in this case, you actually know the destination of that letter. And the general policy is, if you can deliver it, do so. You're probably the only postal employee who knows where it was meant to go."

"That's my point. Can I just call this a fluke of circumstance and deliver it? And if so, to whom? To Scott or to Sunni, since he's in her custody?"

"I'm thinking," Linda said. Though she wasn't there now, I had a mental picture of her in her shiny office in downtown Boston, her red-soled designer shoes on the floor under her desk, her perfect navy blue jacket on the chair behind her. Unlike me, Linda could look as put-together and sharp at the end of a day's work as she did at the beginning. "If Ben were still running the office by himself, or had chosen not to call the letter to your attention, he'd have sent the letter off to a recovery center, to be dealt with by designated postal staff, right?"

"Right, but what if there's some evidence in the letter or

maybe the letter itself is evidence, whether exculpatory or incriminating. You know how much volume the recovery office gets; it could take forever for this letter to come to the top of their list. Meanwhile, anything could happen to Scott. Shouldn't I bring it to the attention of the police who are holding him?"

We went a few more rounds on the protocol for letters written to people in interrogation rooms. Was Scott technically a prisoner, whose correspondence, in either direction, was up for grabs? Unless it was from his lawyer. But Sunni had told me he didn't have a lawyer. The questions made my head hurt. I needed to call it quits until the morning. Tomorrow, I'd look more carefully for a return address or informational postmark on the ordinary, size ten, white business envelope; there was nothing more I could do tonight.

Linda and I ended with a meeting of the minds—I should take the letter, unopened, to the police, in the person of Chief Sunni Smargon, and let her take it from there. Only the police knew Scott's official status and rights.

We signed off with the familiar Skype chirp.

I had one more task to see to before bedtime: Search for Scott James and Quinn Martindale on the Internet and see if the names collided. And a related task, search for a mother accused of murder.

Usually, whatever the question, I'd be on my laptop clicking around the various online-pedias for information, specious or otherwise. Why hadn't I rushed to perform this search? I could only guess that I wasn't sure I wanted the answer. I quit stalling and went for it.

An hour later I was no closer to the truth about my lunch

date. Pulling a Scott James out of the more than half a billion hits was hopeless, as I'd expected. Too bad I wasn't trying to find the songwriter or the snowboarder at the top of the list. It occurred to me that I was bumping against a deliberate play by the man—choosing a name that made it impossible to single him out.

Isolating a Quinn Martindale wasn't much easier, however. I scrolled through the first of only half a million options, many of them female. I flopped back as far as I could on my rocker, nearly slipping off, headfirst.

Another washout was my search for Scott's mother, the murder suspect in San Francisco. If I'd even heard correctly, that is. I scrolled through stories of ongoing investigations, but neither victims nor suspects in homicide cases were identified. Was Scott's mother the woman who was accused of shooting a neighbor in a South San Francisco brawl? Or the woman arrested in a case called the Road Rage Murder on a freeway out there? Without at least one other fact, like the date of the crime or the arrest, or the weapon, I had no way to narrow my search. Not even the San Francisco newspaper site was helpful, reporting only the most recent incidents. The crime I was interested in might have happened last week or ten years ago.

I closed my laptop. The evening stretched before me.

I needed a hobby. In college, I'd given knitting and crocheting a shot, but I was hopelessly impatient to do well at either one. One dropped stitch or twisted loop, and I gave up.

Oddly, I'd never tried stamp collecting, but I ruled it out quickly. A friend at one job I had was a collector and was in a constant state of stress over whether he could afford to acquire a triangular issue, or how much his Falkland Islands sheet was worth. When I'd asked, "Shouldn't a hobby be relaxing?" he'd given me a strange look.

Hobbyless, I settled for a large bowl of ice cream and the opening scenes of a crime drama on television to distract me from the insurmountable task of learning anything concrete about my newest almost-friend. On the television screen, the heroine of the drama, a prosecuting attorney who'd received a threatening phone call, walked into a dark, deserted parking garage late at night, her high heels tapping on the pavement, ominous music in the background. I clicked the remote. OFF.

I got up and paced my small house. Picked a dying leaf from a houseplant that Aunt Tess had nurtured. Put a load of clothes in the washer. Checked the locks on the windows. (Cheesy as it was, the creepy music had gotten to me.)

In Boston, entertainment had surrounded me. I simply had to walk out the door to a concert, an exhibit, a club, a ball game, or a gala sponsored by any of a number of organizations. Why had I even bothered to pack my little black dresses, some sleeveless, to show off the small rosebud tattoo on my left shoulder, others meant to hide it? In North Ashcot so far, I'd gotten by with my uniform during the day, sweats in the evenings and on weekends.

Now I might have to create my own diversions. Maybe Sunni's quilters would take me in. Or maybe I could learn gourmet cooking. Or any kind of cooking.

I had a flashback to a chat with Adam last year.

"You should take cooking lessons," he'd suggested.

"Why?" I'd asked.

"So we'll be able to hold our own with important parties once I'm launched . . . Why are you laughing?"

"I'm picturing Old Ironsides in the Charlestown Navy Yard. You know, launching a big ship."

He'd frowned, an expression I'd witnessed often. "I'm serious. You've seen the lavish spreads the partners in my firm put out. You think that's all accidental? There's this underlying competition to have the most people talking about your dinner party the next day."

"I know some really great caterers."

"Not the same."

"You don't think your fancy friends use caterers?"

That conversation might have launched his eventual plan to have parties without me. Too late now to start a culinary hobby.

An ice-cream snack can last only so long, and I was soon back to my mental list of concerns. The sketchy UAA letter wasn't my only problem. There was the matter of the phone books. I had no idea if and when Sunni would release them to me. If I never got them back, I'd have to arrange for replacement books. Who should pay for them also had to be negotiated. Since it was only a little after nine o'clock, I felt a call to Wendell Graham wouldn't be an imposition. He'd given me his cell phone number to report any problems, and this qualified. The best outcome would be if we could handle this problem locally. If Wendell was busy, I could leave a message, and put half of a check mark next to that item.

I'd entered Wendell's number into my smartphone contacts list during his memorable visit, and now called it up.

I heard three rings, and then a pickup.

"Yes, hello." A vaguely familiar male voice.

"Is this Wendell?" I asked.

"Who is this, please?" Rather formal. Also, higher pitched and younger than Wendell's voice.

"It's Cassie Miller. I wanted to talk to you about a problem with the phone books."

"Hey, Cassie. This is Ross. Officer Ross Little down at the station."

Had I punched the wrong numbers? It wouldn't have been the first time. My fingers were much too wide for the spatial allowance on phone pads. This was one step away from an accidental butt dial.

"Sorry, Ross. I guess I made a mistake. I was trying to reach a friend."

"Who were you trying to call?"

Nice of him to care. "Wendell Graham. I must have punched the wrong numbers."

Ross sighed, making me believe that he was overly concerned about my simple phone call. "No, you didn't do anything wrong, Cassie. This is Wendell Graham's phone. We have it."

A pause, while I tried to figure out why Wendell's phone would be at the police department. Probably Ross was trying to decide how much to tell me. Had Wendell, my erstwhile prom date, lost his phone, or was he also being detained? Finally, Ross broke the silence. "We just reached his family about an hour ago, Cassie, and we'll be releasing the information momentarily."

"Is something wrong with Wendell?" I asked, with friendly

curiosity since we were on a Cassie-Ross basis after our road trip earlier today.

Ross cleared his throat. "We've identified our shooting victim as Wendell Graham."

I drew in a sharp breath, and felt my phone slip from my hands.

6

My phone seemed to take on a life of its own. Or it might
have been the sudden onset of perspiration that caused
the device to slip onto my lap and down to the floor. I retrieved it and addressed Ross.

"It was Wendell's body? The one that was found—?"

Ross sensed my difficulty and broke in. "I'm sorry to tell
you this way, Cassie. Did you know him?"

I shouldn't have been surprised that the twenty-
something Ross didn't know our history. "Yes, we were
friends in high school."

"Oh, yeah, I forgot you used to live here."

"Did you just find out?" I wanted to ask, "Are you sure?"
but it was just as well that I didn't challenge my local police.
I was too confused to take it all in, anyway. Wendell was
murdered. Scott was being questioned. Did Scott even know
Wendell? I remembered what Sunni had told me about

Scott's two names and his telephone number being on a piece of paper in the victim's pocket. Now that I knew who the victim was, things made even less sense.

Ross had continued and I tuned in to hear him explain further: "The victim's younger sister was his only local family, but he had another sister in Maine, and a brother in Florida. We wanted to make sure they'd been contacted before making it public."

"Why?"

"Because the family has to be notified before—"

Apparently, I was pretty far gone, assuming Ross had been following my mental wanderings. "No, I mean why do you think Scott is connected—"

"I really can't discuss anything else, Cassie. I'm sure you understand."

"Yes, sorry." I was about to hang up when another thought came to me. "Can I visit again tomorrow and talk to Scott? He asked me to come back."

"I'll have to check with the chief, but I don't see why not."

Happily, my business persona kicked in, as if I were trying to keep Ross a satisfied customer. "Thank you," I said. "I appreciate that and thanks for letting me know."

I hung up and sat in the dark for a long time, holding my phone. Maybe it would ring and someone would tell me it was all a mistake. I could hit redial and this time I'd reach Wendell. It wasn't hard to reconstruct a world where Wendell was alive and Scott was driving me to the tea shop for lunch. A big rewind.

Before I went to bed, I started the process of deleting Wendell Graham's name and cell number from my contacts list. I don't know why I thought I had to complete that project, but, just as suddenly, I had to stop. I couldn't bring myself to do it. It felt too much like killing Wendell all over again.

I've had a few fitful nights in my life. When the call came that my parents had died in a car accident on the way home from a Christmas shopping trip, I was at the sixteenth birthday party for one of my friends. Thus, two special events lost their glamour forever. There were less traumatic events, like receiving the "It's over" texts from Adam (not even doing me the kindness of "It's not you; it's me"), and various other disappointments, large and small. Now news of Wendell's murder inched its way into my mind, inserting itself onto the list of tragedies, forcing me to accept it, keeping me from sleep. I reminded myself over and over that Wendell and I weren't close anymore and hadn't been for many years, that currently we had only a business relationship, and even that was slight. It didn't seem to matter to my mind and body. I tossed and tossed.

Now and then through the night, I fell into dreamland. Images from my past and present collided and I saw Wendell in his prom tux, fighting with Scott over the phone books. At some point, the inordinate amount of attention I'd already spent on the "why" of Scott's phone book theft took over. In my half-awake state, I dreamed up a story where Scott had learned about an ad appearing in the current issue of the directory, offering a valuable piece of furniture, and he wanted to be the first and only one to make an offer, so he collected all the books before anyone else could see the ad. Cue the fight scene with Wendell, and I'd solved the mystery of who killed Wendell. Except that I went back and forth between Scott-of-course and of-course-not-Scott. Trying my hand at detective work. And fiction.

I arrived at work on Tuesday morning, my head aching, my eyes burning. Two large mugs of coffee had barely made a dent in my state of awareness.

That my first "customer" was a baby wallaby needing weigh-in helped a little. The tiny cousin to the kangaroo was a protected species in some countries, but its caretakers, Carolyn and George Raley, assured me that this particular wallaby, called Aussie, was destined for a zoo within the state and would not be siphoned off as a pet, nor would we all be arrested for endangerment. I was glad I was on hand to deal with the small animal, since Ben was not as open to the various wildlife that passed through our office.

When he first realized I'd been accommodating local service animals, as I now called them, Ben had said, among other negatives, "Next thing you know, this office will be nothing more than an annex to a petting zoo."

"Slippery slope is not a valid argument," I'd said, mimicking a long-ago class in critical thinking. But some weeks, like this one—with two animal appointments already, and Mrs. Spenser's ailing cockatoo due to come in tomorrow— I saw his point.

Ben had agreed to be on call today in case I got the go-ahead to visit Scott. I promised him he'd have to deal only with good, old-fashioned human-type mail and mailers.

The Raleys were always careful not to hold up the line with their weigh-ins, and made sure to have postal business to conduct, even if it was just buying a roll of stamps. But before they slipped away with Aussie today, Carolyn leaned over, her gray waves falling on her forehead, and whispered to me, "Everyone says you were at the crime scene with the killer. Is that true?"

"Tell everyone they'd better not mess with me," I said, with a wink.

In general, Tuesdays were less busy than Mondays, but this morning each customer took a little extra time at the counter to interrogate me or give me a taste of their own gossip. As far as I could tell, the police hadn't released Wendell's name yet, and I wasn't going to be the one who did. I thought of his siblings, two sisters and a brother, as Ross had mentioned. His sister Whitney, I recalled, was a few years older and had already graduated from high school by the time Wendell and I entered as freshmen. It took a moment, but I came up with his younger brother's name, Walker, when I remembered that they were all Ws. His younger sister had been a pesky nine- or ten-year-old who'd followed Wendell and his crew around. I smiled as I remembered how she would pretend to lose something like a string of beads or a stuffed animal and mobilize Wendell and the rest of us for a search.

Sometimes I was glad to be an only child, to avoid not only a clever name game, but especially the pain of losing a sibling.

I developed a standard response for my customers' questions: "I guess we'll have to be patient until there's some kind of announcement." Then, I shrugged and pouted as if I, too, were longing for news. No scoop here.

One customer, the same striking redhead who'd offered

me stale muffins—Wanda Cox, if I remembered correctly— was particularly aggressive, and this time I was captive behind the counter. As I totaled her stamp purchases (who buys thirty-five dollars' worth of small-denomination stamps?), she badgered me with questions.

"I'll bet you were freaked out when your date turned out to be a murder suspect," she said, when I didn't respond to her first remarks.

"Your total is forty-three dollars," I said. I piled her newly stamped envelopes together for the collection box, inserted her loose stamps into a thin paper sleeve, and handed it to her.

"Would you like to talk about it?" she asked, placing a white business card on the counter in front of me. I noticed she'd had time for a mani, if not a pedi.

I slid it back toward her. "Unlawful during business hours," I said, and tilted my head to welcome Mrs. Hamilton, next in line.

I thought how easy it would have been to cash in on Scott/ Quinn's detention and Wendell's murder and enjoy celebrity status in town, perhaps pretending I knew more than I did. I imagined a full calendar of luncheons with so-called friends, movie dates, a book club membership, and my name on everyone's list of party invitations. It wasn't hard to take a pass on the idea.

With the citizens of North Ashcot zeroing in on me as information central, I decided to follow my backup plan for lunch: a peanut butter sandwich, apple, and cookies from home, eaten at my desk. It seemed like ages, not just twenty-four hours, since I'd left for lunch at the tea shop with Scott. I closed the lobby and retreated to my work.

I picked at my sandwich and at routine tasks—checking the vacation-hold log, tracking an insured package that hadn't reached its destination in Minnesota, verifying a new shipment of commemorative stamps. I wanted to take care of as much as possible before cutting out, if the opportunity arose.

When the phone on the desk rang, I jumped, as if it were the middle of the night and I'd been sound asleep. With all my fantasies this morning, that description wasn't far off, though the real time was only fifteen minutes past noon.

"North Ashcot Post Office," I said, a little shaky.

"Cassie? This is Sunni. Can you break away for a few minutes to come down to the station today?"

"Sure. I'll call Ben."

"The sooner the better; but definitely before two o'clock. I can't hold him longer than twenty-four hours." The NAPD had a smart chief. She knew there was only one "him" who mattered at the moment. Only one who was alive, anyway. "Will that time frame work for you?"

"No problem. Thanks, Sunni."

I considered waiting a couple of hours until Scott was released, but what if after twenty-four hours he was charged, instead. And he might have lawyered-up by then, as they said on television. I decided not to take that chance.

Ben was ready for me, as usual. He'd probably been sitting by the phone since before service hours began.

"I'll be there to open at one-thirty," he said. "Do what you have to do to help out that nice young fellow."

Ben's comment took me by surprise. I wanted to ask, "Which young fellow, Wendell or Scott?" but I knew there wouldn't be a short answer.

Whichever side Ben was on, I wished I'd thought to pick up some cupcakes, his current favorite snack. I'd have to remember to stop at Hole in the Wall before I returned. In the meantime, I'd leave my cookies for him.

I finished up one more loose end Ben didn't need to be bothered with, then gathered my jacket and purse. I opened my desk drawer and picked up the letter addressed to Quinn Martindale. Another debate, brief this time, *Cassie v. Cassie*, but I ended up following the policy Linda and I had discussed. *When you can deliver, do it.* I stuffed the envelope into my purse. Surely I couldn't be violating any rule, delivering it to the police.

Confident that Ben would be on time at one-thirty to wield his mighty power at the retail desk, probably in a freshly dry-cleaned sweater, I left the office around one o'clock. My spirits were lifted by the thought that I was on my way to an excellent espresso, though it would have been better if I were headed for the coffee shop down the street and not a coffee system surrounded by mugs with an NAPD shield.

I hoped the walk to the police department would clear my head. I was lucky that the streets were deserted. Everyone was at lunch, I figured, and hurried along to take advantage of the timing. When I got to the corner where Tim Cousins's church-home stood, I recalled his strange visit last evening. It wouldn't have taken much to convince me that the incident was really just part of my dreams. The do-it-yourself builder was nowhere to be seen now, and I wondered if either of us would make an effort to have lunch as we'd promised. My guess: Tim was like all my other new so-called friends, wanting information, and once he'd satisfied that need, one way or another, I'd be history. No love lost.

I was past questioning whether I was on my way to see Quinn Martindale or Scott James. The seven hundred million hits on the latter name must have been a big draw for someone wanting to change his identity.

I flashed back to the crafts fair in the community room over the weekend, remembering how he'd taken great pains to avoid Sienna, the official photographer. When she announced her goal to have photos accepted by a special newsletter in Springfield, he'd offered to give her a break by taking over and shooting photos of her with the crafters and customers. Sienna with the show organizers. Sienna with a woman who bought the largest ceramic bowl in crafts show history. Sienna with everyone but himself. A good way to avoid having your image on file. I never want my photo taken either, so no bells had gone off.

I arrived at the police station, slightly irritated by the man who'd deceived me. Not the first to do so, but the most recent. From now on I'd think of him as Quinn. No benefit-of-the-doubt mental slashes to include his fake name. I was ready to face Quinn Martindale and get some answers.

Now that I knew my way around the police station, I walked through to the area in front of Sunni's office. Two desks on either side of her door were staffed by two of her four officers, the day shift. A civilian was stationed near the entrance, but not during lunch hour it seemed.

I sat on a short bench in front of Ross Little's desk while

he completed a phone call. I'd taken my e-reader with me and pulled it out. Thrillers and spy novels were my favorite genres, but nothing on my device could match the real-life crime drama I was witnessing. In fact, was a part of. I closed the reader and tried to relax.

"Hey, Cassie," Ross said, finally hanging up. "Sorry you had to come all this way." I thought he must be teasing me about the three-block walk from the post office, but it was no joke. "Scott—I guess I should say Quinn—was just released."

I was sure my face showed the disbelief rattling around in my head. "But the chief called me no more than a half hour ago."

Ross nodded. "That was then; this is now. I thought she was going to get back to you, but she had to take care of some stuff at the coroner's office and I guess she forgot. Sorry."

I waved away the apology. "Why was he released?" It was strange to realize that I wanted Quinn to be here so I could get an answer or two. I should have been happy he was free and on his way. I'd have to revisit that.

"A lawyer showed up and invoked a twenty-hour rule," Ross said.

"A public defender?"

"Nooo." Ross dragged out the word. "Big-time guy, Edmund Morrison. We had to admit we couldn't charge Quinn with what we had. The lawyer laid it all out. There wasn't a lot to connect him with the victim or the time and place of the murder. And no physical evidence at the scene."

"I know you can't give me many details, but—"

Ross held up his hand. "You're right. I can't. I shouldn't

even have said that much. I know you're a good friend and all, but it's up to him and the chief what they want you to know."

It was foolish to argue with Ross. In fact, I felt sorry for him. It was hard enough being new in any business, learning the rules, but not necessarily knowing the hierarchy of applying them. I'd been there. In some ways, I was still there.

"Have a good day, Ross," I said, turning toward the door.

He removed his NAPD cap. "You, too, Cassie," he said.

I was gone before he finished wiping his brow, and I was sure I heard a soft "Whew."

I stopped at Café Mahican, a block from the police building. Ben wouldn't be expecting me back for a while, and I needed coffee that was as good as the police chief's. The aroma of dark roast seemed to carry enough caffeine my way as soon as I stepped into the room, and I inhaled gratefully. A small television set behind the baristas' workstation ran continuous loops of local news. The usual features had to do with new road construction, an equipment malfunction at a utility center, a ruling by the selectmen about a new tax. The biggest story might involve statistics from informal voter polls on the betting parlor issue.

Today was different. Like all the other patrons of the coffee shop, I sat facing the television screen, ears tuned to the announcement of the first murder in North Ashcot in ten years. The clicking of laptop keyboards, cell phone conversations, and the hissing of the coffee machine stopped while we listened to Rick, a meticulously groomed anchorman from central casting.

"North Ashcot Police Chief Sunni Smargon told Channel 30's Erin Ryan today that the body of a man found here"—a map of the southeast side of town appeared magically behind the anchorman just in time for him to point to it—"has been identified as thirty-five-year-old Wendell Graham. Erin?"

I heard gasps from many and tried to determine who was most astonished. This was me, ready to ID the killer by his or her reaction to the news.

Erin was in the field, and therefore less well groomed than her counterpart in the studio. Her chestnut hair fell victim to the breezes as she told the story, stretching the few facts Sunni had given out into her full-time segment:

"North Ashcot citizens are stunned today, Rick, as they deal with the news that one of their own, Wendell Graham, a telephone company worker, was shot to death and left in this field."

Behind Erin was the field she indicated with a sweep of her arm, as well as an old building—an abandoned factory surrounded by a chain-link fence, with rubble strewn around the lot. Lighter debris was lifted by the wind and floated around Erin's nicely made-up but sad face. All in all, North Ashcot looked forlorn.

"Chief Smargon says she has no suspects, but our crew caught a glimpse of this man leaving the police department building just before the chief came out earlier."

A small rectangle in a corner of the screen showed an image of a man leaving the back of the police building, but, between the great distance and the man's hat and wide sun-glasses, there was no way to tell who it was.

I was sure that was how Quinn Martindale wanted it.

I hadn't learned anything from the broadcast, but now that the rest of our citizens knew what I did, maybe the newsmongers would get off my back.

Wishful thinking. I had my head in my smartphone for one last e-mail check before I left the coffee shop, and barely noticed that someone with a laptop took a seat at my small table—common practice in crowded coffee shops the world over. When I finally looked up, I saw young Ms. Cox, the woman who'd faced off with me at the post office. She'd edged her computer toward the center of the table and leaned on it. It would have been nice if she'd brought me a fresh muffin from the basket at the counter.

"This thing has really upset the town, hasn't it?" she asked. Strange that a reporter, if that's what she was, couldn't come up with a word or phrase better than "this thing" to describe the violent death of a fellow resident.

I nodded. "Uh-huh," I said and kept my thumbs active on my phone, even though I was now scrolling through yesterday's messages. A universal way of saying, "Please don't bother me," and the reason I always took my e-reader or book on an airplane flight.

"Big news, now that we know who the deceased is. I understand you were close to him as well as to the suspect?"

I frowned at her. If she could have read my mind, she would have seen some nasty phrases.

"And you've come back into town just as all this is happening. Is that right?" she continued.

I collected my coat and purse, reached to the adjacent

supplies stand, and grabbed a to-go cup. As I prepared to pour my coffee into the paper cup, she handed me her card, a third attempt. "I'd love to chat with you," she said.

I headed toward the door, stuffing her card into my pocket, only to avoid littering.

Before I exited I heard the news clip repeat itself. This time there was an added interview with Selectwoman Gert Corbin, my favorite pot holder friend.

"We're all stunned," the selectwoman said to the woman in the field. "On behalf of all the community leaders, I want to extend my condolences to the family of the victim and also assure our citizens that we are bringing all our resources to bear on finding the killer, who will be brought to justice, and we're determined to make North Ashcot the safe place it has always been."

A long, run-on sentence, my grammar teacher would have called it. Like the kind every politician uses so he or she won't be interrupted. I was surprised she hadn't managed to wrap up her thoughts with a reference that furthered her own agenda against the proposed betting club.

I thought how unfortunate it was that our little television channel wasn't carried very far to the east. Linda, tuning into news in Boston, wouldn't have heard our local broadcast; she'd have to wait until I called her this evening, when she'd be forced to rethink her view of our crime rate.

7

I'd hoped to go back to work with questions answered, but instead a few more stumpers had been added to my list. Why hadn't Quinn told me he was going to hire a lawyer, and a "big-time" one, no less? Not that he owed me anything, but I thought a spark was developing between us and I hated to think I was way off on that. Hadn't we essentially planned a second date before we'd finished the first? I remembered his look at the time. Serious, not joking. And hadn't he asked to speak to me specifically when he was first in custody?

Where was Quinn now? Hiding in another state with another name, probably. In other words, in the wind. And, still lingering in my mind: When would I get my phone books back? A coin toss would have helped me decide whether to go home or back to my job. I still had Quinn's letter to deliver, and though that might have passed muster as being "on the job," I couldn't bring myself to approve, especially since there was no telling where he was for sure. My regular duty was calling. And so were red velvet cupcakes.

I walked from the bakery to the post office enjoying the crisp air and the sweet smell of pink icing. I found Ben at the counter with only two customers, the first buying an armload of colorful special-event bubble-wrap envelopes. To speed things up, I stepped to the counter and took care of the second project in line, a tub of bulk mail for Tracy, who owned the beauty salon I'd passed so often in the last two days, walking to and from the police station. I ran my fingers through my hair. Why did I always feel so unkempt in Tracy's presence?

"I'm going to make an appointment soon," I told her.

"Everyone says that when they see me," said the fortyish woman who still looked like a teenager and, even more so, like a popular child actress Aunt Tess used to love. Today Tracy's curls were blue, bordering on purple. "When business is slow, I just walk down the street," she joked.

With the office now empty of customers, Ben and I took seats behind my desk. "I think I'll hang around for a while, in case the police call and need you," he said, stretching his long arms above his head.

Not likely. But the one dozen cupcakes in a pink box might also have contributed to his decision.

"I'll put on some coffee," I said.

Whatever the reason Ben stayed put, it was nice to have someone to talk to. Usually one or both of us were busy, our interactions limited to brief encounters over post office issues we couldn't agree on.

One trivial issue was Ben's old office spindle, a five-inch-long green metal spike on a circular base, from his first post office job. I'd seen the objects in old movies, usually at a cash register in a diner. The clerk would slam the checks onto the sharp point. I never saw the point, as a matter of fact, of mutilating a transaction record.

My main objection now was that the spindle was a hazard. Many customers who came in with children sat them on the counter while we conducted business, and I had nightmares about a child getting stuck with the needle-like object.

"Kids should not be on the counters in the first place," Ben had insisted, in his usual show-stopping way of winning an argument.

We had a truce of sorts, whereby he'd take the spindle out when he was working, and I'd put it in my desk drawer when he was off duty. The North Ashcot Post Office, like the rest of the world, ran on compromise.

The first thing I learned in this afternoon's more leisurely chat was that, as upset as Ben was by Wendell's murder, he'd never liked the guy very much. When Ben had agreed to sub for me this morning, the "nice young fellow" he'd urged me to help was Scott/Quinn. He explained why.

"A lot of times he'll come by and change a fluorescent for me or give me a hand on something," he said. "And I don't think I ever told you about the time Quinn—well, he was Scott then, as far as I knew—came to my rescue on the day after Halloween last year. Some kids had made a mess of the outside of the building."

Color me startled. "Wait. How did you find out Scott and Quinn are the same guy?"

"It's all over town. Didn't you know?"

"Yes, I've known. I didn't know you knew." What would my grammar teacher have done with that sentence, other than circle all the forms of the verb "to know"? "And since when has it been all over town? And why did you label the letter addressed to Quinn Martindale as undeliverable if you knew who he was? Is."

"Well, now, I didn't know yesterday, did I? I didn't know until I had a date last night with a certain person who works in the police building. So maybe I exaggerated on the 'all over town' bit."

More startling: Ben was dating. Maybe he could give me some advice. Back to the leak—who worked in the police building besides cops? Before I could ask, Ben went on.

"And before you ask, I'm not saying who told me exactly."

That didn't mean I couldn't try to guess. "Someone on the cleaning crew?"

Ben gave me a look and pressed his lips together. "Did you want to hear my Halloween story or not?"

"A clerical person?" The only administrator I'd seen was too young for Ben, but who was to say? I ran images through my head. What older women had I seen in the station? "One of the civilian volunteers? The lady who tags abandoned cars?"

Ben made a move to leave. I put my hand on his bony arm. "Okay, I'm sorry. I want to hear the Halloween story."

"It was trick-or-treat night, you know. A bunch of teenagers from the south end of town had TP'd the place, sprayed the front door with some kind of green monster paint, I can't remember what else, but every old trick in the book. Quinn had only been in town about a month as I recall, and he happened by and saw me trying to clean up out there. To make things worse, the kids had hosed the place and the TP was soaking wet." Ben shook his head as if he was still trying to figure out what would make anybody think that was funny.

"And Quinn helped you clean up?"

"Yup. A lot of other good citizens walked on by and said 'Tsk tsk,' you know, but Quinn rolled up his sleeves and dug in. Didn't even ask. Then, this year, he suggested we take some seats and a bowl of candy out there and stay as long as we could without freezing to death. It worked, too. We gave out some candy, and then when it got late and we had to go in, Quinn took turns with me driving by once in a while until we figured the little monsters were all in bed."

"I'm glad to hear that."

I had no trouble picturing Quinn as a good neighbor, pitching in where he could help, making an effort to fit in without being ostentatious.

And I imagined Ben would be very grateful. On the whole, Ben was easy to please and things were pretty simple for him. I had to remember that the next time he irked me.

While Ben and I were bonding during this little break, I took the opportunity to broach a subject I'd been thinking about since I heard the newscast in the coffee shop. The cameras had caught the police department flag waving in the breeze, always a great photo op. The shot jogged my memory: Postmasters had the authority to fly the flag at half-mast to commemorate the death of a local citizen. I remembered a time when I was in the third grade and another teacher, not my own, died after three decades of service in the school district. I couldn't remember details like time of day or why I happened to see it, but I know I was moved by the special gesture of lowering the flag in her memory.

"I think we should wait a bit," Ben said, when I brought it up now, suggesting we might honor the late Wendell Graham that way. I had the feeling he'd have rushed to say yes for Quinn Martindale.

"You're not sure?"

Ben twisted his wide mouth, awakening the surrounding wrinkles. "We should just wait, is all."

"Because of the way Wendell died? Because it was obviously a crime?" I asked, not one to back down easily. Or because he didn't offer to repaint the front door? I wondered. Ben shrugged.

I hadn't researched the practice sufficiently to know whether the manner of death or the popularity of the deceased mattered, as far as the flag-lowering rules went. Wendell was a native son who'd lived and worked in the community all his life. Wasn't that enough?

"What if Wendell was involved in some activities that he shouldn't have been?" Ben asked. "Something that led to him getting shot? We should wait and see."

My head snapped up from its relaxed position. "Do you know something like that about Wendell?" I asked.

"What if? That's all I'm saying."

"Are we talking about shady dealings? Is there someone you suspect of killing him?"

"Never mind," he said.

"If you know anything, Ben, you need to tell Sunni." When Ben didn't respond, I made it more clear, as if he might not know who Sunni was. "The police, Ben. If you know something they don't about a motive for killing Wendell, or anything at all, you need to tell them."

I was about to lay an obstruction of justice charge on him, when the front door opened. Ben unfolded his long legs, got up faster than I could even think of moving, and leaned over the counter, ready to serve.

"Evening, folks," said Officer Ross Little. Only when I stood did I see that Ross had arrived with a dolly piled high with phone books.

"What do we have here?" Ben asked. I realized that I'd never mentioned the missing books to Ben. He probably thought I'd handed out every last one of them while he wasn't around. "Do you know anything about this, Cassie?"

"I'll explain later," I said.

Ben looked relieved to have been handed an excuse to avoid my probing of who he was dating and what he might know about Wendell Graham. So much so that he didn't pay much attention to the oddity of our phone directories being in the custody of a cop.

"I'm on my way home and offered to drop them off," Ross said. "Sorry you had to wait so long."

Ben, not the least bit flustered, opened the door between the lobby and the retail counter. "Just wheel them over there if you would and the new postmaster will take care of them." His chuckle brought on a cough, as usual.

"There's more outside in my truck," Ross said, spilling the books over the floor in their proper corner.

Ben and Ross made two trips to his truck. When the third load was delivered, Ben suggested Ross just leave them on the dolly. "We'll return it in the morning," he said.

"Sure you don't want me to help you stack them a little better?" Ross asked.

"Matter of fact, I was just leaving." Ben put on his jacket and tipped his cap toward me. "Night, Postmaster," he said with a grin. "I'll walk you out, Officer."

Whatever dirt Ben had on Wendell wasn't going to be revealed today. Maybe I should have brought more cupcakes. I still hadn't gotten the hang of the North Ashcot system of bartering.

A small rush of customers forced me to ignore the newly returned phone books and take care of immediate business. Besides, I needed a stretch of quiet time first, to count the directories, check the bundles for any damage, and generally welcome them back, before handing them out.

A phone call came in while I was putting through a medium-sized flat-rate parcel. The caller ID was the NAPD. Priority interrupt. I collected high-schooler Joanie Campbell's money for a sheet of LOVE stamps with one hand, smiled at her, and answered Sunni's call with the other hand. I figured a teenager would surely understand this kind of multitasking.

"Sorry I didn't get to warn you about Quinn, Cassie. It's been a wild couple of days," Sunni said.

"I second that."

"A big-name attorney stomped into my office and showed me some paperwork and demanded that Quinn be released. To tell you the truth, I didn't give him much of an argument. We really had nothing, and I decided that Quinn on the loose might lead us to something. He's in trouble for changing his name without going through proper channels with Social Security and the motor vehicles registry, et cetera, but that's not really our problem."

This was the moment when I could have mentioned the quasi-UAA letter I had in my possession. But I found a way out in her comment that Quinn Martindale was no longer her problem.

"Thanks for that update, Sunni," I said, and agreed that we needed to have lunch soon.

So many potential dates—Sue and Beth, to make up for leaving me stranded; Tim Cousins, who'd banged on my CLOSED sign; Derek Hathaway, who'd rather talk to me and follow me than have tea; a redheaded stalker who might or might not be a reporter; Gert Corbin, of our governing board, who wanted to officially welcome me to town and probably pitch her anti-betting agenda; and now the chief of police. If they all came through, I'd be one busy postmaster.

After Sunni's call, I had to handle an unpleasant incident. A woman I'd never seen before came to the counter with a postal money order for eight hundred dollars. I told her I was sorry, but I didn't have that much cash on hand.

"Of course you do," she said. She tapped the multicolored check-sized piece of paper. "These can be cashed for up to one thousand dollars."

Ordinarily, I would have inspected the paper for legitimacy—the Benjamin Franklin watermarks and the vertical thread of the letters "USPS" and other telltale features—but I didn't have the cash to begin with, so it was a moot point whether her check was legitimate.

"I'm sorry," I said again. "So many people pay with credit

cards these days, I just don't have eight hundred dollars in cash."

She leaned over the counter. If she had been any larger or fitter, I would have felt physically threatened, but she was a short, dumpy woman, older than me by a lot, with wiry gray hair. The only weapons I could see were a handful of long nails in a too-bright shade of red, now shaking at me.

"This is no way to run a business," she told me. "I waited until the end of the day. I don't believe you don't have enough money on hand by now. You're simply a poor manager."

I felt compelled to ask why on earth I would want to keep the cash from her. Instead I thought of all my training in "Dealing With Difficult People," so seldom used until this moment. A small line had formed and I was eager to settle the matter. I pulled out an empathetic smile, suggested that she could visit the bank two blocks away, which would surely have the cash, and offered to call them for her to confirm that they were adequately supplied to meet her needs. As she continued to rail against my management abilities, I handed the unhappy woman a sheet with information on filing complaints. I explained that she could call, fax, send a letter or an e-mail, expressing her displeasure.

She grabbed the form, turned on her heels, and nearly ran down the next customer.

The best part of the incident was that every customer after her was sweeter than sweet to me and sympathized with what I had to deal with.

"You were so patient with her. I'd have clocked her," said a male customer.

"Poor dear. You didn't need that," said a female customer.

And so it went, down the line, with more praise for my management skills than I could have hoped for. In all my years interacting with customers of the post office, the number of such incidents was negligible and the support that followed was always heartening.

The rest of the workday was not as exciting. There were no more questions about my part in the big news feature, just a few expressions of surprise and regret at the death of someone they knew. I assumed that everyone who could had watched the broadcast and heard Sunni's announcement.

Still, when it was time to close up, I wasn't looking forward to leaving the building, lest I be accosted by reporters.

I made it to my car, which was parked around the back of the building. No sign of stalkers, or well-meaning "friends" like Tim Cousins or Derek Hathaway. Given yesterday's town-meeting atmosphere, I wondered where everyone was today. Either they no longer cared about the murder victim in our town, or they'd heard his identity and lost interest. Neither option was one to be proud of.

It also occurred to me that the citizens might be staying home, behind their lace curtains, in case the killer was out and about, seeking his next victim. I locked my car doors and drove off.

I still had Quinn's letter in my purse, all my fuss over what to do with it futile. But now that Quinn was free of police custody, and the whole town, in Ben's words, knew his identity, things were less complicated in a way. I didn't have to worry about sneaking correspondence in to a virtual prisoner. If I could find him, that is. I'd tried his cell phone but it went to voicemail each time.

A few blocks past the police station, I took a sharp left and slowed down as I approached Ashcot's Attic, the antiques store where Quinn worked. The store was dark, a CLOSED sign in the window and their distinctive distressed blue delivery truck in the driveway. I guessed it wouldn't be good advertising for an antiques shop to own a shiny new vehicle.

A small white-panel van with a telltale satellite dish on its roof was parked under a maple tree a few yards from the front door of the shop. The streetlights and the leaves and trunk of the maple made a strange pattern of shadows on the lawn and the storefront. Creepy, almost. Maybe Ben's Halloween story had affected me in more ways than he had in mind. Or maybe it was the young redheaded nag. Or the strange run-in with Derek Hathaway.

I drove on by.

I considered going to Quinn's home, but figured there'd be a news crew there also—everyone but Quinn himself. They didn't have a lot to do, reporters Erin and Rick. The show kept them busy with a book group; sports coverage of local teams; reports by reps from the water district board; civic events and announcements. A murder trumped them all, even off-track betting, and I had to remember that news was their job—we loved news people when we needed them, dissed them when our sensibilities were offended. Not too different from other professions, now that I thought of it.

I made a U-turn and headed to my home. I parked down the block and walked the rest of the way. I figured I could slip between neighboring houses and enter my own through the back door. Time to find out how smart reporters were.

At the end of my street, I saw a familiar white van with a satellite-bedecked roof. Either Channel 30 had a fleet of vans, or the same crew was following me. For a minute I considered knocking on the panel door and confronting them.

Then mental exhaustion kicked in, and instead, I ducked behind an old clapboard cottage and made my way through the two backyards before mine. I entered my home, found my glide rocker with the help of only a hallway night-light, and plopped down on its seat. Safe, at last. One would think I was the one who had spent twenty hours in jail.

It didn't take long for intense curiosity to overcome my low energy, and I ventured farther into my living room. I approached the front windows, pausing at each step to listen for sounds of outdoor activity. I pushed my fingers through slats in the blinds to separate two of them, wondering if the van had moved closer to the house.

No van. No redhead on the loose. Something worse. A man, in shadows, sitting on my front steps, just below the porch.

I pulled back my fingers and stepped away from the window so quickly I nearly fell backward over a small footstool and knocked my black UMass captain's chair against the wall. I took a breath, and moved to the other side of the bay windows, peering through a lower set of slats, to see if anyone had heard what seemed like a commotion inside my house.

My visitor hadn't moved. I studied his shape. Broad shoulders, slightly hunched over, hands between his knees, a ball cap on his head.

Scott James. Quinn Martindale.

I sat on the chair and leaned against the college seal on its crown, as if all the wisdom and learning in the generations of alumni at UMass could come to my aid and help me decide what to do about the man on my stoop. He'd committed fraud at least, possibly murder; he'd stolen from me and, technically, every post office box holder in town. Yet he'd helped Ben clean up a Halloween mess and had been nothing but a perfect lunch date. Until the police had come for him.

I weighed the pros and cons. And opened my front door.

I took one look at Quinn and knew what he wanted most. I couldn't do much about the slump in his shoulders, but I could at least help him wash away a night without sleep.

"Let me get you some towels," I said. "The bathroom's back there on the left."

"That bad, huh?"

"Bad enough."

I dug out the largest sweatshirt I owned, a gray XXL with a maroon UMASS MINUTEMEN logo on the front, and added it to the pile of towels. Pushing the limits of the extent to which I could accommodate a male guest.

"Can't tell you how much I appreciate this," he said. "I'll be out in ten."

Quinn emerged on time, presenting a whole different picture. I'd turned up the heat, poured two mugs of coffee, and placed a plate of cookies on the coffee table in the living room. "Slim pickings," I said.

"I'm the one who barged in on you."

"I opened the door."

"I know you want some answers," he said.

"It's not my business, really."

"I'd like to make it your business, if you don't mind."

I gulped. As a pickup line, that wasn't too bad, especially from a guy who was freshly showered.

8

Here was my chance to ask Quinn, the former Scott James, all the questions that had been nagging at me: about his mother's status as a murder suspect; about his own connection to the murder of Wendell Graham, my onetime boyfriend; about the first-class letter staring at me through leather every time my gaze landed on my purse.

I seemed frozen by his offer to give me some answers. I invited him to have a seat across from me, the coffee table between us, while I prepared my queries.

My first question should have been, "Who are you?" but instead, I came up with what seemed to be the most trivial incident, but had been the beginning of the weirdness of the last two days.

"Why did you go to all that trouble to steal my phone books?" I asked. I could see that Quinn was as surprised as I was at my choice of opening, but he jumped right in.

"It was stupid, Cassie."

"I'm all ears."

"I've been trying to keep a low profile. Actually, to erase all evidence of Quinn Martindale. For now. I took the identity of someone who died decades ago. You'd be amazed how easy it is, once you start clicking around the Internet. You just find someone deceased, with no family, get a new phone, and start there. I thought it was going to be for a short time, so I didn't have to bother building a whole background. Ever wonder why I keep to the speed limit so carefully? I don't want to get pulled over and have to show my Quinn Martindale license."

"I hadn't noticed."

"Sorry, of course not. You've never asked to see my license. And you've only ridden with me once."

"And that wasn't even a round-trip," I said, trying to lighten the mood, put him at ease.

"Thanks for reminding me how that trip ended."

"Now I'm sorry."

He waved away my apology. "A couple of weeks ago, I found out that Fred, my boss at the shop, without asking me, put my photo in an ad he took out in the new directory, the issue that was going to be delivered to the post office last week."

"Without running it by you first?"

"He thought he was doing me a favor, and complimenting me. Said he needed a new cute face"—here Quinn blushed, I was relieved to see—"someone that might appeal to the younger generation. He'd taken a few pictures with his cell phone at an open house we had, and apparently I wasn't vigilant enough and he caught me smiling at a customer."

"At least he didn't put it on a supermarket cart," I said, and hoped I wasn't being overly frivolous.

"It's a good thing there aren't any bus stops in North Ashcot, or I might have found myself on a bench," he said, adding to the humor.

"Or on the bus itself, big as life."

Quinn took a long breath; I felt he was reliving the last week or so of anguish. "I thought if I took all the directories, well, no one would really miss them, and I'd have my anonymity a little while longer. At that point I should have taken off, left town instead. Another new name, whatever, but I was getting settled here, feeling comfortable. And I'd just met you."

I could feel a hard ball of suspicion forming in the pit of my stomach, a frown taking shape on my face. I may even have shaken my head at the part about meeting me, flashing back to the lovely feminine penmanship on the letter now in my purse. Quinn leaned forward, his arms on his thighs, one hand grasping the other. I sat back and folded my arms across my chest, protecting myself from his sincere look, wrapped in my sweatshirt. He pulled back, sat up straight.

"Cassie, I'm not trying to play you. I know you're smart. I did a selfish thing. There was no real excuse." Quinn's voice started to crack. "The worst thing was all the trouble it caused you. I didn't think it would, but, like I said, I was stupid. And I wasn't thinking of anyone but myself."

The doorbell rang and both our heads snapped up. I seldom heard the ring at my home in the evening. Once Aunt Tess was gone, I'd had no visitors other than delivery people.

Quinn stood. "I know who that is. I hope you don't mind. While you were getting the coffee, I ordered a pizza."

"You're kidding. Pizza delivery in North Ashcot?"

"From South Ashcot, actually." He smiled. Not too symmetric a grin; just crooked enough to be interesting. "I found this place that will deliver across the border for an extra couple of dollars. They're very good, made right on the premises." As if that were the most important issue we needed to address at the moment. He got out his wallet, put two twenties on the table, and stood. "That should cover it. If you don't mind, I'm going to make myself scarce."

What kind of alternate universe had I fallen into? Then and there I had a mind to call the police. How could I be sure there was a pizza on the other side of my door and not an accomplice? A hit man. The real Scott James. The real Quinn Martindale. Wendell Graham's killer. All of the above.

I wrestled with a shiver of fear as Quinn walked away from me, crossed the living room floor, through the small dining room, and settled himself at my kitchen table, out of the line of sight of the front door. I picked up the cash and engaged my slat-opening fingers again at the window. I had no view of anyone standing close to my door, but I could make out a red SUV at the curb. I squinted at a logo on the side and an enormous, plastic slice of pizza on the roof. It looked benign, if not classy. I couldn't imagine a hit man going to all that trouble.

I opened the door. The aroma of tomato, sausage, and cheese hit my nostrils and I knew I'd made the right decision.

"Extra-large pizza, four sections of toppings." The announcement came from a pimply-faced kid in a red company parka that matched the truck. He looked past me at the empty (he thought) house and down at the huge box. "Is this the right place?"

I nodded. "I'm having a party later."

"Cool," pronounced "kewell." He seemed happy with his tip and bounded down the stairs two at a time.

Quinn carried the unwieldy box to the kitchen table and I sat there with my mystery guest. In the short time it took me to say, "This was a great idea. Thanks," Quinn consumed an entire slice of pizza from the first section, the "everything" topping. I would have bet that he hadn't had a normal meal since our tiny cucumber sandwiches yesterday. Neither had I, come to think of it. I took a slice from the second section, the extra cheese and mushroom quadrant.

I wanted to hear more. We still hadn't gotten to the part where his mother may or may not have killed someone. I allowed Quinn one more slice and a coffee refill before asking him to continue.

"I'm from Northern California, where I was born—Quinn Martindale's my birth name, by the way—in a town north of San Francisco, across the Golden Gate Bridge. My mother lived in the middle of the city. She's had a rough life, starting with my father, who died a long time ago, killed by his own reckless driving." He took a swallow of coffee before continuing. "Enter my stepfather, I guess you'd call him, even though it was a good thing he had no fathering to do. He married my mother about three years ago and turned out to be just another version of my father, with the added attraction of being a gambling addict. Then last year, he was found murdered—stabbed so many times, they were sure it was a crime of passion, and my mother was charged.

She's now in custody, awaiting trial. I ran away to avoid testifying. If they can't find me, they can't call me."

My facial expression was out of my control. I tried for an empathetic look; a supportive smile; a kind, patient attitude. But I was sure my eyes or the muscles around my mouth gave away how upset I was. I wanted to know why he wouldn't testify. Wouldn't he be eager to help clear his mother? Or did he know something to the contrary?

"Which 'they' are you trying to avoid? The prosecution or the defense? And why?" I asked, before I could stop myself. "Why won't you testify?" I hadn't meant for it to come out so much like an accusation.

Quinn pressed his palm against the side of his head, as if trying to keep it together. I wished I could help him. "You know what? I shouldn't even be talking to you about this. In fact, can we move on? Can you trust me for now, until I can figure out the best course of action for my mother?"

"But . . ."

"Please?" He put his hand on mine and pulled it away immediately, even though I'd made no attempt to move it. Unless my mental waffling showed outwardly. "Let me just say that I need to keep you out of it, for everyone's sake, including yours."

I took a deep, frustrated breath. "Can you at least tell me what this has to do with Wendell Graham?"

Quinn threw up his hands. "I wish I knew. I swear. I'm telling you straight out; I'm not holding back. I have no idea why they questioned me about Wendell Graham. I'm not sure I ever met the man, unless he was in a line with me getting coffee or, you know, crossing in front of me while I was at a stop sign."

"He was found with a piece of paper with both your names on it. Why? How would he know your real name?"

He took a breath, sounding equally frustrated. "I. Have. No. Idea." His knees bounced in a nervous way with each beat, each word of the sentence. He didn't speak in an angry tone; it was at a slow pace, as if trying to find the answer. He looked at me. "Do you believe me on that?" he asked, his eyes pleading.

"I do. And I guess the chief of police believes you, too. Otherwise she wouldn't have released you."

Quinn reached for his third slice of pizza; I was finished eating, having practically inhaled my slice.

"She's okay with it as long as I stay in town, but that's fine," he said. "I'm grateful to that lawyer, wherever he's from. Edmund Morrison, I think he said."

"You didn't hire him?"

He raised his eyebrows. "Me? From what the cop told me, his watch cost more than the monthly budget for the whole force. He's from some big firm in New York."

"Did he interview you?"

Quinn shook his head. "He came in for, like, five minutes, gave me his card, which I have to locate, now that I think of it, and told me not to talk to anyone without him present, and left."

"Did that seem strange to you?"

"More than strange, but here I am, instead of in jail, so I'm not complaining. I should have called him immediately when I got out, but in a way I'm afraid to. What if it was a mistake and they put me back in custody? On the other hand, I don't want to be slapped with a bill that will require me to sell my car, if I can head it off." He finished his coffee and started on the cookies. I'd forgotten how much men as big as Quinn and my dad could put away in one sitting. "I plan to call him as soon as I find the card. And catch my breath," he continued. "These two days have been a roller-coaster ride. Or maybe a crazy trip to one of those carnival fun houses."

I knew what he meant.

My phone rang, making this one of the busiest evenings of the season that didn't involve work. Was more pizza on the way? Dessert? I checked the caller ID, excused myself, and walked into the living room with the phone. I said hello to the chief of police. Alas, no gelato delivery.

"Hey, Cassie, just checking in. Sorry again that you had to make the trip to the station for nothing."

My gaze fell on Quinn, sitting a few yards away in my kitchen, one leg resting on the other knee, sipping from a mug of coffee. "No big deal. It gave me a chance for a nice little walk."

"Did Ross tell you about the fancy lawyer who got him out? Very top tier." ·

"Uh, yes, he did." Why did I feel I was withholding information?

"You sound like you have some company. I'll let you go."

"Well . . ."

"It's okay. Just wanted to check in. Mind if I stop by with my lunch tomorrow? My coffee's better but your place is quieter. At least at noon."

"That would be great, and I'll start with a fresh pot, I promise."

"Just kidding about the coffee. See you then. Have a good evening."

I hung up, as nervous as if I'd lied under oath.

* * *

Quinn and I moved back to the living room and took the same easy chairs across from one another, the coffee table between us. The street outside was quiet. Not that it was ever as busy as traffic on the Fenway in front of my Boston apartment, but on some nights here teens turned out to cruise the neighborhood. Reveling, North Ashcot–style.

We shared a little more of our lives beyond phone books and murder investigations, and Quinn became the first person in town to learn about Adam.

"Looks to me like you miss Boston more than you miss Adam," he said, after sharing one innocuous back-home anecdote of his own.

"What makes you say that?"

He looked around, pointing here and there. I followed his direction, from the paperweight on an end table—a glass encased rendering of the Swan Boats on the Charles River—to a framed certificate verifying that I'd bought a brick for the courtyard at the USS Constitution Museum to a coffee table book on the collection at the Museum of Fine Arts.

"And then there's the mirror in the bathroom."

"With the Plymouth lighthouse scene across the top."

"And the pens, the Old North Church magnet on the fridge, the mugs—"

"I get it," I said, laughing. "And"—I pointed to a small bowl of red candy-covered nuts—"you forgot the Boston Baked Beans."

He popped a couple of "beans" in his mouth. "Always loved these. Didn't know they were really from Boston."

"A lot of the things you're pointing out were gifts," I

explained, bordering on defensive. "I'm showing my appreciation by displaying them."

"Are they from Adam?"

"No. Good point."

From what I'd told him, Quinn had deduced correctly that my home now reflected my taste and not Adam's. In fact, most of the Boston paraphernalia had been hidden away in my apartment, since the items only contributed to Adam's disapproval of my touristy décor, which was even worse in his mind than my college-dorm taste. More grist for my "Letting Go" mill.

For his part, Quinn kept to his pattern of engaging me in stories about jobs after college, and threw me only small bones now and then about what his life was like pre–North Ashcot.

He told me one typical frat story from his college days in Berkeley, and admitted to his part in keeping the tie-dye T-shirt tradition alive on campus. He then pointed to a small toy mail truck among my windowsill ornaments and asked for my favorite post office story. Lucky for him, I loved to tell mail tales.

Around eleven, we decided it should be safe for Quinn to sneak out and head home. Even so, I helped him work out an inner belt route from the back of my house to where he said he'd left his car. It was a cold night so we doubted anyone would have windows open or be sitting on a porch.

"Let's hope I'm not back at the police station, arrested for trespassing," he said. I took it as a good sign that we could joke about his situation, at least for now. There was still the matter of who murdered Wendell Graham, and I was sure Quinn wouldn't feel really comfortable until that mystery was solved. Neither would I.

"One more thing," I said. I'd extracted the errant letter from my purse as Quinn was putting on his jacket, stuffing his arms, still encased in my UMASS sweatshirt, into the sleeves. "I forgot to give you this. It came to the post office yesterday, when you were . . ." I searched for a neutral word. "Unavailable."

"Forgot" wasn't exactly the right word either, but every time I'd thought of it this evening, I found an excuse not to hand over the envelope. The pizza would get cold, for example, or the phone might ring.

Quinn took the envelope from me, glanced at it, and put it in his jacket pocket with a simple, "Thanks."

What? Just like that? Sharing time was over? Didn't I deserve to know what I'd been sweating about for so many hours? If I'd known I was going to be shut out of this letter-opening event, I might have kept the piece of mail longer and made a more active attempt to identify its source. Maybe even used the steam-from-a-kettle technique my college roommate had taught me.

"I hope I haven't inconvenienced you by forgetting to give you that letter sooner," I said. *Hint, hint.*

"No. I'm the one who should thank you for letting me drop in tonight. You saved my sanity." He laughed and tilted his head. "I think. I know I had a really nice time, in any case."

"Me, too." *Except for these last two minutes.*

"Do we dare try lunch tomorrow?"

"Sure, but maybe we should drive separately," I said.

Quinn smiled, and went down my back steps. At the

bottom, he turned and touched his cap, a salute of sorts. I felt like a teenager ushering her boyfriend out the back door before her parents caught on.

It made no sense, but, in spite of the way he kept things close to his vest, I trusted Quinn, and felt closer to him than to anyone else in North Ashcot.

Besides, now I had a few more details than I had earlier today. I could narrow my search a bit with confirmation on the place: San Francisco; a date: a year ago; and a scenario: a woman accused of stabbing her husband multiple times. Curiosity was an annoying addiction.

After a half hour, I'd ruled out the newlyweds in a town north of San Francisco who'd attempted to kill each other, and an older couple who'd gone on a shooting rampage. A better possibility reared its head: the case of a woman who lived in the Sunset District of San Francisco, close to the Pacific Ocean, who had been taken into custody when her husband was found in nearby Golden Gate Park, the victim of multiple stab wounds. Police were looking for anyone with information. Her adult son was unavailable for comment.

Aha. I was sure I'd just shared a pizza with her adult son. It took me more time than it should have to realize that the stabbing had occurred only last week. Wrong time frame. I closed my laptop and called myself a failure at effectively utilizing search engines.

I was headed to my bedroom when I remembered I hadn't checked my messages. My routine had been thrown off by the busy social evening. And it wasn't over yet. I had three messages and three more lunch invitations. Derek Hathaway was "eager to catch up" with me after all these years; Tim Cousins finally had a little free time to give me "a proper welcome to our little town," as did Selectwoman Gert Corbin whose secretary had called: Could someone please call the office to schedule a date? In other words, my people should call her people. I didn't think so.

Two unappealing men and one woman who didn't care enough to handle her own lunch dates. No thank you. I'd been meaning to get rid of the landline handed down by Aunt Tess—who needed them anymore?— and now moved the chore to the top of my list.

Another fitful night. Last night, questions had kept me up; tonight, it was some of the answers that wouldn't let me sleep. I'd almost dozed off when I realized I'd double booked myself for lunch—with Sunni, and then with Quinn. Even aside from the annoying message-leavers, my social life was booming. If only it wasn't all wrapped up in law enforcement, murder, and legal issues.

The last dream I remembered on Wednesday morning was another twisted scenario where my phone books had been delivered with a special postmark that would one day be ranked high value on the collectibles list. I shouldn't have been surprised, since I'd read a blog article right before falling asleep. The article chronicled a recent convention of postmark collectors, a group who were less well-known than stamp collectors, but no less avid. I needed to monitor my bedtime reading more carefully.

One of the collectors in the (real) photograph I'd seen, looking a lot like Quinn, snuck into my dream and walked away with phone books that had an outline-type postmark in the shape of California. Never mind that there was no postmark on the real phone books, or that nothing else in the dream made sense.

In that way, my dreams matched my real life.

9

The first thing I had to take care of on Wednesday morning was the disposition of the newly recovered phone books; the second was to unbook my lunch date with either Quinn or Sunni.

The first was easy. I spent about fifteen minutes before opening the doors, making sure the directory count was correct at two hundred and fifteen books, and that none were damaged to the extent that they couldn't be used. I'd checked the offensive ad for Ashcot's Attic and felt bad that I didn't have time to open each one and scratch Scott's name from the listing. I did note that his boss had been right: Scott James was definitely cute.

Following strict policy, I should have put a notice in each post office box, asking the customer to come to the counter, where I'd hand over a directory. But I decided that, since I was already a few days late with distribution, I'd cut that corner. I placed a pile of books on the counter with a sign that invited box holders to take one, and replenished the pile through the morning. I trusted North Ashcot citizens not to cheat and take a book if they weren't box renters, or to take more than one book. After all, our crime rate was negligible. Except for this week's murder.

The second chore, straightening my lunch calendar, was harder to accomplish. Sunni or Quinn? How to make the decision? I could decide based on chronology—"first come, first served"—and keep my date with Sunni, the first to ask. Or I could follow the "keep on the good side of the law" principle, which still brought me to lunch with Sunni. Factoring in the nosiness principle— did I want to know more about Quinn and his life before North Ashcot, or more about the current investigation into Wendell's murder? That line of thought ended in a tie.

My final choice: I'd start with Sunni, and if she wanted to talk about her quilts or the kite festival instead of the murder investigation, I'd plead upset stomach and call Quinn as backup. The fact that it took so much thinking on my part to arrange lunch was a clue that I didn't get out much.

To complicate matters, my counter was very busy for the first half hour or so and I didn't have a minute to make a call to either of my potential dates.

Continuing the trend of animal week, Mrs. Spenser's cockatoo had an accident on the table that held the postal forms, requiring special cleanup. Happily, Mrs. Spenser's young granddaughter offered to take care of the mess. I handed her cleaning supplies and a pile of new forms and she assured me we'd be back in business in no time.

When Sally Aldritch came by with another large "media

mail" box for her son, I gave her a look that sent her ducking back and out the door. I figured she thought I was giving her a sign that in our midst today there was a mystery shopper—like an undercover cop, only a postal worker who'd come to check on operations and potential postal code violations. I wouldn't have been sorry if Sally had been afraid that she'd be led out in handcuffs. Maybe the frightening image would keep her from further testing my leniency.

I could have told Sally about the time I was enlisted to monitor a certain post office with respect to the conduct of a postmaster, only to learn that he'd been living in the building. It was a large enough facility that he had his own office, and he slept, ate, and lived in that room after hours. The stiff penalty might have sobered Sally to the realities of trying to put one over on the USPS.

The last customer before a break in the line was none other than my least favorite redhead in her green parka.

Wanda Cox came to the counter with a flat-rate envelope that I suspected was empty, a prop that she was willing to pay for to get my attention. If there were a postal inspector in my office that day, I knew he wouldn't care about someone willing to spend more money than necessary. After the transaction, real or not, Wanda did her best, given her small, short frame, to lean over for an intimate conversation. I noticed for the first time how young she was, probably nine or ten years my junior.

"Look, how about I buy you lunch, and we talk, just for as long as it takes to eat a salad. Huh? Can you give me that?" she asked.

"I'm booked. In fact, I'm double booked." It felt good to say that with a free and clear conscience.

"After work then. Coffee?"

"I'm booked." Conscience almost clear, since I planned to have lunch with Sunni and coffee with Quinn, if it worked out for him.

She slid her card toward me.

"I have one already."

"Did you even look at it?"

By reflex, I looked down, ready to say, "Yes, now go away." This time I read the name. Wanda Graham Cox.

"Please go"—I looked again—"Wanda Graham? Are you—?"

She nodded, seeming on the verge of tears. "I'm Wendell Graham's little sister and I need your help."

My knees went limp and I had to grab the counter to keep my balance. The little girl who constantly lost her stuffed animals was back. How could I help her this time?

I took advantage of the break in the line to make two calls, one to Sunni and one to Quinn, cancelling lunch with both, through their voicemail. I fumbled around with phrases about something that had come up unexpectedly and I'd call later to reschedule and sorry, sorry, sorry.

I'd agreed to meet Wanda shortly after noon at Betty's Diner, even though there was a good chance that Sunni would end up there with an alternate lunch partner. I wasn't worried that Quinn would appear in that public a place any time soon. He'd taken home the leftover pizza from last night and I imagined it would be gone by noon if he hadn't eaten it already. A smile crossed my face as I thought of our impromptu dinner, quickly followed by a frown as I recalled giving up the UAA letter without the satisfaction of learning its contents.

At noon, I closed up and struck out for Betty's, in the opposite direction from the police department, but not much longer a walk for me.

As the only eatery in town that wasn't fast food, Betty's was line-out-the-door busy. Wisely, they'd recently added a small takeout annex next door, and provided seating outside in a covered area. Tall heat lamps stationed around the perimeter made the patio bearable most of the year, including today. The only things outdoor diners lacked were the signature red Naugahyde booths and throwback jukebox that the indoor folk enjoyed.

I sat across from Wanda and searched her face for the little girl I knew, the one with skinny legs who showed up whenever her mom needed a break. It was clear that she loved to be with her big brother and his posse whenever she could. She'd wander into the Grahams' basement rec room and happily serve us sodas and snacks. Wendell feigned annoyance, but it was clear that the two shared a special bond. And the rest of us just thought she was cute, sometimes taking advantage of her good humor to send her on an errand or ask her to sweep the field before a pickup game at the park. Water girl. Bat girl. Errand girl. Groupie. That was Wanda.

"You're remembering when I was a kid and pestered you and the gang," Wanda said, catching me in the act of putting braids on her again.

"I suppose so," I admitted.

"People always said Wendell and I looked the most alike of all us," she said. "There were four of us, but Wendell and I . . ." She stopped to catch her breath.

"I remember." It was a strange feeling, eighteen years later, to be meeting the sister of a high school boyfriend, let alone one who had been murdered. While we waited for our salads, I apologized for brushing her off.

"It's just that the reporters wouldn't leave me alone, and I really had nothing to tell them," I explained. "I thought you were one of them."

"I guess I was testing you," Wanda said, playing with her paper napkin. "I had to know if I could trust you, if you were the same Cassie that I looked up to. If you were just another gossiping pseudo-friend, I wasn't going to bother. I need the old friend of Wendell's who was willing to play my silly games."

"I lost my teddy bear," I said, mimicking a kid's voice, getting a big smile from her.

"I didn't want to just come out and yell, 'Hey, I'm different. I'm not one of those reporters. I'm Wendell's little sister.'"

"Still, I didn't have to be snarky. I'm so sorry for your loss, Wanda. I'm sure it's a terrible sadness for all of you."

She shrugged. "The family fell apart when Mom died. Except for Wendell and me, everyone split and we hardly keep in touch. Dad moved to Florida to be with my brother Walker, and my sister, Whitney, never came back from school in Maine."

"It must be so hard for you now." Were there any other trite phrases I could call up? I could say, "I'm here for you" or "You have my sympathy," but I balked at those. At times like this I forgave all those well-meaning people who uttered the same platitudes when I lost my parents.

Wanda overlooked my clumsy words and returned to who in her family left town, when, and why. "I always thought you and Wendell would stay together," she said.

I gasped. Silently, I hoped. Then, salads to the rescue. "And, here we are," our waitress said. "Sorry for the wait."

I was grateful for the intrusion, and for the loud clatter of dishes and conversation that gave me time to recover from the thought of Wendell and me together as adults. More welcome distraction came, as patrons walked within inches of us. Betty's was set back from the sidewalk, so close to foot traffic that every passerby could reach into our bread basket and help himself to a free sesame roll if he were so inclined.

"It was a teenage thing," I said, finally. "Wendell and I actually dated only part of our senior year." I didn't mention that it ended around the time of the ugly green prom dress.

Wanda looked surprised. "It seemed like forever to me. I guess that's how things look when you're little."

"Everything's bigger, longer, more intense," I agreed. I had an image of her tugging on Wendell's shirt, asking him never to change.

For a few minutes we were silent as we dug into our salads. I snuck a glance at my watch, conscious of being on my lunch hour. I made the mistake of looking around the room at one point and caught Derek Hathaway smiling my way. He formed a phone with his thumb and little finger, and mouthed, "Call me."

I decided that mouthing, "I don't think so," back would be rude, and simply ignored the request.

Wanda still hadn't told me what she meant by needing my help, as she'd put it this morning. Maybe she'd meant simply that she needed to talk about her brother with someone who knew him at a happy time in their lives. I could do that.

"He never married, you know," Wanda said.

Uh-oh. Did Wanda think Wendell had hung around North Ashcot waiting for me to return? She seemed smarter than that, but the trauma of her brother's death could have sent her back to a time when her little-girl self envisioned the best part of her life lasting forever. Wendell and all his friends would never grow old and she and all her toys would always be loved and protected by all of us.

"What do you do, Wanda?" I asked, universal code for "Do you have a legitimate profession?" as if we were on a blind date, getting to know each other. Anything to move forward.

"I'm a graphics designer. Freelance. A lot of my work is designing covers for e-books."

"I guess I'd have known that if I'd read your business card."

We'd finished our salads, chatted about how important a cover was, even for a book that was distributed only online, and received our check. Still no clue what if anything Wanda wanted from me.

I made a move to gather my jacket and purse. "I'm due back at work," I said, though I had a half hour left. It wouldn't be the first time someone left the most important nugget until the last few minutes of a meeting or a phone call. I wanted to give Wanda an opening while I still had time to listen. "Is there something specific I can do for you, Wanda?"

Her face turned sober and she looked straight at me. The noise from the kitchen stopped, as did all the chatter around us and all the motion past our table. I heard only Wanda's pleading voice.

"Cassie, I need your help finding my brother's killer."

I blew out a deep breath. I was sorry I asked.

Wanda walked me back to the post office. It was more of a stroll, with Wanda explaining to me how busy the North Ashcot Police Department was, with a series of vandalism incidents at the high school and a rash of vehicle pranks and break-ins along the back roads.

"They're really not equipped to handle a murder case," she said. "The last one was not even in this century."

I bristled at the implication that Sunni and her force were unqualified, that they might be more concerned about graffiti and slashed tires than the murder of one of our citizens.

"Chief Smargon has the training and she has her priorities straight," I said, stretching what I actually knew for sure. "And if she needs to, she can get help from other towns, or even the state."

Wanda used her trendy short boots to kick some leaves, a favorite pastime in North Ashcot at this time of year. "I tried to tell her I suspected my brother had fallen in with some questionable characters, and she said she'd look into it, but I got the impression she was blowing me off."

Maybe Wanda wasn't so far off about Wendell's current

buddies. I thought of Ben's reluctance to consider lowering our flag in Wendell's honor and his hint of a shady involvement that should be investigated. On the other hand, "questionable characters" without names and documentation wasn't much of a lead for the police to follow.

"Is there something, or someone, in particular you think the chief should be looking at?"

"I'm not sure, but I know that Wendell had a lot more money in the last few months than he ever did. He bought a new car and he's been fixing up our old house. He still lives there and hasn't been able to afford an upgrade until, all of a sudden, he's hiring carpenters, redoing the bathrooms. I have my own place, but I go to the old homestead pretty often and I see the difference."

"Maybe he got a raise or a promotion, or . . ."

She shook her head. "I'm talking very high-end stuff. He couldn't make that kind of money working for the phone company. And it's certainly not an inheritance."

"You really think your brother was breaking the law in some way?"

She kicked another leaf. "Wendell always felt he was the loser in the family. It was such a letdown for him after being so popular in high school. Whitney and Walker went off to college and now they have really good careers and families. Even I make more than he did, though my little foray into marriage"—she spread her palms—"thus the Cox on my business card, didn't work out so well." Wanda took a long breath, perhaps revisiting her marriage. "Believe me, I don't want to think Wendell was into something illegal. It's taken me a long time to look at things realistically, but now that he's been"—

she stopped, as if unable to say the word—"murdered, I have to consider that might be why."

It was a lot for a little sister to bear. It was even a lot for a former-if-brief girlfriend to think about. "Is there anyone new in his life, someone who might have enticed him into a scheme of some kind?"

It took all the limited word power I had to dance around crime-related words like "bribes," "kickbacks," "payoffs," "fraud."

"He didn't have much of a social life at all. The only person I can think of is an old classmate. They weren't especially friendly in high school, but he's been seeing a lot of this guy in the past few months, maybe a year. His name is Derek Hathaway. I'm not saying he's a criminal or anything, but he is super rich. Did you know him?"

I managed a combination nod and frown, not too obviously skewed, I hoped. "He's in construction, isn't he?"

"He's a developer, actually, according to Wendell. He has buildings all over Albany."

Why did I not have any trouble picturing Derek Hathaway at the top of an illegal enterprise? Just because he was rich? Not fair. I found myself defending him.

"You haven't told me anything about Derek that makes me think he or your brother was engaged in anything sketchy."

"Well, that's what the cops are supposed to do, aren't they? Investigate and find out if there was anything going on?" she asked, her tone heavy with frustration.

We'd come full circle. "I'll tell you what: I'm on good terms with Chief Smargon," I said. At least before I cancelled a lunch date with her. "Do you want me to try to find out how the investigation is going?"

"Of course that would be great, but I also think you could be a big help to her. Detective work is your thing, right?"

I stopped walking and so did Wanda. "What? Where did you hear that?"

"I've kept up with you, Cassie. Every now and then, you've made the local news for some postal reason or other, and then there was that big fraud case, where you busted it wide open."

I shook my head more than was necessary for a simple no.

Wanda had latched on to my fifteen minutes of fame. A few years ago, my diligence with regard to metered mail from my office in Boston paid off. My discovery had led to the arrest of a businessman who'd been using a stolen postage meter to the tune of thousands of dollars a month. Heads rolled, people went to jail, and I was a hero. For fifteen minutes.

I had a vague memory of talking briefly to a North Ashcot reporter who called me at the time. He'd gotten the story from our public affairs office, noticed that I was from his hometown, and wanted embellishments from me. I gave him the correct spelling of my name but little else. He filled in the rest from his creative imagination.

"You've got it all wrong. I was just doing my job then," I explained to Wanda. "Checking my collection box to be sure the permit number was legitimate. Something every postmaster is supposed to do. I found a discrepancy, followed it through, and reported it. Not exactly leaping tall buildings."

"Isn't that what detective work is? I read that you had to track down where the unauthorized mail was coming from and stuff like that, too."

"Wanda, that was still a long way from a murder investigation. And your brother deserves the best investigators we have."

"That's what I'm trying to make sure happens," she said.

We'd resumed walking and had reached the post office, with a few minutes to spare before I had to open up. I turned to face Wendell's grown-up sister.

"I'm not sure what I can do about this, Wanda. I'll see what I can learn from the chief, and I'll let you know if I find out anything."

She reached over and hugged me. I felt tears coming on—for both of us. I was sorry for Wanda, for Wendell, for all the losses in our lives since we were both naïve kids.

"Thanks, Cassie. I knew you'd come through."

I gave her a comforting pat, suppressing my question. "Come through how?"

10

I couldn't remember a more distracted afternoon of retail work. Loose threads of nagging questions floated in my mind no matter what else I was doing. I came close to giving one customer twice as many commemoratives as he'd paid for, and almost charged another person forty dollars for a sheet of twenty one-dollar stamps. It was a good thing my patrons were on the ball and corrected my errors.

I felt as though someone had forced me to make a quilt, then gave me patches of fabric with threads hanging from every edge, each patch with a different, unfinished pattern. And my sewing machine was broken. If I had a sewing machine. I knew I had to stop thinking of quilting and find myself a viable hobby before Sunni swooped in and gave me one of her old machines. I'd never known a quilter who had only one sewing machine.

As I hefted another pile of phone books onto the counter, I realized the burning issue of directory theft that began the week was the only incident now resolved. Nearly fifty customers had picked up their directories this morning, none of them seriously inconvenienced or wise to the fact that their books had taken a weekend vacation trip first to Quinn's house and then to the police station.

All the loose ends in my mind began to take shape into a long list. Whether Quinn's mother had murdered her husband in San Francisco. Why Quinn ran away rather than testify. Why Wendell had Quinn's names and address in his pocket. What the UAA letter I'd passed on to Quinn contained. Whether Wendell was involved in a criminal enterprise. What Ben knew about Wendell. Who Wendell's killer was. And finally, what Derek Hathaway had to do with anything.

I stopped counting before I ran out of fingers. Since simply telling myself to mind my own business hadn't worked, I needed to attack the list. I knew Wanda expected more of me than I could give, but I owed her my best shot. It was the least I could do.

The last thread seemed the easiest to take on. After all, Derek Hathaway had already invited me to lunch. When the lobby was empty at three o'clock, I steeled myself for a call to him. I put on my headset to free my hands, and lined up chores I could do while carrying on a conversation. I found Derek's card in a pile of unsorted papers on my desk, along with the betting club literature that Selectwoman Gert and her friend Coach had handed me—all material that accumulated each time I emptied my pockets. I punched in

Derek's number in Albany, the only information on the card. No title or company name. I wondered if he had separate cards for different purposes and had judged that I needed to know only his phone number. Either that, or he assumed everyone knew who he was and what he did; all anyone needed was a line to his office.

As expected, "Hathaway Enterprises" answered and I left a message with a professional-sounding woman. I could tell she didn't recognize my name, so who knew when, if ever, the great man would receive the message and return my call? I reminded myself that the reason for contacting Derek was simply to satisfy Wanda. His was the only name she'd been able to come up with as someone tied to Wendell in his recent dealings. If lunch with Derek didn't work out, too bad. I could at least tell Wanda I'd tried.

My first customer after that break was another lunch date left hanging, Tim Cousins, who'd tried to work his way into the office on Monday night. I greeted him as he hoisted a heavy, dented tub onto my counter. He wore a paint-splattered formerly white hat and the same dark parka I'd seen him in the other night.

"Doing a favor for my friend," he said. "I think this is all legally metered and all." He paused for a long breath. "Hey, I'm sorry I hassled you Monday night. I was just, you know, freaked out by the murder."

"We all are."

"I'll bet it's really hard for Wendell's sister Wanda right now. I saw you with her today."

I nodded. "Uh-huh."

Why was I surprised? Everyone saw everyone in North Ashcot. It annoyed me, however, that in one private moment for Wendell and his killer, no one had been watching. Where were all the busybodies then? What were the chances that no one had been snooping around Wendell, collecting gossip, during the murder? Maybe they'd seen the murder take place, but were too afraid to come forward. My opinion of my fellow townsfolk was deteriorating.

"I wonder if she has a clue about who might have killed him," Tim said, leaning on the white plastic tub. "Wanda, I mean."

I extracted the tub from under Tim's arms and moved it to the floor where I could rifle through the flyers more easily. "Everything seems to be in order here," I said. "I'll have your receipt in just a minute." I was getting to be an expert at not buying into the gossip game.

A short line had formed behind Tim, and I shifted my gaze to Mrs. Hagan, the next customer. Tim moved to the side and eventually walked off. For a minute, I thought he was going to invite me to lunch first, like every other curious citizen in town. If he was put off by my surly manner, so be it. I made a point to be sweet to Mrs. Hagan, though, who was free of animals today and simply needed extra insurance on whatever was in her large padded envelope bound for a post office box in Albuquerque, New Mexico.

Mrs. Hagan was in a sharing mood. She pointed to the zip code on her envelope and said, "My niece went to college out West ages ago and never came back."

Smart girl.

The next time the phone rang, I saw NAPD in the caller ID window. *Uh-oh.* Could one be arrested for breaking a date with a police chief? I tried to remember what excuse I'd given her in my message. A vague "something's come up" I thought. I hadn't exactly lied; something really had come up.

"Did you enjoy your lunch with Wendell Graham's sister?" Sunni asked. I stuttered through another excuse until she stopped me. "Don't worry about it. Wanda can use a lot of support right now and I'm glad she feels she can talk to you. I suppose she wants me to deputize you."

Too close for comfort. I was glad to see a customer arrive at that moment. I had to put the chief of police on hold even though it might mean another punishable offense.

I dealt as swiftly as possible with a young man's special delivery letter to the Division of Motor Vehicles in Utah. Each time I sent through a personal mailing like this, it occurred to me how much trust is placed in the postal service. Many people in town knew that Josh, standing in front of me, had just returned from being best man at his friend's wedding in Salt Lake City, but how many knew that he'd had some kind of run-in with the traffic laws? I made it a point to handle the transaction with a smile and no comment, and clicked back for Sunni.

"It's busy here right now," I said, which was more of a lie than "something's come up."

"Can I take you to dinner?" I offered.

"Sure. Shall I be prepared to defend myself against incompetency charges from Wanda?"

"She's grieving," I said.

"She should focus on that."

"I'll pick you up around seven and we'll head to a place in Pittsfield. Italian okay?" I asked.

"Okay, except let me drive. I have a hard time giving up control."

"I'm good with that," I said, wondering if we were still talking about cars.

Just my luck that three more customers came in, turning my "busy" fib into the truth.

When Ben stopped by a little after three, I thought I'd messed up another date. Lately, it had been hard to keep straight which appointments I'd made and which ones I'd broken or forgotten.

"Just stopping by," he said, clearing it up for me. Ben didn't walk behind the counter, but stayed in the lobby and leaned over next to the scale.

"Something on your mind?" I asked him.

"I know it was kind of unfair of me yesterday, when I started to talk about Wendell and the whole flag-lowering issue."

"Whatever do you mean by 'unfair'?" I teased.

Ben grinned. "I don't like speaking ill of the dead, is all, and it's not as though I know anything for sure. So can we just forget I said anything?"

"Or you could tell me, and then I could forget it."

Ben laughed. "Boy, you young people sure are quick on your feet." His turn to tease.

"Will it make a difference if I tell you that his sister already has suspicions that Wendell was involved in something illegal?"

"That true?"

I crossed my heart. "You must be the only one in North Ashcot who doesn't know I had lunch with her today."

"Oh, I knew that. Timmy Cousins told me. He didn't know what you talked about, though. But what could it have been besides her brother?"

I was hoping my entrée to the subject, creds from Wanda, might entice Ben to share what he knew. If he knew more than Wanda. If Wanda was right. If. If. If. I was not enjoying the role of detective.

I had a real job to do and I was falling behind. Not that I would ever be late with my collections. But, this week so far I'd been delinquent in so many areas—keeping up with memos and updates from management, freshening the postal products displays, making sure the lobby was neat and clean, digging out the seasonal decorations. Besides those regular duties, I was still fielding queries from my former job in Boston, and had a backlog of several e-mails to answer in that regard. I was tired thinking of it all.

"Help me out, Ben. Wanda wants me to look into things. She's hurting and a few insights into her brother's life would go a long way toward helping her make sense of his death."

"I know they were pretty close, the brother and little sister," Ben said.

I nodded. "From back when I met her, when she was just a kid."

"Oh, yeah, I forgot about you and Wendell way back when."

I let out a resigned sigh and waved my hand. "That's okay. Everyone forgets I ever lived here."

Ben reached his long arm over the counter and rubbed my shoulder. "Things have been tough on you, too, huh?"

I hadn't meant to whine, but a supportive hand on my shoulder felt pretty good.

"Part of it's Boston's fault, you know," Ben said.

I looked up and met his watery blue eyes. "Meaning?"

"A lot of people around here resent Boston and the east coast of Massachusetts. If you were going to go AWOL after high school, it would have been better if you hadn't headed for Boston. Chicago would have worked. Or even some place in New Mexico."

"Because?"

"People see the capital as draining our resources and neglecting our needs. The state legislature is supposed to be for the whole state, right? But we don't get our fair share; funds are diverted to take care of Boston and Cambridge, all those famous cities to the east, as if the Berkshires and Western Massachusetts didn't exist. A few years ago, the state dismantled towns out here to reroute water for Boston. And the Big Dig? Let's not even go there."

"How come I never realized this?"

"You were a kid when you left."

"Thanks, that was useful. Now I'll just think of myself as a traitor and not expect much."

"Yup. You should have found a college in Vermont or Rhode Island. Reentry would have been easier." Ben laughed at his own wit. "Back to Wendell Graham and his hobbies."

"I don't want to pressure you, Ben. It's Sunni's job to figure all this out anyway." I moved away from the counter and took my seat at my desk. The next minute, Ben came through the door from the lobby and took the seat next to me.

"You're going to find out sooner or later. Might as well hear it from me. Though it's really not worth all this fuss."

Ben planted his feet on the side of my desk and used the leverage to push his long body back, to the limit of the swivel chair. I'd seen him perform this maneuver successfully many times, but I still worried that one day he'd push too hard and end up head over heels on the floor.

"Comfortable?" I asked.

He smiled. "Better than my expensive recliner at home, but don't tell my niece. She bought it for me. So, there was a time a while back, maybe last year, when one of the phone company customers had a problem with his bill. He was charged for two lines and he was only using one. He went on a mission to find out what happened, even though the charge for the extra line was cancelled. The guy ended up blaming Wendell for fooling around with his lines."

"You mean, like listening in?"

Ben shrugged. "Could have been."

I didn't get it. "Wendell was wire-tapping a telephone company customer?" The image of Wendell in a trench coat and fedora, prowling around undercover as a spy, wasn't working for me.

"Could have been that, or maybe using the guy's line for something else. There's a lot you can do on a rigged phone line. I remember Wendell was a wreck, but then Timmy got involved and the whole thing went away."

"Tim Cousins?"

"Yeah, I call him Timmy. He was just a little kid when I met him. I knew his father."

"Does Tim work for the phone company, too? I thought he was an architect."

"You're right. It was his father who worked on phones. Passed away now. But Timmy was having phone lines installed in his new place at the time. It all got straightened out as far as I know, and I can't imagine it had anything to do with Wendell's murder."

"I wonder why Wanda didn't know this."

"It's not like anyone went to jail or anything. It was over in a flash, is the way I remember it."

"Wanda didn't mention Tim; she thought Wendell might be involved in something with Derek Hathaway."

Ben rolled his eyes. "You mean just because he owns a piece of everything from here to Albany and back?"

"Apparently so."

The arrival of a customer cut our conversation short, but I felt we'd probably taken a small incident as far as it could go. Ben jerked up from the chair. "Hey, Buster," Ben said to one of our senior customers, "caught any big ones?"

Buster plopped his package on the counter. "Yep, and here they are. I'm sending them to my buddies in Maine, where it's too cold to fish."

Ben pretended to smell the package, and there ensued a little fishing/post office/old guy humor. I was elated when Ben turned and released me for the day. "I'll take this," he said. "In fact, I can close up if you want. You look like you could use a break."

Nothing sounded better than a little downtime before dinner with the chief of police.

* * *

I left the post office before four, carefully planning my schedule before Sunni would arrive for the drive to Pittsfield. Thanks to Ben's generosity, I'd have time for a stop at the market and a phone call to Linda. I hadn't spoken to her since Monday, and unless Wendell's murder made the news in Boston—the evil Boston, as I'd been made aware—she wouldn't know about it. The idea of forgetting everything and taking a nap also sounded good.

I had mixed feelings about dinner with Sunni. I had to figure out how to interrogate a professional interrogator without her knowing it, even though she'd already admitted she expected it. Talk about impossible. I might as well just ask her my questions outright. Either way sounded daunting. I hadn't anticipated how tricky it would be to be friends with a cop. We were still feeling our way around these obstacles and I hoped the relationship would survive.

I stopped at the market on the way home for some real food, and contingency snacks in case the trend of having visitors continued. I ended up buying a chicken, once again longing for the time when I could pick up a cooked chicken dinner, complete with mashed potatoes and vegetables, within a block of my apartment. I figured it wouldn't kill me to prepare a chicken from scratch, and it might even taste better. For backup, I piled my cart with cans of tuna, cookies, crackers, and an assortment of cheeses. I threw in some ginger ale, in case my digestive system couldn't handle the shock of good nutrition.

Each time I pulled into my driveway, as now, I had the same thought: One of these days, the garage would be free of furniture and packing boxes—some on the way in, some on the way out—and I'd be able to use my garage for its original purpose of storing a vehicle.

Loaded with bags, I walked around to my front steps, careful not to trip in the dark. I felt him before I saw him—Quinn Martindale, taking the tall paper bags from my arms.

Maybe I didn't need that downtime after all.

11

Quinn, who'd probably been waiting—for the second night in a row—on my front steps, traded me three bags of groceries for one UMASS sweatshirt, mine, looking cleaner than it ever had.

"I wanted to get the hoodie back to you as soon as I could," he said.

"I've really missed it," I said.

We fell into a comfortable banter while Quinn helped put things away. He picked up the chicken, tossed it like a football, from one hand to the other. "My specialty," he said. "Need help cooking this?"

"Sure, great," I said, then realized I already had dinner plans. "Uh . . . maybe tomorrow night?"

"Sorry," Quinn said. "I didn't mean to invite myself."

"You just beat me to it," I explained and told him my reason for putting him off this evening.

"You're having dinner with my jailer," he said, but with a smile.

I set out my newly acquired crackers and cheese and convinced him that we had time for a snack before I had to leave. And, yes, he could slip out the back if Sunni arrived early to pick me up.

"Aren't you concerned that someone might have seen your name and number in the directory? Someone at the telephone company office, for example? I would have expected you to split as soon as you learned your contact info was out there in the phone book."

"Don't leave town," he said, in a voice that I assumed was meant to sound like Sunni's. "Remember?"

"She said it like that?"

Quinn nodded. "Even though she spent some time checking out my mom's situation, and admitted that it's clear I'm not a suspect back there. I guess she's still trying to find an angle, something to charge me with until she can find a connection between me and Wendell Graham. I can see her point in a way. Why would the guy have my names on a piece of paper in his pocket?"

I didn't know, but it occurred to me that I should have asked Wanda that question. I was pretty sure I'd have a chance to talk with her further, like when she'd ask me to report on my progress as an investigator.

"Do you know Wendell's sister, Wanda, by any chance?" I asked Quinn.

"No. Should I?"

"She's a graphics designer. I thought you might have run into her. Maybe she made business cards for Ashcot's Attic?"

He shook his head. "Nothing. But, you know, this has been a good lesson for me. I'm not sure I'd leave town anyway, even if the entire North Ashcot police force weren't on my tail."

"All five of them?"

"Two at a time," he said. "The worst thing that can happen now is that someone comes from San Francisco and slaps me with a subpoena. I'll just go back and do what I have to do." My confusion must have shown, because he waved his hand. "Let me start again. My mom is innocent, but she told me things about her relationship with her new husband that might sound like she had motive. The prosecutor is bound to ask me that question and my testimony would go against her. I also have some credibility issues if Mom's defense attorney were to call me. As her son, I'm a very unreliable witness anyway, as far as a jury is concerned."

"It sounds like lose-lose."

"You got it. Which is why I'm here. To make it harder for the prosecution, which stands to gain if I have to testify. But now I'm thinking that they're not going to take a chance on cross-examining a witness when they don't know what the witness is going to say. So unless I go around telling everyone what I just told you, they have no idea how I'd answer their questions."

"No wonder I didn't go to law school. Too complicated. And meanwhile, the trial is going on?"

"It is. Leaving town, taking a new name for a while, was my idea, and I'm starting to think it wasn't a very good one. I get reports almost daily from my mom's attorney, a man I know I can trust."

"Was there anything in the letter I gave you that would help you figure out what to do?" *Hint, hint.*

"As a matter of fact, it might have. I have a contact now and I'm working it out." He might have noticed my frown and heard my sigh of frustration at the wishy-washy answer, because he added, "I know I'm being vague, but I have to be right now."

He hung his head in a way that said he was considering saying more. At least that's what I wanted to think. "Okay," I said, unable to stay ticked off.

"It's ironic, isn't it—fleeing one murder trial where I could be a witness, and I end up with the threat of another where . . ." he began.

"Where you might be the defendant," I finished. There seemed no hope of having my curiosity satisfied. At least Quinn hadn't ignored my question completely. But what was I doing entertaining someone so slick at revealing only as much as he chose? Was I that desperate for company?

"I've thought about it a lot," Quinn said, back to his initial track. "It's crazy. And I was so careful not to interact with law enforcement around here. My driver's license is the same, as I've told you. I didn't change the registration. I just made sure I kept to the speed limit, and I was lucky enough this past year not to run a light or bump into anyone. Things were going fine."

"Until a murder victim shows up with your contact information in his pocket."

Sitting across the coffee table from me, he threw open his arms to encompass my living room. "But then there's this. And I'm glad I met you."

I covered my embarrassment by refilling our coffee mugs

and helping myself to a slice of Jarlsberg, but he might have heard my low, "Same here," followed quickly by, "Do you mind sharing with me what you did in San Francisco? Work-wise, I mean."

"Hey, we've shared a sweatshirt," he said, arms open again. "I was a computer programmer."

"Connected to the telephone company in any way?"

"Do you mean could Wendell have wanted my expertise or to consult on some telephone matter? Nope. Except that I had a phone, of course. I worked for a big grocery chain, writing code for inventory control. That's why I chose an-tiques out here. You know all those spy novels and witness protection dramas—they always tell you to avoid what you did in your other life. If you were high tech, go low tech, et cetera. If you were great at football, go for baseball."

"Or knitting," I suggested.

He laughed, which was my goal. "I'm also kind of a handyman, woodworking type, so being around old furni-ture has been fun."

"Are you back at work now?" I asked Quinn, flitting back to the present.

"Fred told me to take the week off. I hope it's not his way of firing me, but I don't think so. He's a good guy."

Quinn caught me looking at my watch. I regretted that he had to leave, not only because I was sure he had an excel-lent chicken recipe.

"I probably should get ready," I said.

He rose. "Sure. You have an important date. Maybe you can ask her if she still thinks I'm guilty of anything."

"Not you, too." I explained how Wanda had pressed me into service to find out how the investigation was going.

"I never meant to put the heat on you," Quinn said. "I was teasing, really. I hope you don't think I've been hanging around just because you have the police chief's ear."

I assured him I didn't think that. I just had to convince myself.

In the few minutes before Sunni arrived, I had a quick conversation with Linda, across the state, via Skype.

"You are really stirring things up there," she said. "I can't wait to meet this fugitive of yours."

"He's not exactly—"

"I know. I'm sorry. And I'm really sorry about Wendell. I feel bad about dissing him last time. I hope they catch whoever did that to him. Are you working on it?"

"Me? What do you mean?"

Linda shook her finger at me, a possible disadvantage of visual phone calls. "Come on. When did you ever let a little detective work get by you?"

"Join the club that thinks that."

"I can't believe you don't recognize the talent you have. Remember that lost revenue program we had, where we tried to uncover ways we were losing revenue? Didn't you take the prize for the most money recovered, from misuse of media mail, money order fraud, and I forget what else."

"That was just part of the job."

"Yes, but you excelled at it. Do you mean to tell me you're not putting those talents to use on an investigation of the murder of an old friend? In a town where there are four cops?"

"Well, not technically, but—"

"Aha."

My turn to shake a finger at the face on the screen. "And there are five cops." I had to admit to Linda that I was sort of involved. "Only peripherally," I said.

"Of course," she said, in a tone that sounded incredulous. "But after your dinner with the police chief tonight, it will be centrally, I'll bet."

"We'll see."

Linda shared news of her own recent date, the real kind, where you had dinner at a nice restaurant at the top of a skyscraper, and ended at a club with dancing. She'd met this new guy, Noah, at a retirement dinner for one of our old bosses. She'd already sent me a smartphone photo of him, the lights of Boston in the background.

I listened to a few water-cooler tidbits about people I'd worked with. I decided not to share the insights I'd picked up from Ben about how small-town North Ashcot viewed big-city Boston. She had enough to hold against my home-town without more ammunition. But, apparently, selfish as the big city was, there were more opportunities for meeting people with only one identity.

The twenty-minute ride from my house in Sunni's black Explorer was quiet, with intermittent talk of the weather (too cold for this time of year), movies (holiday shows were mostly kid-flick fare), an upcoming referendum on more STOP signs in town (sure) and one on a betting parlor (no way), and Sunni's daughter who'd be going off to college next year. I wondered if I should warn the young woman that she shouldn't pick a school in the parasitic city of Boston if she ever wanted to come back home.

We arrived at Russo's early enough to choose seats against the wall, Sunni's preference. I imagined she was always surveying her environment. The restaurant was a noisy little Italian place in a cluster of eateries just off the main street in Pittsfield, the largest city in Berkshire County. The funky décor included the high tables and chairs that seemed to be so popular in restaurants and coffee shops these days. Climbing up was easy for someone of my height—it was more like sliding across. But not so for Sunni, who, once she reached the red vinyl seat and shoved herself back, claimed she wasn't planning to descend except to go home.

"I don't think I've ever seen you out of uniform," I said.

She fluffed her brown-red hair. "It happens."

"Nice sweater set. It's almost the post office blue."

"I know it's a fifties look, but they're back. In case you hadn't noticed."

I had noticed, and commented on how much snazzier the bolero-type cardigan was. "It's not my Aunt Tess's sweater set."

After a brief chat about wardrobes, Sunni dropped her casual tone. "Let's get right to the business stuff," she said. "That is, my business, not yours."

Uh-oh. A warning. "Sunni, I assure you it's not my intention to interfere with your business."

She looked doubtful, then patted my hand as if I were an unruly kid. "It's not that I couldn't use a little help, Cassie, and real leads or information, delivered to me directly, would be most welcome, but nothing is served by rumors and innuendos, and those seem to spread like wildfires in the hills. And as far as snooping around without a badge and weapon . . ." She trailed off with a "needless to say" gesture.

"I understand completely." I hoped Sunni didn't think I'd spread any rumors. She needed only to ask my frustrated customers to learn that my lips had been sealed in that regard. Whatever the citizens were spreading, they didn't hear it from me.

"I know you're close to Quinn. I'd like to think you and I are friends, too, Cassie, but when it comes to the law and major crimes . . ." She opened her palms, which I took to mean that, once more, I could fill in the rest.

"I'm glad we're friends, and I wouldn't do anything to jeopardize that." Or get myself arrested, I added to myself.

"Or get hurt in any way," Sunni added, as if she'd heard both my spoken and unspoken thoughts.

Once that was settled, I realized, my true intentions for the dinner flew out the window.

We ate caprese salad and pasta (I decided against a chicken dish, hoping that I'd have one tomorrow evening), and affogatos for dessert. We talked about her quilting (she'd just finished a special one for her daughter's future dorm room) and my adjustment to managing my own post (slow), books we'd read and television shows we liked (crime drama for both of us), and a new set of shops coming to downtown. It also turned out that neither of us wanted a betting parlor in town.

"Not unless they triple my staff," Sunni said. "And my ammo budget."

It was nice to be in agreement. No talk of Wendell Graham, Quinn Martindale, or murder.

Anyone listening to our conversation would have thought we were just friends.

Wasn't that what I'd hoped to find back home in North Ashcot? A friend to share the small things with. A meal, a conversation, a few laughs.

Why was I disappointed when that's how the evening turned out?

Back at home, I found myself in withdrawal. I'd spent so much of my time and mental energy the last three days on the phone book theft, the Scott/Quinn revelation, Wendell's murder, being stalked for gossip, meeting Wanda again after nearly twenty years. And, not to be neglected, new feelings for Quinn Martindale—mixed as they were, since I had no reason to believe he really was who he now claimed to be. I told myself that, by this point, Sunni would know the answer to the last question, and that she would have found a way to warn me about hanging around with him if there was anything to worry about. I hoped I hadn't missed a cue.

It was too early for bed, so I took out my laptop and clicked around, but even my Web browsing, which a week ago might have included a frivolous game or two, now consisted of serious searches.

I found Wanda's card and typed in her website address. I opened her home page—Wanda Graham Cox, Freelance Graphics Designer—and admired the head shot in the upper left corner. Wanda's red hair was cut shorter than she wore it now, in an attractive, mature-looking bob. Her wide smile spoke of friendliness and confidence. Seeing her full name reminded me of her brief mention of a failed marriage. She didn't seem to have any scars from it. I rubbed my arm as if to check for scars from a failed engagement.

Wanda's professional offerings were many and her samples impressive. Covers for e-books, website design, flyers, banners, logos and letterhead for small and large companies. The little girl who lost her toys every day had done very well for herself. I had the sad thought that her brother, who must have been very proud of her, could no longer let her know his feelings. I didn't look forward to telling her that, despite my chummy dinner with the chief of police, I was no closer to knowing how Wendell's murder investigation was proceeding. In fact, I suspected it wasn't proceeding at all.

While I was at it, I did another search—for Edmund Morrison, the lawyer who'd bailed Quinn out, though not literally. I sifted through the search engine hits and settled on a likely candidate, Edmund A. Morrison, "of counsel" at a large Albany law firm with a long list of partners. The firm listed many associates and of counsels, which I knew could mean many things, from a young lawyer on probation to a retired lawyer who was still consulting. Given the photo posted, of a gray-haired, bespectacled man, the latter seemed more likely. I scrolled through Morrison's publications and credentials, Yale Law School among them, then clicked on his image and sent a screen shot to Quinn with a simple note: "Your lawyer?"

If someone knocked on the door and asked me why I was researching our murder victim's sister and our only suspect's lawyer, I'd have been at a loss to explain. Maybe Wanda and Linda were right. Maybe I was a detective at heart.

I hoped not.

I got a text reply from Quinn immediately.

Yup. That's him. U up?

I felt that familiar twinge at what seemed like an invitation. It took longer than it should have for me to decline a late-night visit. Too many questions, doubts, and potential dangers. My warning system kicked in.

Turning in now, I responded, not sure what I was missing.

My house needed a good cleaning, but all it got tonight was a once-over, with a little dusting here and there, a run through with my handheld vacuum, and a quick straightening up in the kitchen.

I felt I'd done all I could for the day, at least trying to keep all the promises I'd made, while staying on the good side of Chief Sunni Smargon. I rummaged through my to-be-read pile of books and chose a mystery novel that I knew would end well. The victim would not be a completely innocent, all-around nice guy; the killer would be caught; justice would be served; the protagonist would live to solve another crime. A different world. I sat in bed reading until my eyelids were too heavy to continue, and switched off the small lamp on my night table.

I'd nodded off—or had I?—when I heard the noise. Were the crashing, clattering sounds in my dreams or in my driveway? My bedroom was in the back of the house, one

JEAN FLOWERS

half flight up from the street, at the level of my front and back porches, overlooking a small yard. Along the edge of the house was a pathway with several trash cans for different categories of waste. The noise seemed to come from there.

Though the ruckus stopped in the next few seconds, I got up and went to the window, peeked through the drapes at the backyard, and saw nothing unusual. I chalked it up to a raccoon or a skunk, hopefully not the rabid animal waging war in Mr. Jayne's backyard, as I'd heard about from one of Sunni's officers. While I was up, I wandered through the house, peeking through all the windows. I saw nothing out front except my old Jeep in the driveway.

Too sleepy to worry any longer without a good reason, I trudged back to bed.

12

I woke up in good spirits on Thursday morning, despite the gloomy weather. Rain or snow on the way? It was anybody's guess. I resolved to take the warning from Sunni seriously and pay strict attention to my postal duties today. Wanda would have to understand that I had orders from the chief of police herself to back off.

I looked forward to a nice chicken dinner with Quinn this evening. As for lunch, who knew which of my fans would pop in at the last minute and claim their date? Derek Hathaway, the richest guy in town? Tim Cousins, the young man who was so eager for gossip? Or Gert Corbin, the government official who probably wanted me to continue whatever Aunt Tess had started by way of support for her campaign?

I donned a brand-new navy blue cardigan, a warm scarf, my navy parka, and I was ready to go. I gave one last look at my house, which I felt was fit for company, especially since the sun would be down long before dinnertime, hiding the dust. I'd always counted on that when entertaining.

Keys ready, I headed down the porch steps, approached my Jeep. And groaned. A flat tire? Really? My right front hubcap rested unnaturally close to the concrete. Good thing I had a spare, and an even better thing that my father had forced me to learn to change a tire before I had my first drivers ed course. No worries.

Also, I was glad I'd gotten an early start this morning, though this wasn't the way I'd planned to use the extra time.

I tried to remember where I'd been in the last twenty-four hours that was rough enough to bring on a flat. Only around town as usual. Not even as far as Pittsfield, where Sunni had taken her car last night. I walked around to the trunk. And groaned again. Another flat. My right rear tire had bottomed out also.

It didn't take a genius to think of checking the two left tires. Now the groans were less casual. I toured once around the Jeep, looking more carefully, noting the slash marks on each tire. I thought of Ben's story about the Halloween gang that had struck last year, but I didn't remember any real damage that had been done, just a nuisance attack. This felt more personal. Designed to keep me from work at least, or something more sinister at worst.

My back to my house, I walked to the edge of my driveway and surveyed the neighborhood. As if someone would be hanging around, his knife on display, admiring his handiwork and the homeowner's distress. I glanced behind me, then to the sides where small pathways separated my house from my neighbors' houses. It seemed no one was up yet.

I tried to convince myself that harmless teen vandals were having a little fun at my expense. The queasiness in my stomach and the tremors in my hands as I tried to calm my nerves told a different story. If this wasn't for fun, what was it for?

I considered running back into the house and locking myself in. I also considered running down the street, away from the house, from the car, from North Ashcot.

In the end, I stayed put and called the police department, having decided they should see it before a tow truck did.

While I waited for Ross, I walked around my property looking for a clue. As if I'd have known one if it were in front of me. Unless the slasher had dropped a glove full of DNA, or hurt himself and left his bloody fingerprint behind. Not likely. Nevertheless, I searched the small area—under my car as far as I could see, up and down the two pathways on either side of my house. I found a candy wrapper; indeterminate pieces of stiff plastic, one possibly from a six-pack of soda, another a blister pack, and still others that could have held together the countless items that came shrink-wrapped; a metal nail file that could have been mine.

On one side, stuck in a tuft of weeds, was part of a strap of nondescript color that looked like it was ripped from a backpack. From the size, I guessed it was a kid's. It was hard to picture Operation Tire Slash associated with a cute grade-schooler, with a lollipop in one hand and a knife strong enough to slash my tires in the other.

It might just as easily have fallen off last summer, I reminded myself. Or it might have blown into the thin strip of grass overnight, from several houses down the block. I was realizing more and more how difficult it was to be a detective, how personal stress might influence "guesses," and how far off one could be.

Dangling at the end of the strap were three doodads, in Aunt Tess parlance. It occurred to me how often I lapsed into her figures of speech and weird jargon. We'd spent a lot of time together in her last days—making me wish I'd come back to be with her long before she was near the end—and I'd picked up some ancient expressions. Maybe hanging on to them was keeping her close.

I'd resisted acquiring doodads, or whatever they were called now, though even my classiest friend, Linda, had a couple hanging from her tote. One I was tempted to emulate was a small photo of her standing in front of the first post office where she worked. The photo was encased in clear plastic, the office identified on the back.

"Post office memorabilia don't count as doodads," she'd advised me.

The set of objects I inspected now comprised a flashlight that was not much bigger than my thumb; a pair of miniature neon green flip-flops; and a small key, not for a life-sized door, but something that might symbolize the key to one's heart. No identifying marks that I could see.

The gloomy weather had settled in my body and I quit my search. I took the strap and my heavy heart to my front steps and waited for help. If things continued this way, I'd have to buy a chair for my tiny front porch. Maybe Ashcot's Attic had an appropriate one.

* * *

"Might be some kind of personal message," Officer Ross Little said, articulating my worst fear. He looked at my face and tried to smooth things over. "Not personal like you. I mean, personal as in, they wanted to aggravate some person. But not necessarily you."

Strangely, I knew what he meant, and it did make me feel a little better.

Ross walked around my car as I had, stooping now and then, writing in a notepad, then slapping the pad against his hand. Thinking.

"I wasn't sure I should bother you with this," I told him.

"No, no, you did the right thing, Cassie. Someone will be coming by here to see if there are any prints or anything we can use. We'd like to go over the whole car, just in case."

"Sure." I handed him my keys.

In case what? My car was rigged to explode? I pulled my scarf up around my neck, above the collar of my parka. The temperature seemed to be dropping by the minute.

"You don't have to stay," Ross said. I have everything I need from your statement, and I can call the auto shop for you when I'm done. Can you get a ride to work?"

Ross seemed genuinely concerned about me, possibly from having seen me carless, stranded, for the second time this week. "Sure," I said again, though I was far from it. With all the interactions of the week, was I any closer to being able to pick up the phone and find someone who'd drive me to work? Maybe a little.

I almost hated to leave before Ross did another search.

What if I missed something important? But I knew I should get to work and let the police take care of my problem. Unlike murder, car vandalism was probably a specialty of the house. Like rabid skunks. I almost felt bad that I'd blamed last night's clatter on an innocent animal.

I pulled out my cell phone. Quinn and Ben were the only ones I knew who would be willing to chauffeur me. Did I want Ross to know what my relationship was with Quinn? Worse, for him to speculate and come up with something it wasn't? I hated to bother Ben, who was not a morning guy. He'd claimed he'd never have retired if he could open at ten or eleven every day.

But Ross already knew Quinn and I were connected in some way from all the events of the week, including prison visits, so to speak. In for a penny, I thought, and dialed Quinn.

Quinn took his own tour around my sagging Jeep, keeping his impressions to himself. He and Ross said barely more than "good morning" and we took off. True to his driving policy, he kept to the speed limit. As far as his meticulously full stops at the STOP signs, all of my Boston friends would have been disgusted with him.

"Stop signs are only a suggestion," I'd heard from more than one of my city colleagues.

I reached into my purse for a mint and pulled out a long, thin piece of canvas with doodads on the end.

"Oops. I forgot to hand this over to Ross."

Quinn turned to look at what I was holding, still with both

hands on the wheel as we drove on an open road. It was as if he were saying, "See how I'm obeying the law, Officer. My hands are at ten and two o'clock."

"I found this in the grass between my house and the one next door on the left. It's probably nothing but trash," I explained.

"You never know. Leave it in the cup holder. I'll take it to Ross."

"Thanks." I had an "I'm glad I met you" moment. I was in a mood to take what I could get by way of friendship.

"I don't suppose you have a clue how this happened? All four of your tires?" Quinn said.

"I wish I knew. I heard some noise last night before I fell asleep but I don't think it came from out front. I was sure it was from the side or out back."

"That could have been the getaway route. Are there trash containers back there that he might have knocked over?"

"Uh-huh."

"Do you think it's someone who knows you're investigating Wendell's murder? Are you getting too close?"

"I'm not investigating. And I'm not close at all."

We both laughed at the internal contradiction. "Reminds me of that lawyer joke," Quinn said. "The defense lawyer says, 'My client is innocent of letting his dog loose, and if he did let it loose, it was of grave necessity, and my client may not have a dog.' Something like that."

I laughed. "I know the one you mean."

"Seriously, Cassie. You're seen with me, with Wendell's sister, with the chief of police. Someone could misinterpret your role in all of this."

"And how would four flat tires stop me?"

Quinn shrugged. "What if the killer thinks you're on to him or closing in, and wants to scare you away?"

"It's scaring me all right."

"Enough so you really will stop thinking about it, stop trying to help the police department, stop trying to work on closure for Wanda, and maybe for yourself?"

"It's just tires," I said.

Even with Quinn's overly careful driving, I made it to the post office in time to raise the flag, stuff the PO boxes, and open the doors to the retail counter by nine o'clock. To my surprise, none of my customers mentioned either my slashed tires or the fact that I'd been dropped off by Quinn Martindale. I decided the key to maintaining privacy in North Ashcot was to arrange for all embarrassing or confidential moments to occur early in the morning.

A highlight was a visit from a young llama. His keeper, an old-timer who lived in South Ashcot, learned from Carolyn and George Raley that the North Ashcot Post Office had an animal-friendly scale. He introduced himself as Vic, and his llama as Llarry—with two L's, he explained. He raised the animals and shipped the wool around the world. From now on, he told me, all his mailing business would be conducted in my establishment. South Ashcot had lost his considerable business.

When my first break in the line came around ten-thirty, I thought I was doomed to lunch by myself. None of my potential dates had made an effort to schedule. My relief was short-lived when I checked my cell phone messages.

Derek Hathaway's secretary had called to ask me to please meet him at Betty's at twelve. I wavered between ignoring the request, which left no room for confirmation (didn't everyone know I couldn't leave my post until noon?) and taking a chance on learning what, if anything, had been going on between Wendell and Derek. I told myself it was a simple way to follow up on Wanda's tip that Derek was a new presence in her late brother's life.

While the office was quiet for a while, I pulled a white tub from a shelf—a container of what we called "unattached items." I'd already weeded out obvious trash, like coffee cups and crumpled paper napkins that had been dumped in the collection box, but it always amazed me how personal belongings ended up there. Teddy bears were a constant presence, as were CDs, books, and packages of cookies for Santa. Some of the items in the tub were incoming; that is, they'd arrived at the North Ashcot Post Office separated from their packaging. Others had simply been dropped into our collection box, accidentally or on purpose.

"Or maybe they're meant as gifts to postal workers," Linda had said more than once in our Boston office, as she was sorely tempted to confiscate a lovely silk scarf or a bestseller she'd been wanting to read. "Too bad it's against the law to give us presents."

Once in a while Ben or I could identify and return an item, like a child's sweater with a label sewn in, or the red sneaker with running lights that we'd seen on Mrs. Hagan's granddaughter. Today I pulled out several items of clothing and a small camera—maybe deliberately discarded in favor of cell phone apps? I had some discretion as to how to dispose of such objects, but, for the most part, I took a conservative route. If neither Ben nor I had a hope of determining the owner, they'd be sent to the mail recovery center, where they would eventually be discarded or auctioned off.

I was fingering what looked like a computer part when the phone rang. Derek Hathaway's secretary canceling our lunch? No such luck. Officer Ross Little, instead, letting me know that my car had been towed to the auto shop.

"Sorry they can't give you an exact quote on how long it will take to replace the tires. They suggested that they look for other damage also, that might not be visible. I told them okay. You good with that?"

"I'm good with that. And thanks, Ross. I really appreciate all you did."

"My pleasure . . . well, not a pleasure, but you know."

I did.

The rest of the morning passed routinely with packaging items for the recovery center and dealing with the usual round of mailings, including two international packages that had to be rewrapped.

Sunni called just before noon, concerned. Ross had described my prework adventure.

"Who do you think did that?" she asked. I almost told her it was her job to find out, but I suspected that was my fear talking.

"Some vandals, I guess. A couple of mothers came in with their kids and told me there was no school today because of a teachers' conference."

"A possibility."

"Do you know of others?"

"Not specifically, but I want to reiterate my warning to you."

I figured it would be counterproductive to pretend I didn't know what she meant. I tried not to read too much into the fact that Derek Hathaway came through the front doors at that moment.

"Oops, customers arriving," I said. "I'll talk to you later."

Derek walked to the counter, leaned over. "Are you ready for some Derek time?"

I nearly gagged, but managed, "I thought we were meeting at Betty's?"

"I know you don't have a car, so I came to get you."

Color me red. Had I really forgotten that my car was in the shop? The next question was more frightening.

"How did you know?" I asked Derek.

"It's all over the news. Your Jeep was seen being towed to Marley's." He paused and laughed. Derek's laugh was not so much light and fun as dark, bordering on mean. "Just kidding. So, are you ready?"

What were the chances Derek had slashed my tires, just so he could pick me up and take me . . . where? To the woods where Wendell had been killed? Was I being paranoid, or wiser than oh, so many victims of serial killers? I thought of a famous one who lured young women to ride with him by having one arm in a sling, looking helpless. Dozens of well-meaning girls stopped to help him and never came back.

I took a breath, came back to reality and reasonableness. "I'm ready."

For what? I wished I knew.

* * *

"We can go right in," Derek said, bypassing the line at Betty's. "I made a reservation." I supposed there was no point in reminding him that Betty's didn't take reservations.

Once Betty's had come into view, about a quarter of a mile down the road, I'd relaxed in Derek's luxury town car, thinking it was hardly likely that he'd kill me in this part of town. I'd wondered if Wendell Graham had gone through the same kind of reasoning.

Derek had been quiet on the short ride to the restaurant, asking only about Ben's adjustment to his new status (no problems; he's been a big help) and mine also (no problems; all is well), and whether I planned to stay in North Ashcot permanently (hard to tell).

Now we were settled at the best table in the establishment, of course, far from the din of the kitchen and the drafts from the front door. As soon as our server set down our plates with the special of the day, which Derek had preordered, Derek dug into his agenda.

"Did you happen to read that brochure on the betting club?" he asked, after a healthy bite of crab salad.

I thought back. Hadn't it been Selectwoman Gert and Coach, whoever he was, who'd given me the literature? It was possible I had that wrong. I'd gone from near-zero personal interactions last week to a record high this week. At this rate, the town would have to hire more gossipers just to take care of my news.

"I honestly haven't had a chance," I said. "It seems the office has been busier than ever since the terrible tragedy this week." A lame segue if I ever heard one, but it was the best I could do to introduce my own agenda.

My attempt didn't work. Derek continued on his own

train of thought. "When you examine the very reasonable arguments, I think you'll agree, it would be a very bad move to bring that kind of activity into North Ashcot. We don't want the type of person it would attract in our town." In case I still hadn't been persuaded, he added, "Have you ever been to Las Vegas?"

"No, but it was good enough for Frank Sinatra."

"My point exactly."

"My mom and dad idolized him."

Derek shrugged his shoulders. Had I really caught him? "I didn't think you lived here anymore, Derek. Are you planning to move back to North Ashcot?"

"I still care about my hometown, Cassie. As I told you, my ex-wife and daughter live here."

"I understand you were friendly with Wendell Graham. That you two reconnected recently?"

"We saw each other now and then, yeah. It's bound to happen when you come back to a town like this. You know that, right, Cassie?"

Why did I cringe every time Derek Hathaway said my name? "His death must be hard for you. I'm sorry," I said.

"It was quite a shock, yeah. I can't say we were close, but he was a classmate after all."

"But you also had some business together lately, isn't that right?" I asked, all casual.

Derek sat back in the seat, puffed out his chest as far as he could. "What makes you think that?"

I buttered a piece of warm cheese bread. "Small town."

"Why are you interested?"

"Just curious."

"You know what they say about the curious." He laughed, with the same unpleasant tone. "But, hey, this was supposed to be a friendly little reunion lunch." He raised his coffee cup and motioned that I should do the same.

I turned my cup toward him. "All gone," I said.

13

I exited Derek's car and walked toward the side door of my building, collecting a few stray wrappers on the way. I'd never understood why my elegant colonial, so beautifully landscaped, flag flying high, didn't inspire people to take care of the sight and dispose of their own trash.

I replayed my lunch, asking myself several questions. Why did Derek care so much about my one vote on the betting club referendum? He'd brought it up twice more before we left.

I wanted to tell him I had no desire to encourage a betting club. It would have ended the topic, but I felt it was none of his business which way I was leaning. In fact, his and Gert's opposition might just push me the other way. I looked around in case the man named Coach, who'd accosted Gert in the post office, was around to provide some balance. Perhaps Derek was grandstanding in case voters were listening.

A bigger question in my mind was why did Derek avoid talk of Wendell? If Wanda was telling me the truth, her brother and Derek had renewed contact and appeared to have business dealings. I wished I'd asked what kind of business a big developer and a small-town telephone company worker could have together. I doubted a guy in Derek's position would have to manage the day-to-day operations involving wires and phones.

I supposed I could give Derek the benefit of the doubt and conclude that he was grieving over Wendell's death, and it bothered him too much to talk about anything to do with his friend. Possible. But hard to swallow.

Even more puzzling was my own behavior. Hadn't I very recently received a "hands-off" warning from the chief of police and, maybe, a definite in-my-face warning in my driveway this morning? What had I been thinking, directly interrogating a very rich, very powerful man? This was not a case of mail fraud, which I knew a lot about; or of a few extra stamps here or there; or trying to stuff nonmedia items into a low-rate package. This was a murder case and I had no business even being curious.

I tried to strengthen my resolve and clear my mind of all but postal matters. I entered the building, walked to my desk, and glanced toward the front doors, where someone was waiting for me to open. I still had fifteen minutes, but an exception was called for.

Quinn Martindale stood with his back to the building, hands in his pockets, jockeying from one foot to the other, as if he were continuing a run, but more likely to keep warm. I gathered he hadn't noticed that I'd entered through the side door. I was still expecting a fully cooked chicken dinner tonight; the least I could do was open the doors for him a little early.

"I want to show you something," he said, once inside. He held out the piece of backpack strap I'd found by my wounded vehicle this morning. "I forgot to pass this on to Ross, so I did a little digging of my own."

We sat on two folding chairs in the lobby. I congratulated myself on not violating the "Employees Only" rule for who was allowed behind the counter, even though his Scott James persona had already done that last weekend when he'd entered and carted my phone books away.

"You ran fingerprints on the doodads and ID'd the tire slasher?" I joked, because it would have been too depressing to be serious.

"Not quite. But getting close," he said, surprising me. Of the three doodads that still dangled from the strap, Quinn singled out the small flashlight and held it so I could follow as he ran his finger along the edge. "It's still scratched up, but I cleaned it the best I could and now you can sort of see a logo that's a stylized tree."

"Your restoration talents at work," I said.

Quinn smiled. "I guess so. I was pretty sure it was swag from Take a Hike, that sporting goods store in South Ashcroft. I gave the store a call to see if I was on the right track. The guy said yeah, they did at one time give the flashlight I described to all the Scouts in the area. Sort of goodwill, a gesture of support. And promotion, of course."

"This is amazing, Quinn. We should take it to Sunni."

He handed me the strap and hanging doodads. "I think you should be the one to give it to her, not me."

"But you're the one who figured it out," I said, ready to give it back.

He shook his head. "That doesn't matter."

"But it's a fantastic lead. Are you sure you don't want to take it to the police?" I hesitated to come right out with a reminder that he needed brownie points with the NAPD even more than I did.

"I'd just as soon they forget about me," he said.

I put what I hoped was a useful piece of evidence in my pocket. "I understand." Next thing I knew, I had the nerve to ask what had been a nagging question. "Who knows your real name at this point?"

"'Who knows?' is the answer. To the best of my knowledge, only you and the cops know. I didn't even tell my boss. He's not aware of the phone book fiasco, even though he did see how upset I was that my photo was out there. He just thinks I'm shy."

"Ben Gentry knows," I said. "But I don't think he knows you took the phone books. He was too distracted with other things the day the books were returned to us. He's never asked how they got to the police station en route."

"So I guess I'm still Scott James to most people. The chief said it was up to me to clarify things with the RMV, but I'm hoping not to have to hide behind that name much longer. I'm not driving with an expired license, just so you know. It's just that you're supposed to notify them if you change your name. On the other hand, it's sort of part of changing your name to notify them, so it's a circle and I'm just riding it for now."

"I wasn't worried." And I certainly didn't need all that explanation, but I was glad he thought he should tell me. Now, if he would just tell me what was in the undeliverable letter that I so kindly delivered. The letter with the peacock blue ink. I cleared my throat and took another direction. "Do you have any idea how Wendell knew both your names?"

"I've tried to figure that out. He did work for the telephone company. He might have seen the directory before it was out. But so what if he saw my picture? He didn't know me before I came here. What would make him take notice?"

"We may never know," I said, wistful, not for the answer, but for the loss of Wendell.

"Maybe it will be cleared up once we know who murdered him."

"Maybe." I rubbed the flashlight doodad, as if it were a genie-bearing bottle. "I'll stop by the station on my way home and turn this in. I won't mention your name."

"Much appreciated. Are we still on for dinner?"

"I'm counting on it," I said.

I felt only a flicker of my old worry: Was I entertaining and becoming close to a murderer? To the son of a murderer? Both? Whenever the thought came up, I dismissed it more quickly each time.

Ben, who I now considered my savior and best friend, called around three.

"I just woke up from my after-lunch nap. I'm bored."

Talk about an honest guy. No pretense about why he was calling. "Too bad you don't have an old job you can pop in on at any time."

"You busy?"

"Not too many customers right now, but there are still some unattached items to deal with."

"Plus some sweeping up?"

"Definitely some sweeping up."

"You can plan on leaving in about a half hour."

I blew him a kiss, thinking how good it was that he'd never know.

I called the auto shop and, as luck would have it, my car was ready. Things were looking up all around, once my Derek Hathaway lunch was over.

"No damage other than the tires, that the mechanics could see," the secretary told me. "Too bad, though, huh?" I didn't respond. "I mean too bad it happened," she explained.

"Yes, too bad," I said.

"One of the guys can drive it over now, if you want."

Apparently, the auto shop was much better staffed and equipped than the police department, with more personnel and more supplies, like extra tires. In a town like North Ashcot, where there was no public transportation except to take seniors to medical appointments, it made sense. Everyone depended on cars and pickups, so it wasn't hard to keep a decent-sized staff of mechanics on the payroll and busy full-time.

With such a low crime rate, however, what was the point of a large full-time police force? I wondered if things would be different now that a murder had entered the crime statistics. How many major crimes would it take for Sunni to get approval for more resources? At least she had better coffee than the auto shop, though that was just a guess on my part.

For now, I was happy to be getting my Jeep back.

* * *

Ross was on hand, as usual, to accept my piece of strap.

"I forgot to give this to you before I left this morning," I admitted.

"Hmm. It might be nothing. Or it might be something."

"I think it's something," I said, and pointed out the flashlight logo. I felt like a fraud, claiming to have thought of checking, and, further, to have contacted Take a Hike. Too bad brownie points weren't transferable.

I drove away on my new tires, confident that the PD would take it from there, and headed for a stop at the market. If I didn't know better, I'd have thought there was a team following me around. This time it was Tim Cousins, our architect in residence, in the produce aisle.

"I heard about your Jeep," he said, shaking his head. "Bad news."

"Did Derek tell you about it? Or was it Gert?"

"Huh?" he asked.

"Never mind."

"Probably some kids," he suggested. "But, all four of them? That's something else. Any idea who's involved?"

"No idea," I said. Didn't he have beams to paint? Church pews to convert to living room furniture? Incense to burn?

I wished he'd stop checking out items in my cart. Was he counting them? Would he report that I had enough veggies for two? Would everyone soon know that I was expecting company for dinner tonight?

"Do you have any news on the investigation into Wendell Graham's murder?" he asked.

"No, do you?"

He gave me a funny look, perhaps finally understanding that I'd had my tongue in my cheek during our whole conversation. As soon as he indicated that he was turning right toward Canned Goods, I turned left toward Bakery.

Working side by side, finding the proper utensils and cookware (me) and cooking (Quinn), was more fun than I'd had in a long time.

"Did you ever notice this?" he asked, holding out the blue-and-white pot holder with Gert Corbin's name on one side.

"Yes," I said. "It dates back to before I got here."

"Was your aunt a fan of the selectwoman?"

"I'm not sure. I think she kept everything that ever came into the house."

"Or she just needed a pot holder," Quinn said. "Have you seen this?" He'd turned the pot holder over to reveal the writing on the other side: *Endorsed by Raymond Levitt, Mayor of Albany, NY.*

"Strange. Wouldn't anyone in Massachusetts endorse her?"

"I guess New York matters more in the scheme of things."

I thought of Ben's lecture to me about how small-town North Ashcot looked askance at all things Boston. I shared Ben's city-versus-town argument with Quinn, explaining how small towns got short shrift when it came to resources.

"Good to know," he said. "Helps me plan my next move."

I didn't know what to make of the fact that I cared what that would be.

"Let's eat," I said.

* * *

In the middle of an incredibly tasty curry chicken dinner, the phone rang. If it hadn't been Sunni Smargon, Chief of Police, I wouldn't have answered.

"Do you want the good news or the bad news first?" Sunni asked. "Never mind, I'll tell you the good first. The store was very helpful and we have the kid who slashed your tires."

"He admits to it?"

"She."

"A girl slashed my tires?" I wasn't proud of my leaning toward a stereotype, assuming the little criminal was male. Why couldn't a girl bend over and use a knife on my tires? Probably because we don't think of girls as being violent, but with so many real-life cases to the contrary, it was a foolish assumption.

"She admits to it. But there's something funny about her confession. That's the bad news. This is a reasonably good kid. She's an honor student, not from the richest family in town, but she's never been into vandalism before."

"You think someone paid her to do it?"

"I'm not thinking anything at the moment. The store had a record of all the kids in town who got flashlights. Not very many. It turned out they weren't a mass distribution item, but given to certain kids who completed a project. So, right away, we have a Girl Scout, literally, and one who is smart and has good follow-through. There were only four girls on the list, and we were able to narrow it down quickly."

"What happens now?"

"We'll be talking to her parents. I'm hoping she'll open up and tell us what's really going on. I'll keep you informed."

Unlike with the murder case. "Thanks," I said.

"It was a girl," I told Quinn, sounding as if I were announcing a birth. "Which sort of surprised me."

"Not me," he said. "From the other gizmos hanging on the strap—flip-flops and a small key the size of a charm. Much more likely to be a girl. A boy would have a knife, maybe, but that's it."

"Not even a little soccer ball?"

"Not unless he's five years old."

We were a pretty good detective team, I thought.

We talked and ate and talked more. Quinn seemed more relaxed now that at least someone (the cops and I) knew his secret.

"I tried to get ahold of that lawyer, you know."

"Edmund Morrison? The lawyer who got you out of custody."

"Yeah, I just wanted to find out who sent him and why. But I couldn't reach him. I left messages and a secretary said he'd get back to me when he could, but I'm not holding my breath."

"He's probably pretty busy."

"I just don't like loose ends."

I didn't blame him. I felt I had more loose ends than a tailor's shop. I told Quinn about my lunch with Derek Hathaway, his strange fascination with the betting club, and his near denial of any kind of relationship with Wendell Graham.

The topic we saved for last was the most serious.

"I'd like you to pull back a little," Quinn said. "In fact, make that 'a lot.'"

Uh-oh, I sensed that I'd had my last home-cooked meal in a while. "I'm sorry if I've seemed pushy with you."

Quinn blinked and shook his head, causing a pleasant movement of his longish hair. "I meant, stop investigating. I'm worried that the little message delivered through your wheels today might have to do with the fact that you've been hanging around Wanda, questioning Derek, for starters."

"It was a Girl Scout," I reminded him.

"Maybe not."

"You said you don't like loose ends. Don't you want this all cleared up? Isn't it enough to have one murder trial hanging in the balance, and affecting your life?"

"Of course, I want it all cleared up. But not at someone else's expense." He looked straight at me. "Not at your expense."

"Dessert?" I asked.

Quinn left early enough for me to make some calls. I dialed Ben first, and got a woman's voice.

"Is Ben there?"

"Hey, Cassie, it's Natalie."

I'd met Ben's niece once or twice when I first moved back. She lived in Boston and had just started nursing school near a large hospital. I wondered if her uncle had given her the "Boston-Is-Bad Talk." Knowing him, he might be accusing her at this very moment of taking the water from under him and his neighbors, just to be sure the big city kept on rolling.

"I didn't know you were visiting. How nice."

"Just since yesterday. A friend is getting married in town. I'll be staying the weekend. Besides, I have to check up on the old man, you know."

I laughed. "You'd better not let him hear you call him that."

"No kidding. Wait a sec. I'll put him on."

"Sorry to call so late," I said, when Ben took the phone. "I just want to be sure everything went smoothly this afternoon. Is there anything I should know about before I raise the flag in the morning?"

"Nope, everything's fine. Oh, yeah, except we're out of those hot-rod commemoratives. Put in an order, would you?"

An odd request, and an odd way for him to make it, as if I worked for him and not vice versa. I cleared my throat. "Sure. Anything else?"

"I think that's it. Make sure you're in by about two-thirty tomorrow."

"What? What are you talking about, Ben? Is there something different about tomorrow morning that I shouldn't go to work as usual?"

"That's correct. Thanks for asking. I'll see you then."

Now I was really confused. Was nothing normal these days? Was I about to find out that Benham Gentry was a fake name, that he'd burned flags and had been on the run since the seventies?

Then it hit me. His beloved Natalie was visiting. She probably didn't know that Ben was on his way out of the postmaster job. He wanted his niece to think he was still in charge. That was probably why he called yesterday, asking to come in. What other reason for this little dance? I knew he cared a great deal about Natalie, and had had a lot to do with raising her, so it couldn't be that he didn't want to spend time with her.

"Okay, boss," I said.

"You got it."

"I'll see you at two-thirty. Call if you need anything."

I wondered if I'd find it so hard to leave my post when my time came.

I stopped for a cup of coffee, then made my second call, to Linda, and asked that very question.

"It's sad, in a way," she said. "I don't see myself hanging around, begging to work more. I've got a ton of things I'm going to do once I don't have to dress in blue."

"You don't have to dress in blue now. You're in the main office, where no stamps are sold, no services provided."

"Metaphorically speaking."

I'd debated about telling Linda that my car had had an adventure today—major surgery on its wheels. "Not now" won over "share everything," on the basis that I didn't want to give the upsetting incident any more sway over me and my friends than it already had. Besides, it was over.

The last call of the evening was incoming, from Wanda. I thought of ignoring it, since I had no information for her, but she'd just keep trying and I'd never get to sleep. Besides, I did really feel sorry for her. I picked up.

"Hey, Cassie, just checking in, you know."

"I've been thinking about you and wish I had something positive to report." Again, I decided to skip the fact that I had new tires.

"I wanted to tell you that we're having a service for my

brother on Saturday and I hope you can come. Nothing big; I'm sure it will be mostly family. Walker and Whitney are flying in tomorrow. I know Wendell would want you there if you can possibly make it."

"Of course, I'll be there. Just tell me where and when and if there's anything I can do."

Wanda gave me the details, then broke down. I couldn't help but join her.

I made a tour of my house before going to bed, checking the locks on all the doors and windows. I positioned my cell and its charger on my night table, within easy reach. Nothing wrong with having two phones handy, just in case. I returned to the front windows and peeked out at my driveway one more time. All was quiet and my car seemed to be standing tall.

I caught myself just before saying good night to my Jeep and wishing it well.

14

I'd been tempted not to set my alarm, to sleep late, since a little surprise time off for me just happened to serve Ben's needs. I hated to waste the morning, however. I thought of all the things I could do before two-thirty—learn to sew, for example. Failing that, I could read or shop. There was a good-sized mall one town over, where I could browse in person. Imagine actually trying on a skirt before ordering it. Was that what my parents and Aunt Tess had done before the Internet became the worldwide mall?

My favorite photo of my mother came from a shopping trip we took together to New York City when I'd just turned thirteen. I snapped her picture as she was walking down a major avenue carrying three large shopping bags in each hand, all with the store logos facing front. Big smile on her face, though most of the purchases, as I recalled, were for me.

While waking up with my coffee and toast, I scanned

this week's paper for events. I played tourist for a few minutes and checked out the "Things To Do" section. Not exactly what my old Fenway neighborhood would offer, but certainly enough to keep me busy for a morning. It had been years since I'd visited the Susan B. Anthony museum, in her birthplace of Adams, Massachusetts, almost next door. I also considered a walk down our own main street, maybe checking on the progress of Tim Cousins's home-building project and being neighborly for a change.

Finally, I decided what I'd do with my windfall of free time. I went online and found the address of the telephone company's North Ashcot Central Office. For old times' sake, I told myself, to see where Wendell had spent his career. It's not that I was investigating—even though, if Wanda was right about her brother's lack of personal life, it was a good bet that Wendell's murder was tied to his work life. If I happened to meet one of his colleagues who wanted to chat, so be it. You couldn't be arrested for that.

Dressed in my not-blues, lest I be mistaken for a postal worker, I followed the instructions from my GPS to the western edge of town, where a nondescript two-story building was situated among a few other industrial-looking properties. Beige in color, or noncolor, the telephone company building was surrounded by a high fence, except for a small entrance on one short side of the lot. Also surrounding the facility were rows of various-sized conduits, which, I assumed, held myriad strands of wires and cables. The windows were narrow and multipaned, the bottom ones barred and opaque.

I parked on the street, so as not to get involved in the barbed-wire section, and approached what looked like the front entrance, set back from the street. It was not a pleasant walk from my Jeep (the tires of which were the newest things around as far as I could see) to the doorway, past trash, bits of glass, and pockets of mud. Wendell's place of employment was about as unfriendly and unwelcoming as he had become, at least to me.

So this was a central office. If its appearance was meant to discourage attention, the designers had done well. Five steps up from the street level was an entryway with a double glass door, a large EMPLOYEES ONLY sign filling most of it. In case that wasn't clear, two other signs were more explicit. THIS IS NOT A PUBLIC OFFICE, read one, and DO NOT ATTEMPT TO PAY BILLS HERE, said still another, discouraging not only visitors but rate-paying customers in no uncertain terms. I wondered if Wanda had ever ventured out to visit her brother at work. I doubted they had a Take Your Sister to Work Day.

Any hope I had of entering the building and chatting with Wendell's coworkers was buried in layers of cement and security. There wasn't even a doorbell, only a keypad and card slot. I wondered why they'd bothered to feature the company logo above the door. In case employees couldn't tell which was their building?

One thing that surprised me was the size of the structure. I would have expected that newer technology would fit into a smaller space. Maybe everything was now accommodated in one corner of the building, and the rest of the area was empty or used for storage. If I could only get a peek inside, I wouldn't have to make up the building's history.

I knew I should be relieved that such an important part of my hometown's communication system was so well protected. I simply wished they were aware that I was no threat and would make an exception for me.

I returned to my car, looking back over my shoulder now and then on the chance that a human would show himself on the property. From the number of cars in an adjacent parking lot, it seemed that a couple dozen people had shown up today. None were hanging out windows or having a smoke outside. No greeter, as in big box stores these days.

I got in my Jeep and drove back toward town. I had come to a STOP sign when I ran into an opportunity, figuratively speaking. A telephone company truck was parked in the next block, ahead of me, beside a telephone pole, of course.

Why hadn't I thought of this before? Where there was a utility truck, there were humans. Workers. Telephone company workers. Who needed an entry code to an ugly building when there were workers in the field? I could have saved myself a trip to the rough edge of town and simply cruised the streets until I found a truck. Like the one in front of me.

I drove through the intersection and slowed down by the orange cones, lowering my window on the way.

"Good morning," I said to the nearest man in an orange vest and yellow hard hat. Not the man who was perched in a red cherry picker at the top of the pole, or the third man, who was shuffling tools around in the back of the truck. I was looking at the poster boy for a telephone company promo. A tall, fit guy with a perfect smile, exactly the right amount of stubble, and clear blue eyes that said, "Trust your important calls to me." Mr. Comm, I named him.

Once he realized I wasn't moving on, he asked, "Can I help you with something?"

"I just came from the central office, hoping I'd be able to talk to someone there, but I couldn't find a way in." *Impenetrable* came to mind.

"That's not a public office," he informed me. Something I'd gathered from all the signs and bars on the windows, but I felt no need to be sarcastic.

"Is there a phone number I could call to talk to someone inside the telephone company?" Oops, the sarcasm escaped.

"Nope." No smile; apparently Mr. Comm didn't see the irony. "What is it that you need?"

I took a deep breath. "Well, I'm a friend of Wendell Graham. I'm trying to help his sister by getting the word out about his memorial service tomorrow." I paused. It took all the strength I had to shove thoughts of Wanda and what she'd think of this ploy to the back of my mind. "I assume you knew him?"

"Oh yeah, yeah. Awful that he died that way. Nice guy. He came into the field a lot. When's the service?"

I gave Mr. Comm the details and a big smile. "You know, as long as Wendell and I were friends, I've never understood exactly what his job was."

He smiled back. "Graham was an installer, like us"—he waved his hand toward his two coworkers—"connecting lines, disconnecting lines, hooking lines to central, unhooking lines to central. The usual."

"There a problem here?" We'd been joined by a decidedly not camera-ready worker. A heavier, older guy whose orange vest hadn't seen a washing machine for a while, and whose hard hat was dented all around.

"No problem," I said.

"This here's Jimmy, Graham's replacement," Mr. Comm said of the newcomer to the conversation.

"That was very quick work, bringing you in so soon after Wendell's death," I said, pretending to shade my eyes from the sun, when I was really hiding from Jimmy's sharp, dark eyes.

"It's an important job. Can't keep customers on hold no matter what happens." Even murder, I supposed he meant.

"I guess it will take you a while to get up to speed."

"Not really," Jimmy said, in a "what's it to you?" tone.

"He's a veteran," Mr. Comm said. "He's been in Albany for almost twenty years."

"What's your interest in all this, anyway?" Jimmy asked, cutting Mr. Comm off.

"Like I told"—I paused while Mr. Comm filled in the blank and said I could call him Kyle—"Like I told Kyle, Wendell's sister asked me to be sure everyone he worked with knows the arrangements for tomorrow's memorial service."

Jimmy gave me a skeptical look. "You don't say."

"I can give you the details," Mr. Comm offered.

"We have work to do," Jimmy said. At least he touched his hat to me while he waved me on.

With the window down, I was getting cold anyway.

It was clear that I couldn't be trusted with even a little free time. I sat in Café Mahican, distressed at how I'd wasted my morning so far. I couldn't let go of the fact that Wendell's killer was still at large. Even more puzzling was why I thought I could be the one to solve the mystery.

What if the killer was a drifter, now long gone, as some gossipers had theorized in my post office that first day? A stranger, on the way from crime number one, happens to pass through North Ashcot and decides to commit crime number two, with Wendell in the wrong place at the wrong time.

How many murders fell into that category? Random shootings or stabbings, never solved. I smiled as I thought of all the television dramas I'd watched in my lifetime, and how not a single one of them was ever due to a random act or even the cliché "robbery gone bad." Fifty minutes and the connections were made, the means, motive, and opportunity checked off, and the guilty party nailed.

I had to admit it wasn't just Wanda's plea that had motivated me to insert myself into this investigation. As poorly as I was doing in terms of results, at least I wasn't sitting idly by, and for some reason, that mattered. I wondered how Sunni and the real cops would have handled the boys in hard hats at the utility truck. Would they have asked better questions? Was it just the intimidation of a badge that got them answers where I got nothing? Or did they have special courses in psychology, beyond the management seminars I'd been to? How did they handle dead ends, uncooperative citizens, fortressed buildings? Slashed tires?

I felt sure that Derek was involved in some way, though I couldn't imagine that he himself wielded the gun that killed Wendell. I pictured him stripping bills from a wad in his pocket and paying off a minion. All this, without a shred of evidence. Conviction due to creepiness.

Some detective I'd make, lining up suspects according to whether I liked them personally. In my mental lineup, developer Derek Hathaway, architect and builder Tim Cousins, and Selectwoman Gert Corbin were on one side, and all my friends—Quinn, Wanda, and Ben on the other.

I thought of another case, across the country in California, and the defendant on trial, Quinn's mother. I had a surge of sympathy for Quinn, unable to imagine my own frustration and anxiety tripled, or more, if someone as close as my mother were involved.

I checked the time on my phone. Wanda had called me while I was driving from the central office and asked to meet me at ten-thirty, which turned out to be almost perfect timing.

At ten thirty-four, Wanda walked through the door of the coffee shop, past several empty tables, made a detour to the coffee bar, then took a seat across from me. She gave one last shiver and rubbed her hands together.

"Freezing, huh?" she noted. "Sorry, I'm a little late. Had to drop off a project for a client."

Wanda had tucked most of her hair into an olive green knit cap, which she left on, a good choice until she had a hot drink to provide some warmth. "Unseasonably cold," the weather girls had warned today, as if we'd expect a coat-free stroll any day in November.

I told Wanda about my feeble attempt to garner information at the central office and from the vested boys on the street. "I'm sorry I have nothing to report."

"I do," she said, as her name was called from the bar.

I could hardly wait until she returned with her drink. She seemed animated enough that I guessed she had good news. I allowed her time to use her cup as a heating pad.

Once warmed, inside and out, Wanda started in, leaning

as far as possible across the table. "I was going through some of Wendell's things, the ones he left at my apartment. He always stashed a few things there in case he didn't feel like driving home. He'd crash on my couch and . . ." Wanda stopped to compose herself. "Or, like the time they were painting at his house and he couldn't stand the fumes, so he stayed with me for a couple of days."

I put my hand on hers. "Take your time," I said. Eager as I was for whatever Wanda had come up with, I understood her need to slow down. It had been less than a week since her brother, and best buddy it seemed, had died.

"Thanks. I'm okay." She reached into her tote and pulled out a few pages of text. "I found these e-mails he'd printed out."

She placed the pages on the table, facing me. She'd circled the name at the top, the "from" person. Derek Hathaway. As if I would have missed it. I peered at the message.

The e-mail was to Wendell Graham, copied to Gert Corbin, dated a few days before his murder. The subject was simply: Lines.

The text began with, "New opportunities" followed by a list of names:

Barry Chase
Margaret Phillips
Tim Cousins?
Scott James/Quinn Martindale?

No further text, no other explanation.
Without thinking, I put my finger on the last named per-

son. I felt my stomach flip and my eyes widen. Wanda was more verbal. "What does he mean by that?" she asked. "Scott's your friend from the antiques store, right? Does he have a partner named Quinn or something? And who are Barry Chase and Margaret Phillips?"

I ran Wanda's questions and my own around in my head. How did Derek know about Quinn's dual identity? Other than that he knew everything, from the first day we met this week, to news of my slashed tires.

"Let's start from the top of this list," I said, hoping Wanda would let the answer to the Scott/Quinn question slide. I wished I'd cleared up with Quinn just how long he wanted to stay under the cover of Scott James.

I wondered what the question marks meant, next to his name and Tim's. Maybe Tim also had a fake name. Or maybe Tim was his fake name. "I'm sure I've never come across Chase or Phillips," I said. By which I meant they did not use the services of the North Ashcot Post Office.

"Barry Chase owns the barbershop in South Ashcot, I think. Wendell preferred him to the guy in town. But I think he's retired now. I don't know who Margaret Phillips is. We can check her out. Everyone has a website these days."

Except me, unless you counted the main site for the whole postal system, in which case I'm one of the statistics.

Wanda pulled out her laptop and searched for Margaret Phillips. "That was easy," she said, after only a few clicks. "I assumed she was in South Ashcot since neither of us knows her and Barry is from there. She's the librarian in South Ashcot."

"What do you suppose the 'lines' are that Derek mentions?" I asked.

"The first thing that comes to mind is clothing lines or lines of merchandise, but since this message is to my brother, it must mean telephone lines."

"I agree, but surely Derek wasn't ordering telephone lines for these people."

"Maybe he's informing Wendell that these are opportunities for new customers? Tim is in the middle of building his house, so that might make sense."

"But it doesn't tell us why Derek would be involved. That has to mean something." I didn't tell her that I had no good reason for saying that. "Then there's the matter of—why copy one town official and not all of them? We have to figure out how Wendell, Gert, and Derek are connected."

"How shall we proceed?" Wanda asked, as if I were the chief investigator of a team of two. I couldn't blame her. I was certainly acting that way.

"I'll talk to Scott and see if he knows what this is all about," I said, careful not to out Quinn without his permission, though my good friend and ex-postmaster Ben Gentry hadn't needed my help to figure it out.

"I can swing by the barbershop. They'll know how to contact Barry Chase. And since I'll be in South Ashcot, I can stop at the library, too, and try to catch this Margaret Phillips. Maybe you can stop and chat with Tim Cousins. We'll meet and compare notes afterwards. Then we'll decide when and how to confront our elected official."

"That sounds wonderful," I said. "How about asking the chief of police if we can take a cruiser on our rounds."

"Yeah, and maybe she can deputize us," Wanda said.

At first I thought she was just kidding.

15

Whatever Wanda's assignment for me was, I knew I'd be starting with the question-marked Scott James/ Quinn Martindale. As soon as my partner-in-crime-solving left the coffee shop, which was now filling up with patrons willing to define lunch as coffee and a scone, I called Quinn and asked him to meet me there.

I felt guilty as I planned to do what I criticized in others—taking up a table and a seat and soaking up Wi-Fi for a long time, on the financial strength of one cup of coffee. To assuage my conscience, I returned to the counter and ordered a cappuccino, a muffin, and a parfait glass with fruit and yogurt. Now that I thought of it, there was nothing wrong with calling that lunch.

Quinn arrived in record time. The sign of a bored man. "How come you're not at work?" he asked me. "If I knew you had the day off—"

"I don't have the whole day. Ben needed something to do this morning."

"Man, I get that. If I don't go back to work soon, I'll go nuts."

The barista, a fashionably bald young man with chiseled chin hair, called out, "Small macchiato for Scott." Quinn responded quickly and picked up his drink. I thought it impressive that he was comfortable with both names, but I couldn't decide whether it was good or bad that he traveled back and forth so easily.

"You said you wanted to show me something?" he said when he returned to the table.

Wanda had thoughtfully printed out a copy of the e-mail for me; I placed it on the table, facing Quinn, and pointed to the sender. "First, it looks like Derek knew both your names."

"We were already aware that Wendell knew them." He took a sip of coffee, then a deep breath. "That's what got me messed up with the police, remember? That paper he was carrying with both names." I nodded. Of course I remembered that. "So maybe Wendell told Derek," Quinn added.

"Or the other way around." I tapped the e-mail, hitting the date this time. "This dates back a few days before Wendell was shot. It looks more like it was Derek who found you out, however he did it, and then told Wendell that you were a good 'opportunity' as it says, for a new line."

"So Derek is feeding Wendell new customer information? That doesn't make any sense."

I'd been hoping he, or someone, would see the "sense" that I couldn't see. I sat back, defeated. Why would Derek bother with something so mundane as someone's telephone line? The kickback potential was nonexistent. Still, something wasn't right with Derek. "I don't know what Derek is up to, but he seems to have intimate knowledge of all that goes on in this town, and I can't believe he has nothing to do with Wendell's murder."

"He doesn't even live here," Quinn reminded me.

"It doesn't seem to matter. I think his vested interests are still here." I cleared my throat, ready for a new topic. "Who knows your birth name, Quinn? Wanda? Your boss? I'd just like to know when I can use it."

"I understand, and I apologize. I shouldn't have dragged you in. You didn't ask to be involved in my crazy life."

I hadn't meant to come off so whiny. "I'm not asking to be excused."

"And I can't thank you enough for that, even though I have no right to ask you to stick with me." He smiled and put his hand on mine. I caught a look that I trusted. "At this point, I have no way of knowing who can ID me as Quinn Martindale. I haven't told anyone, not even my boss. I'm sure Derek found out by logging into the same resources I used to get a new name in the first place. The only question is why he looked into me."

"And what he's going to do with the information," I added. I told Quinn the plan Wanda and I had worked out, to talk to Tim Cousins, plus the two people in South Ashcot who were listed in the e-mail, and Gert Corbin, who was copied on it.

We sat in silence for a few moments. Around us was the aroma of the best coffee in town, outside of the police station, plus the sounds of chatter, the clacking of keyboards, the hissing of the espresso machine, and background tunes from the nineties.

"I don't like it," he said.

I figured he meant the music, which I wasn't crazy about either. "It was not a good decade for music," I said.

"I'm not talking about the music." He put his hand on the much-examined copy of the e-mail. "I'm talking about this. I don't like any of it. It's dangerous. I don't like the idea of you pursuing it."

"Think of what it will mean to you if we find Wendell's killer."

He shook his head, releasing the usual wayward lock of hair. "It's not worth it. We have a man murdered; when you start looking into it with any seriousness, you're going to meet more than just Boy Scouts. You've already had a taste of what could happen, with your tires."

I tried to wave off the tire incident. "If you're trying to scare me—"

"I am," he said. "But I have a feeling you don't scare easily. I just wish I could help."

"I don't think so. It's still important that you not raise your profile around here."

"I'm hoping that won't be the case for much longer."

"Is there news about your mother?" I thought of the peacock blue letter, the contents of which I still knew nothing about, except a vague "it might help."

He hesitated, started to say something, then stopped. "Nothing I can share just yet."

"That's not comforting to me."

"I know, and I'm sorry. But I wish you would please think about putting an end to your part in this investigation—"

"Please don't use that word," I said. I looked around, surprised not to see my friend, the chief of police, standing over me, arms akimbo, as she had appeared in my mind, throughout my conversation with Wanda and now with Quinn.

"You're making it very hard for me," he whispered.

"Likewise," I managed.

Home, changing into blues, I thought how much more stressful my so-called free morning was. The activities and interactions had taken more out of me than a normal day of work. I couldn't wait to get back to selling stamps and the satisfaction of moving someone's precious cargo on to the next step in its journey. A small birthday wish from North Ashcot to a big city in Texas, a large box marked for delivery to a town as small as ours, in upstate New York. All important, and all seemed no trouble at all compared to my current personal to-do list.

To keep Ben happy, however, I still needed to stay away from the office for a couple of hours. I puttered around my house, getting caught up on chores. I hung a print that Linda had sent weeks ago, of Boston Common at twilight, in the snow, and straightened out piles of magazines and assorted bills and paperwork. In one of those piles, I came across the literature thrust at me by Coach and Selectwoman Gert, about the proposed betting parlor. I'd meant to toss the two brochures at work, but must have inadvertently stuffed them into my briefcase. Now I talked myself into perusing them, in deference to my duty as a voter.

I settled on my couch and opened the "pro" brochure I'd

gotten from Coach. I'd finally learned from one of my chatty customers that the man had been coaching football at Ashcot High for years. The one high school that served students from both North and South Ashcot was physically located in South Ashcot, which would explain why Coach wasn't familiar to me.

His side of the argument was very persuasive. The trifold pictured a beautifully furnished setting, resembling what might have passed for a gentleman's club years ago, but showing an equal number of females in attendance. It was hard to tell for sure, but it seemed the establishment on the page wasn't an artist's sketch, but a real facility, located on fairgrounds in California. The prose was intended to entice those looking for opportunities to place bets while watching international horse-racing events on one of their big screens or seated in front of an individual monitor.

I read through the hard sell. *Do you enjoy fine dining? Our pleasure to serve you, either at a casual café environment or an upscale restaurant. Don't know which race is which? Click here for a list, from all over the world. Need help with the jargon? Here's a glossary of terms.* I ran my finger down a list of words that were familiar, like "filly," a female horse under the age of five, and unfamiliar, like "stewards," who were the officials designated to uphold the rules of racing at the track and accountable to the state's racing commission. A "pick six"? Bet the horses that come in first in six consecutive races. Six times more difficult? I couldn't be sure.

I faded out at the math, just after learning that a furlong was one eighth of a mile, originally the length of a plowed field.

On the "con" side was Selectwoman Gert's brochure, much less colorful, without the support of big money, I guessed. The cover photo was a long shot of an area of an unnamed town with unsavory characters milling around, and undesirable features like trash in the streets and graffiti on the storefronts. Bullet points gave facts and figures on the increased crime rate reported in every city that had established such a parlor. References were sorely lacking.

If I had no other sense, and voted on the basis of who had presented the more appealing case, I'd find myself voting to rush the betting parlor initiative through for North Ashcot.

A knock on the door stopped me before I rashly signed a petition welcoming the parlor into our little town. Skittish from my tire incident, I peered out the front window before opening the door. Tim Cousins stood there, holding what looked like a cup in his hand.

Hardly anyone looked less threatening than the friendly, smiling architect/builder at that moment. Added to that was the fact that he was on my assignment list from Wanda: "Tim Cousins?" was a suggested new opportunity for one of Derek Hathaway's lines, whatever they were.

I opened the door.

Tim thrust out an empty measuring cup. "I wondered if I could borrow a cup of sugar?"

I gave a quizzical look, half smile, half frown, and asked, "What?"

Tim laughed. "Ha. Just trying to find an excuse to visit and this is all I could come up with."

"Pretty sad." I didn't reveal that he'd made my life

easier—now I wouldn't have to take the initiative to quiz him regarding the "new opportunities" memo.

"Yeah, sad, that's the truth. But you're always so busy. When I heard you had the morning off, I decided to appeal to your generous nature." Another quizzical look from me brought further explanation. "Ben said you were off and you'd probably be home."

I'd have to speak to Ben, who apparently thought, first, that my whereabouts should be public knowledge and, second, that I didn't get out much. Not that he was wrong about number two.

It was hard to resist a guy who'd go to all this trouble to be neighborly. It helped that today he was dressed for a business meeting. "A little formal for North Ashcot," I remarked.

"I just drove back from Springfield. My day job, you might say." He straightened his tie. "I decided not to change, thinking maybe it was my dirty overalls that put you off."

I assured him it wasn't. When I offered him a cup of coffee, he nodded and seemed like a kid who'd finally been accepted for the softball team. Also the frenzy to get information from me seemed to have died down, not just from Tim, but from the townsfolk in general.

In fact, I was getting the sense that the townsfolk had already lost interest in Wendell's murder. Maybe Wanda was right, and even the police no longer gave it much attention. I saw no outward sign of an investigation, but then I had no idea what one would look like from the outside. Would I see cops poking around in trash cans? People being stopped on the street and questioned? Probably not. I wondered how I could find out from Sunni what exactly they were doing all day, without disobeying her orders to me. Or aggravating her, as I might be if someone asked what I did all day.

"I don't have any sugar for this," I said to Tim, handing him a full mug of coffee with an image of Faneuil Hall on it, another of my Boston memorabilia.

"I don't use sugar," he said, in the slightly Southern accent I'd noticed at our first meeting. He turned his measuring cup upside down on my coffee table.

We were off to a good start this time. I was almost sorry I would eventually have to pump him for information.

Tim was in the mood to talk about his building project. A beautiful old white clapboard church almost directly across the street from the police station had gone up for sale a couple of years ago, and he stepped in.

"The church was only about fifteen years old but a rich parishioner decided he wanted his own legacy and donated money for a new one in South Ashcot, where he'd moved to. Must be nice, huh? You move around the state and build your own churches on the way."

"It's your gain. You seem to be enjoying yourself."

"No question about that. I carpentered and painted my way through college and architect school; now this one is for me. I'd be glad to give you a tour sometime. There's a cool loft that I haven't figured out what to do with yet. Maybe I'll make it an office, or a playroom. Depends on my mood when I think about it."

"If I built my own house, or turned a church into one, I'd invite the whole town to see it," I said.

"Not a bad idea, when I'm finished. Don't ask how many more years that will take." He picked up the betting parlor brochure that was still laid out on my coffee table. I'd been in the process of trashing it when he knocked. "I see you're into this referendum."

"Not really, just cleaning out some junk mail of sorts."

Tim flipped the trifold open and closed, seeming to pay no attention to the content. Maybe he was already very familiar with it. "Do you have a strong position one way or another?" he asked.

Uh-oh. Tim was going to pitch his position on the betting parlor. "Why do you ask?" I tried to keep my voice light. "Last I heard, voting was a private matter." If anything could be private in North Ashcot.

"Just wondering. I see that you've become a force in town."

I crossed my arms in front of my chest. Could it be that I felt defensive? "What do you mean by that?"

"Well, you hang around with the chief of police, and then I see you having lunch with Derek Hathaway." I'd started in on a verbal defense when Tim interrupted me. "I'm sorry, Cassie. I definitely started out on the wrong foot here. Again. I'm a little jumpy. I'm trying to avoid getting snared into one of Derek's schemes, and, frankly, looking to see who can help me. It's my roundabout way to ask if he's approached you also."

The perfect segue. "You're asking me if Derek invited me to join him in some new opportunity?"

Tim looked around my living room as if he thought it might be bugged. "Not so new. Derek approached me last year, when I first started my home project. He was careful not to be too specific, but he told me not to make too many commitments to the phone company before he talked to me.

Said he had connections and could get me a good deal. Did he offer you the same thing?"

I reread the e-mail in my mind. I was sure it was headed by "new opportunities," not something a year old. But maybe the people on the list were new, not the venture itself. I didn't feel comfortable sharing the e-mail with Tim at this point. To what extent could I trust him? For all I knew, he'd been sent by Derek. Was I being asked to be a partner in some scheme? Being tested? Or was I the next victim?

"Not exactly," I answered, finally. "But I've heard about a new venture. I'm too confused to have an opinion. What else do you know about it?"

"Not a lot, but you know when you have the feeling someone is recruiting you? Like, 'Boy, have I got a deal for you,' but you know if you get involved, it will come back and bite you at the end."

I did know what Tim meant, and I was beginning to think that Wendell had been an important part of the deal, helping Derek disseminate it. Whatever "it" was. The e-mail after all was from Derek to Wendell. Was Wendell one of the schemers, or was he trying to get out of a deal when he was shot?

"As my dad always said, 'If it sounds too good to be true, it probably is,'" I offered.

"Words to live by," he said.

My best bet was to stall on telling Tim what I knew until I talked to Wanda, who was scouting out a former barber and a librarian in South Ashcot.

Time was on my side. I looked at the clock. "Let's chat about this another time, Tim. I have to get ready for work."

He frowned. "Okay. You're not just blowing me off, again?"

I crossed my heart. "I'm not."

He zipped his jacket and added hat and gloves. "Thanks for the coffee." He headed for the door, turned, and said, "You'll tell me if you hear anything?"

I nodded but didn't cross my heart.

What Tim didn't have to know was that I was already dressed for work, and had only to drive the few miles down the road. But I had some things to figure out before I continued the conversation with him. I sat for a few minutes thinking about his visit and what I'd learned. Not a lot, considering we were talking in circles. He wanted to know what I knew and vice versa. The only thing that seemed certain was that the deal Derek had going—whether a legitimate business enterprise or a scheme that wouldn't have a happy ending for others—involved telephone lines.

I did the math. Derek's "opportunity" involved telephone lines. Wendell's job was about telephone lines. Like the Hollywood-type workman I'd talked to, Wendell installed or deinstalled lines for the phone company. Wendell was shot. I had a flashback to chemistry word problems when I never knew what to put on the two sides of an equation to make it balance. Just like now, when I had no idea where to put the equals sign among all the characters.

One thing that seemed sure was that all the bits and pieces were consistent with Ben's hesitation to sign off on flying our flag at half-mast for our telephone lineman.

16

I arrived at the post office parking lot in time to meet Natalie, Ben's niece, who'd come to pick him up. Even bundled into a thick gray parka on one of the coldest days this season, Natalie looked like a model for winter clothing at a classy ski resort. Her short, trendy boots seemed to perfectly match the turtleneck peeking up from her jacket; her gloves matched the band around her head. I, on the other hand, looked like a woman who'd wear anything to keep warm, happy if my accessories didn't clash too badly with each other.

From her devotion to her uncle, I knew that Natalie was as nice a person as she was a beautiful young woman.

"We're going to Pittsfield for dinner," she said, after we shared a friendly hug. She gestured toward the post office building. "I called Uncle Ben to tell him I was on the way. He'd been reading something about privatizing the post office and couldn't contain himself." She continued in a deep, Ben-like voice. "'It threatens our mission to provide service to every citizen, no matter where they live.' You'd think he wouldn't care that much anymore. But he loves the postal service, and can't stand the thought of complete retirement."

"He's been a huge help to me. I mean, he's the boss, but—"

Natalie put her hand out to stop me. "It's very nice of you to let him think that," she said.

"No, I meant—"

She patted my shoulder and we continued walking toward the building, heads down against the nasty wind and the beginning of a rainstorm. "Really, thanks, Cassie. It means a lot. To both of us."

I entered my building with increased faith in those at the younger edge of the millennial generation.

The lobby had been empty when Ben and Natalie left the building for their dinner date, but quickly filled up with customers trying to meet the deadline for express delivery and special handling packages. I processed more than the usual number of international money orders, vacation holds, and bulk and business mail material. Plus, I had a shipment to Boston to prepare for myself, a box with one of my scales that needed maintenance. My short workday flew by.

The office was bird- and animal-free for the first time this week—I'd hoped for another visit from the baby llama named Llarry, but his owner, Vic, told me the little guy was under the weather. I wondered how one could tell when a llama was not feeling well.

To my disappointment, Fred, Quinn's boss at the antiques shop, stopped in with a tub of mail. I remembered that Quinn was essentially on leave from his job, however, so this was to be expected. On the plus side, I had a visit from Gigi, our local florist, who often stopped by on a Friday with a mason jar of blooms. Today's was bigger than usual, with white Asiatic lilies, carnations, and snapdragons.

"A customer called to cancel a wedding shower arrangement," she said.

"Too bad. I guess?"

"I didn't ask." She shrugged. "You never know what can happen to engagements."

I kept from her the fact I did know, only too well, what could happen with engagements.

Gigi continued, "But I'd already put this together and thought you might need a little something this weekend. I know Wendell Graham was a friend."

I took them gratefully, moved by her thoughtfulness. I was a customer of hers in that I'd had flowers sent from her shop to friends in Boston, but I barely knew Gigi and was all the more thankful for the gesture. Sometimes it paid to be so easy to find.

The workday ended with a visit from Wanda, who appeared just in time to stand at attention as I lowered the flag. Her hometown elementary school training had served her well. Even before she spoke, I could tell by Wanda's demeanor that she hadn't fared much better than I had as far as interviewing the people on the Derek-to-Wendell e-mail list. Nippy as it was, it hadn't started to rain yet and we decided to walk to Café Mahican.

Wanda got us started on the way. Like Natalie, she was

well put-together and I felt more like her dowdy mother than her brother's friend, barely ten years older.

"First, Barry the barber sort of captured me and talked about his new retirement routine, meeting some of his old customers for lunch, watching sports on TV at any time of day, not worrying about new environmental rules." She stuffed her gloved hands in her pockets. "He went on about how more and more regulations about brushes and towels appeared every day, and the last inspector dinged him for tossing a used paper towel in an open container. Or a closed container. I forget which is forbidden. Who knew there were so many rules for cutting someone's hair? Especially a guy's." She removed one hand from her pocket and used her index and middle finger to mimic cutting motions through the air in front of her. "Easy peasy," she said.

"Did you have a chance to ask him if he knows Derek?"

"Oh, yeah, a couple of times. He said he used to cut Derek's hair and his father's, who's also Derek, but now that the son was a big shot, Barry never saw him anymore. He figures Derek the son goes to some artsy—his word—salon in Albany."

"It sounds as though he had no clue why he'd be on anyone's list in an e-mail like the one you found."

"That's what I felt. I was kind of sorry to decline his invitation to have a beer with him, but I'd had enough."

"You did well," I said.

"I had some better luck with Margaret Phillips. She's the reference librarian at the South Ashcot library."

"Great," I said, really cold now, and wishing we'd driven the few blocks.

"No, not great. Sorry, didn't mean to get your hopes up.

But at least I got a response from her. She was very defensive and said things like, 'I'd never get involved with that man.'"

"Nothing about what she wouldn't get involved in? Or why she called him 'that man'?"

Wanda shook her head, and shivered at the same time, from the cold, I decided, and not from something Margaret had revealed.

"She wouldn't even step away from the desk for a minute to talk to me. We had a few words between customers, but I don't think we even made eye contact. So, I was a bust. Oh for two. What about you?"

As we entered the coffee shop and began removing layers of clothing, I told her about Tim Cousins's visit, feeling almost guilty that he'd come to me, sparing me the burden of having to track him down, while Wanda had had to commute to her assigned suspects.

"I don't trust him one hundred percent," I admitted. "But he intimated that something funny was, or is, going on with Derek."

"The only person left is Gert," Wanda said. "Shall we toss a coin for who gets to confront her?"

I scanned the seating arrangements in the room, most of them occupied with patrons, laptops, and piles of winter clothing. I spotted a few people I knew, then gasped in surprise at a couple in the back. I nudged Wanda and nodded my head toward a corner of the café, where Gert and Derek were engaged in animated conversation. "We may not have to toss that coin."

Wanda followed my gaze. "Whoa. Problem solved."

Or just beginning, I thought.

Café Mahican, with its high ceiling and large open architecture, was big enough to accommodate individuals or pairs of people who might come and go without seeing each other. Wanda and I seemed to be in sync with the idea of being one of those inconspicuous pairs. We took seats near the front of the café, as far as possible from Gert and Derek, realizing we'd opened ourselves to cold currents every time someone entered or left. We needed time to strategize.

"Now what?" she said, before I could ask her the same thing.

"I don't know. I can't decide whether I'm happy or unhappy that they're right there."

"Me either," Wanda said.

"Some detectives, huh?" We gave each other silly grins, partners in crime, bonding. I looked toward the back of the room, where, in the short time that we'd been sitting at our table, digging our wallets out in preparation for ordering, Gert and Derek had spotted us and begun a show of smiling and waving us over.

"We need a plan for how to approach them," said Wanda, who didn't have the advantage of facing our targets.

"Maybe not," I said.

Derek, with a long stride for a small man, was on top of us before Wanda could say "soy latte." He went straight to her and offered his condolences.

"Your brother was one of a kind." He tsk-tsked. "We all loved him," he said, giving Wanda a hug. "I have business in Albany tomorrow, or you know I'd be the first one at his memorial service."

Business on a Saturday? I supposed it took a lot of work to become rich and successful. Maybe the poor guy never got a day off. I wondered if Wanda, only nine or ten at the time, remembered how incompatible Wendell and Derek were in high school when Wendell was a sports figure, a star, and Derek was a runty nerd. As I'd always maintained, high school is a predictor of nothing.

Without asking permission, Derek gathered up our coats and scarves. "You don't have your drinks yet," he said. "Let's get you settled over there with Gert, and I'll take your orders."

I felt my face flush. I wanted nothing more than to reject this enforced meeting with a pushy man, just on principle, but I thought of the telephone-line e-mail Wanda had found, and told myself that this might also be the best opportunity I'd have to clear up a few things, get some answers. If I dared ask the questions, that is.

Passersby might have thought we were the best of friends, perhaps members of the same bridge club, who met every Friday. The four of us chatted, shared a plate of pastries that Derek had brought over with our drinks. I saw a few people I knew from their post office trips, and nodded to them while allegedly participating in the alleged conversation with alleged friends Derek and Gert.

"I don't remember a colder November," said one of us.

"Uh-uh, I don't either," said another.

"I'm looking forward to the holidays," said the third.

"News says it's going to stay cold another few days," said the fourth.

"The fund-raising auction for the middle school starts next week," said one.

"I hope they have those wonderful ornaments the children make," said another.

"Wendell Graham left some strange e-mails behind," I said. "One of them is from you, Derek. Something about telephone lines?"

Wanda stared at me. My comment had put an end to the smaller-than-small talk. I wasn't sure where my courage came from. Or was it stupidity? It was definitely disobedience as far as my instructions from Sunni—my sort-of friend but very real chief of police.

What was I thinking? Was I finally fed up with being pushed around? Starting with Adam in Boston, continuing with Derek. I knew that guilt had been part of my makeup ever since I learned that Wendell had been murdered. I could have been nicer to him, reached out to him as soon as I came back. Maybe he would have confided in me about any difficulty he was having. Maybe I could have helped him. Maybe, maybe. Now it was too late. Whatever combination of confusion and anger and frustration in me had built up, it had burst out now and was staring everyone at the table in the face, and they were all staring at me.

Derek and Gert looked flustered, unbelieving. Wanda did, too, but she came to my aid.

"That's right, Cassie," Wanda said. She turned to Gert Corbin, who was trying to swallow her recent bite of Danish. "And I believe you were copied on it also, Ms. Corbin?"

Thanks, Wanda. Gert recovered quickly. I imagined people in the political limelight had a lot of practice at hardball questions. She dabbed at the corner of her mouth and rolled her eyes. "Really, if you had to remember every detail of every e-mail you received or sent . . ." she said in a too-loud voice. She put her hand to her forehead as if trying to stem the tide of an oncoming migraine at the very thought of all that remembering and all those pesky details.

I was aware that some of the conversations around us had come to a halt. I heard no more clanging silverware, shuffling feet, or lighthearted laughs. Even the background music seemed to have decreased in volume, making everything we said that much louder. I felt all eyes on our table and heard the unspoken questions. A lot of them were mine.

"Indeed," Derek said. Not as impressive.

A cell phone rang, and people at two or three other tables near us checked their pockets and purses, seeming glad to get back to life as normal in Café Mahican. Lucky for him, it was Derek's phone that rang. "I'd better take this," he said. He gave us the look he might give if we were standing in his office and he was asking for privacy.

Gert made a move to leave, setting a good example, and Wanda and I followed suit and gathered our things.

"We'll pick this up another time," I said to Derek, nudging him slightly as I made my way past him. I wondered if I'd have been so brave if we hadn't been surrounded by a roomful of patrons, many of whom were young, looking like they'd just come from the gym or a martial arts class.

Derek covered the mouthpiece on his phone and addressed me: "I thought we understood each other," he said.

"Thanks for the drink," I said.

Before I could get my bearings, Gert slipped out the back door. Wanda and I retreated to the restroom, where I noticed her hand was shaking as she tried to manage the water faucet. "I can't believe you did that," she said.

"I can't either. Thanks for your support. I have no idea what I would have done if I'd been left hanging there."

We took some deep breaths and even managed a sort of victory smile, or at least, a starting-gun smile.

"What do you think will happen now?" she asked.

"We wait," I said, wondering what condition my car would be in tomorrow morning. Or if either of us would see tomorrow morning.

I hated the idea of being afraid around my own home. I'd felt perfectly safe in the heart of Boston, New England's largest city, for almost twenty years, and now as I turned the key in my door in North Ashcot, about two hundred times smaller, chills ran through me. I expected—what? A bomb? An intruder lying in wait? A shotgun rigged to go off when I opened the door? Worse were fears that I had endangered Wanda. Or Ben. Or Quinn. I pushed those thoughts as far back in my mind as I could, and forced myself to walk through the door. The icemaker in my fridge chose that moment to kick on. I jumped, then chided myself for my childish behavior.

It didn't help that the rain was now coming down in earnest, beating against my car in the driveway and my front windows. Not until I'd switched on all the lights and checked all the doors and windows was I able to let down my guard. I changed into sweats and looked through my CDs. My favorite country and western ballads wouldn't do: too much sadness and loss, whether of partners, pickup trucks, or dogs.

I wasn't in the mood for classical music, either: not nearly distracting enough. I chose a CD with workout songs from the seventies and prepared my dinner to the sounds of Stevie Wonder, the Grateful Dead, and Creedence Clearwater.

I put together a potpie with leftover chicken and frozen veggies, wondering, of course, where last night's chef was dining now.

When the phone rang, I jumped and nearly tipped over my coffee.

"Hey, Cassie." Sunni's voice. My stomach clutched.

"Hey," I croaked. Had she heard about the dramatic end to my coffee klatch with Wanda, Derek, and Gert? I managed a smile as I made up a new practice: the police arresting people by phone.

"Are you in the middle of dinner?" she asked. More fuel for my theory that Sunni's five senses were supernormal.

"Yes, but nothing special."

"Want some company?"

"Sure," I said. "If you don't mind leftovers."

"I'll bring dessert."

"I'll be waiting," I said.

I hoped she'd also bring some news. Anything that would allow me to retire from investigating. And feel safe in my hometown and in my home.

I rushed around picking up the clutter in my living room. Scattered gloves and stickie notes here; magazines and folders there. I cleaned up in the kitchen, then changed from my scruffy sweats to clean jeans and a nonlogo sweatshirt. Not that I was concerned that Sunni would be judgmental about my housekeeping standards, but folding laundry, scrubbing a baking dish, and wiping down the counters had used up my nervous energy. If my North Ashcot life continued at this intensity and rate of stress, I'd have to invest in a treadmill.

Sunni took longer than I expected to get to my house. I guessed traffic could pile up around this time of day, and the heavy rain added to the mess. I heard Linda in Boston laughing, saying, "Yeah, probably three cars at the same intersection, right?" Though she didn't know it, I laughed with her. My own private standup gig.

I'd added enough ingredients to stretch the chicken pot-pie to two servings and made quick biscuits to fill in the gaps. Nothing to do but wait, and no chance of being able to focus on reading. I sat in my glide rocker and pecked away at a crossword puzzle, trying to guess a five-letter word for the capital of an African country, and what the chief of police might have in mind this evening.

Would Sunni focus on our personal friendship? She might offer to introduce me at her next quilters' meeting or suggest a drive to Springfield for a movie or to the outlets for shopping. Maybe I could offer to show her around Boston on a day trip, for a show or exhibit. We could meet Linda, have girl-time.

Or would there be a heavier agenda? I'd welcome information about the Girl Scout who'd confessed to attacking my tires, for example. Sunni might have a pipeline to Quinn's mother's case in San Francisco. Or news in the Wendell Graham murder case right here in town. Wouldn't that be a thrill?

By the time the doorbell rang (causing another jerky response) I'd imagined that Sunni had heard about and come to discuss my confrontation with Derek and Gert. I walked to the door, ready to offer my hands for cuffing.

The first good news was that Sunni was in civvies. I took her dripping yellow anorak from her and noted her outfit—turtleneck, black jeans, and a dark blue down vest. Not an official visit, then. I hadn't had to change from my UMASS sweats.

My guest held out a pink box. "From the new line of tiny Bundt cakes the bakery started. I picked out four different flavors." She pulled out small plastic containers, labeled *Lemon, Red Velvet, Pecan Praline,* and *White Chocolate Raspberry.* Something for everyone.

We were off to a good start.

Dinner talk was a cut above the forced chatter at Café Mahican this afternoon. I felt only slightly guilty not sharing the e-mail Wanda had found and telling her about the resulting outburst in the café. It was much easier to have Sunni relaxed and off the job. She loved the idea of a trip to Boston, and we made plans for a visit to the Gardner Museum in my old neighborhood, which she recalled visiting years ago.

"I hope they still have the Raphael room set up," she said.

"We can check online."

"Good idea." Sunni filled her fork with raspberry cream and uttered a sound of approval. "Boston's not that far away."

I nodded. "Not even three hours."

"I don't know why I haven't made the trip more often. I used to do it all the time. I guess it's habit. You get into a rut and leaving your everyday comfort zone seems to take too much effort."

"I get that," I said, regret sneaking into my mood. "It's the reason I didn't make the same trip in this direction all these years. I wanted to visit my aunt especially, and it would have been nice to keep up with old friends"—the picture of Wendell and Wanda came to my mind unbidden—"but when it came to actually getting myself in gear and getting on the road, I could always find an excuse."

Sunni sat back, tucked her legs under her, and uttered a sigh that seemed to take her far away. Maybe the response was to another bite of white chocolate raspberry cake; more likely from images of her own opportunities whose time had passed.

"I suppose you'll miss Quinn," she said, coming back to the here and now.

"Miss him?" Did Sunni think Quinn visited every night? Could she even know he'd cooked the chicken she'd enjoyed this evening? "We had coffee this afternoon," I admitted.

She unwrapped herself and sat up straight. "Uh-oh. You don't know."

I straightened a bit too and threw up my hands. "You've lost me."

She took a long breath, and looked up at the ceiling, as if there was a helpful tip written there. "Quinn Martindale went back to San Francisco this afternoon."

I dropped my fork. It landed at my feet, scattering bits of sugary pecans over my hardwood floor.

It took a long time for me to retrieve it and clean up the mess with my napkin.

17

When I was ready to come up for air, Sunni was placing a clean fork on my plate. She handed me a glass of water.

"I'm sorry, Cassie. I thought surely . . ." Sunni looked like she was about to slap her own face or, at least, bite her tongue.

"Not a problem," I said, aware of my shaky voice. "Of course, I can see why you'd think he'd told me. But it's not like we were . . ." What were we exactly? I wasn't clear myself; how could I explain it to someone else? "We weren't that close," I said. "The first time we did anything socially was that lunch last Monday."

"You mean the one where Ross and I came and took him away and left you stranded?"

There was no good response to that except to laugh,

which we both did, heartily. It was the perfect way to ease the tension.

I caught my breath, and tried to pay attention while Sunni explained.

"He stopped by the station on Wednesday morning to see how soon he could leave. We were still tracking him, so to speak, digging around for updates on his mother's situation in San Francisco. I was impressed that he didn't just split, but I asked him to wait a couple of days, and he did. He came back again this morning and I told him he was a free man."

"You said it started Wednesday morning?" It wasn't lost on me that I'd given Scott the mysterious letter in peacock blue on Tuesday night.

"Uh-huh. Of course, I thought you were in the loop the whole time. But, anyway, I've been convinced he's done nothing illegal, technically, and he certainly didn't kill Wendell Graham. There's nothing tying them together except that one slip of paper in Wendell's pocket, and the fact that those phone directories were in Quinn's home. We know why Quinn stole the phone books, and even though we still don't know why Wendell was walking around with Quinn's names, that's not what I'd call evidence of wrongdoing." Sunni talked at an almost breathless rate, and now paused. "If it turns out there was another connection between Wendell and Quinn, and we learn about that, we'll take it from there. I finally reached that lawyer who came through for him—well, I reached his secretary, that is—so I can always get him back if something shows up."

My mind flew to the e-mail. Could that be the other,

important connection? Quinn's name was on a list that seemed to be some kind of assignment from Derek to Wendell. What if there had been a confrontation between them when Wendell tried to carry out whatever the mission was?

I tried to recall Quinn's reaction when I showed him the e-mail. Nothing that indicated he was aware of it. It couldn't have been the outing of the e-mail that sent Quinn running; he'd already started the process of splitting. Did he think the e-mail implicated him one step further than that simple slip of paper?

"I'm curious," I said. "If you don't mind my asking, about what time did Quinn come into the station today?"

"It was around lunchtime. I'd just sent Ross out for sandwiches since I had a lot of paperwork to catch up on."

Lunchtime. Right after our conversation in the café. Right after Quinn had expressed concern that I was endangering myself by looking into possible motives for Wendell's murder. He'd been so solicitous, even offering to help or at least make sure I came to no harm. And then he ran.

I considered telling Sunni about the e-mail now. Would she reprimand me for not convincing Wanda to turn it in? Would she send for Quinn? Did I want some kind of justice or did I want Quinn back? I had to stop making his exit personal. My head hurt. Every mistake or misjudgment I'd ever made came back, full force, to flood my mind.

In the flood, Adam made an appearance, the ultimate rejection, the clue that something was wrong with me. He'd walked out on me without even a face-to-face. Not that I was shocked, but I'd expected a civilized final conversation.

I flashed back to the last texts between Adam and me. I

received the first one a few minutes after I came home from work one evening and saw that all the things he'd left in my apartment were gone—a spare shaving kit, a few T-shirts, a pile of business magazines, a pair of jogging shoes, even his favorite mug with a large green dollar sign. A faded rectangle on the wall of the entryway was all that was left of a Fenway Park print we'd bought. Apparently he'd always considered that print his own.

I'm sure u agree, he wrote in the text. Time 2 call it.
Call what? I answered. This isn't a game.

LOL. It's not working.

Can we talk?

Nothing 2 say.

Still would like a face2face.

I wish u all the best. A.

Thus ended a four-year relationship that included a three-month engagement.

And now Quinn. Without even a text message. Well, it was a good thing I didn't need either one of them. I'd been taking care of myself in one way or another since I was sixteen years old.

Sunni was waiting patiently for me to return. She'd been sipping coffee, taking small bites of her sampler plate of Bundts, allowing me time. I was trying to decide whether to 'fess up about the e-mail or change the subject altogether, perhaps to the exhibits that would be at the Gardner next month.

"More coffee?" I asked. Stalling was my best talent.

Sunni seemed to misinterpret my offer as a request to her. She took my mug from me, headed for the kitchen, and returned with refills for both of us. Such a thoughtful person deserved more than I was giving her. I'd hoped to have her as a friend without involvement in her profession, but it wasn't working out that way at the moment. I knew if I wanted to keep her trust at all, I had to be forthcoming now. Otherwise I'd lose her for good. Another loss was the last thing I needed.

I took a breath. "I have something to show you," I said.

I held my breath almost the whole time Sunni was reading the e-mail, contorting her face now and then, and I thought for sure she was going to lash out at me. I braced myself.

"I don't know what to say, Cassie. Wanda must have thought this was significant, or she wouldn't have given it to you. Did it occur to you to suggest that she take it to me?"

I shook my head. "I honestly didn't think of that. I promise. Wanda brought it to me only this morning. If you'd seen this, would you have changed your mind about letting Quinn go?"

"Probably not. It's no better than the piece of paper with his names on it in Wendell's pocket. And it's only peripherally useful to begin with. But that's not the point."

"I realize that, and I don't know what I was thinking, except I assumed Wanda and I should check it out before bothering you with every little thing."

"Are there other little things?"

I spilled out everything I'd done today, from trying to

visit the central office of the telephone company to checking out the names on the e-mail list.

"That's it," I said. I was willing to tell her what I'd had for breakfast, if that would convince her of my willingness to cooperate. One tiny omission was the brief interaction Wanda and I had had with Derek and Selectwoman Corbin. A small voice in my head said it was a bad idea to keep this from Sunni, but in the end, I convinced myself that there had been no real significance to the meeting. It was what Aunt Tess would have called a kerfuffle—a small fuss—plus a sense of underhandedness in the air.

"I hoped we could be friends, Cassie, regular friends, not coworkers on police matters."

"We can be, Sunni." I folded my hands together and held them out. A gesture of supplication if there ever was one. "Please, cut me some slack, just for this case. It's not all my fault that I'm involved." I ticked off the excuses. "I happened to have lunch with Quinn. Once, and it was the wrong day to do it. My phone books were in his house. Wanda came to me and asked for help. For one reason or another, people in town sought me out, either giving or seeking information." I threw up my hands. "I didn't ask for any of this." I sat back, feeling like a ten-year-old telling her parents she didn't start the squabble, her brother did. What hope did I have that the chief of police would take me seriously?

I looked over to catch Sunni's smile. "You left out how Wendell was your prom date."

I hoped the smile meant I was forgiven. Assuming the best, I uttered a weak, "Thanks."

"Let's look at this again," she said, picking up the e-mail. "Something struck me when I first read it."

I moved to the edge of my chair, leaned closer to the table. Sunni ran her finger down the text, stopping at Barry Chase.

"He's a barber in South Ashcot," I said, not mentioning that Wanda had already interviewed him.

"Yes, I know that, but I've seen the name recently in another context." She looked to one side then the other, lips tight, foot tapping, thinking. "I don't know. Maybe not. It's one of those names that could just as easily be the name of a new game app on my nephew's smartphone." She gave me a smile. "Barry Chase, very common. Like Cassie Miller."

"Not like Sunni Smargon," I said, continuing the light moment.

"Definitely not like Sunni Smargon."

We sat back on our respective chairs. Finished for the evening, I thought, until it struck me. I'd also seen the name Barry Chase and seen his photo on a business card. "I think I have it," I said. "Isn't he one of the named partners in the firm where Edmund Morrison is a lawyer?"

"The lawyer who got Quinn out of my custody. That's exactly right," Sunni said. "And now I also recall that he was a big contributor to Gert Corbin's campaign for reelection. I couldn't place it until you mentioned his firm. Thank you, thank you." Sunni pulled out her phone. "And . . . just let me check." she said, typing madly with one finger. "I know I have it here somewhere. Yes, that's also the firm that represents Derek Hathaway. Derek gave me his card a few months ago for some other legal matter and I stored it in here."

"Wow," I said, picturing all the loose ends closing in on each other. "What does it mean that a lawyer from Derek

Hathaway's firm, who helped get Selectwoman Corbin re-elected, is also the one who got Quinn freed from your custody?"

"Maybe nothing. It's a small town," Sunni said.

"Not Albany."

"Good point."

"So can you look into this?" I asked.

"You mean instead of you?"

"No, I—"

"I know you mean well, Cassie, and you have actually been a great help, but it's a dangerous pursuit. These people are not players in a ball game. One of them might be a killer. Didn't that tire-slashing party on your Jeep teach you anything?"

"No, because I don't know how it came about, other than a sweet young girl confessed."

"A subtle reminder that I haven't given you an update?"

"Could be."

"Okay, it is a little strange. You certainly have a right to know that. The girl who confessed? Her mother is very sick and they don't have a lot of money. A guy offered her cash, told her it was a prank, no one would get hurt, just a little inconvenience to a good friend who liked to play games with him. When we explained that was not the case, I could tell she was really upset, and not just about getting caught."

"I don't suppose she knows the man."

Sunni shook her head. "Someone came up to her at a ball game in the park and made this offer. She couldn't resist, et cetera. She described him as medium this and ordinary that; not much help. I'm willing to bet it wasn't Derek Hathaway, by the way, if that's what you're thinking. If he's involved, he's insulated himself. I can't see him trolling the park for young girls to do his bidding."

I could, but I decided not to pursue the idea. "I get that you think my tires were slashed because someone thought I was snooping around too much. But isn't that a little juvenile? I mean, why not really threaten me?"

"You'd rather someone put a gun to your head?"

I shivered. "Of course not, but—"

"You know, I took a workshop last summer. A wellness program for cops that they make us attend every so often. They talked about various sources of stress and how to deal with it, but they never mentioned what to do with well-meaning citizens who want to help."

I gave Sunni an apologetic look.

"So, the sooner we solve this case, the sooner I'll get rid of a lot of stress. Tell you what, let's brainstorm on what this e-mail could mean. We can start by assuming as you did that the 'new opportunities' has something to do with Wendell's job with the phone company, and probably has to do with new lines being installed."

I thought back to my ad hoc interview with Mr. Comm, the guy I met on my way back from the central office. "The phrase that keeps coming back to me is 'connecting lines, disconnecting lines, hooking lines, unhooking lines,'" I offered.

Our brainstorming began, but not before another round of coffee. With my permission, Sunni raided my cabinets for snacks. It seemed a long time since the chicken potpie. She came back with pretzels, corn chips, and small chocolate squares.

"I left the dried fruit behind," she said.

"Good choice."

"There's a lot you can do on a phone line that isn't registered properly," Sunni said, settling back on her chair. She grimaced at the taste of a stale pretzel. Too bad we'd already demolished the miniature Bundt cakes. Too bad they were so small.

Sunni used her smartphone to make notes; I chose the old-fashioned pad of paper and a ballpoint, randomly choosing a pen from a mug. The logo on the pen was ASHCOT'S ATTIC, Quinn Martindale's former place of employment. I stuffed it back in place and took one Linda had sent me from the Boston Public Library.

"Could Wendell have been hooking or unhooking lines to Derek's advantage?" I asked.

"Hacking phones and e-mails is a national pastime, and not just in this country. There was a big case recently, I forget where exactly, where a reporter was accused of eavesdropping on the phones of sports stars, politicians, celebrities, to get scoops."

"Not too many celebrities in North Ashcot," I said.

"Except for us," Sunni said, primping her hair and smiling, reminding me how much I liked our chief of police and looked forward to a deepening friendship.

"You said it." I took a satisfying bite of corn chip before I shared a sudden brainstorm. "On TV, the drug dealers are always using burner phones to do business, so their calls can't be traced. When they're through with the number, they click on something and the burner number goes out of service. I think it even wipes out all the numbers called."

"You think Derek might be dealing drugs on special telephone lines instead of buying dozens of burner phones every month? Why?"

I shrugged, hoping Sunni didn't think I had intimate knowledge of drug dealing. "Because it's less expensive?" I suggested.

"If that's what's happening, that would make the people listed on the e-mail about 'new opportunities'"—here Sunni drew quotation marks in the air—"potential users? Other dealers? What?"

"Prospective new users or something similarly unsavory would make sense in the case of the South Ashcot librarian, Margaret Phillips. Wanda said she claimed to want nothing to do with Derek. She'd be likely to squash any suspicious invitation immediately, if she's like the librarians I know."

"You mean smart," Sunni said. "It wouldn't hurt to talk to her; I'll take a little trip to see our neighbors to the south."

I nodded. "Our 'new users' hypothesis doesn't make sense for Barry Chase. If he's Derek's own lawyer, why would Wendell need to be involved at all? Derek and Barry could deal directly."

"In more ways than one. I see what you mean. And who knows about Tim Cousins and Quinn? Maybe they're already in the business." When I didn't respond, Sunni moved on. "What else could it be, besides a drug business?"

I ran all my favorite TV crime dramas through my head. What were other popular themes and motives for crime? "Blackmail," I blurted out.

Sunni tapped her smartphone, the updated version of chewing on a pencil while deep in thought. "Blackmail which way? Say, Derek is looking for people to blackmail.

He wants a special line—one that's rigged, or can be tapped, whatever—to blackmail people, and Barry, Margaret, et cetera, are potential victims."

One of us had to say it. "Quinn obviously fits the bill here," I said.

"Aha," Sunni said, as if she hadn't thought of it herself. "So, Derek finds out that Scott James has something to hide. He uses his lawyer to get Scott/Quinn Martindale out of custody so he's free to be blackmailed. Or he's already being blackmailed, and Derek doesn't want him spilling the beans."

"But the lawyer is also on this list. Does Derek have something on him, too?" I asked, rethinking my whole blackmail theory.

"I don't know, but let's put a star by that possibility, even though we're getting away from the telephone lines. You don't need a telephone line to blackmail someone. It almost makes you long for the good old days. Remember the phreakers?"

"Sure," I said. "They'd game the telephone system for perks like free long distance and conference calls. It was like do-it-yourself wiretapping with a little homemade device."

"And the crime was 'theft of service,'" Sunni said, adding the technical, legal name.

"It's overwhelming. There are so many ways scammers can use the telephone to cheat people or steal from them. They offer travel packages, loans, warranties, free trial offers, investment opportunities. They make pleas for relocation assistance, charitable donations."

"They even claim to be local police or federal agents," Sunni said. "There was a case right here in town not long ago where a woman got a call saying her unpaid parking fines or traffic tickets would be forgiven if she'd send x amount of money to some address."

"Wouldn't she know if she had an unpaid ticket?"

"Sure, and this one did. The scammers call around until they get a hit. They know that *someone* will be ripe for the offer."

"Scary."

"We tell people over and over to hang up and call the FTC if anything questionable is offered or solicited over the phone. I don't know the data, but I'm willing to bet that only a small percent actually report that kind of crime."

"Do we think Derek and Wendell were involved in anything like these scams?"

Sunni shook her head. "Not really. Not classy enough for Derek, for one thing."

I supposed she was right.

We sat back again, seeming to have wrung our brains dry with guesses and second guesses.

"Thanks for letting me brainstorm with you," I said. "Not that I had much to add, but I feel like I'm helping."

She gave me a squinty-eyed look. "Just for this one case."

"Of course."

"Don't act all naïve. I want to protect you, Cassie. Did you ever read what's on the side of our cruisers?"

"Protect and Serve."

"Right. North Ashcot hasn't lost a postmaster yet, and I don't want it to happen on my watch."

I couldn't object to that.

18

The rain had stopped by the time Sunni left, before nine o'clock. The trees on my street had settled down after hours of fighting the wind. I thanked my guest again for the sweets and for protecting and serving and we parted on good terms. We planned to go separately to Wendell's service in the morning and perhaps have lunch together afterward.

I'd started to clean up from our meal and snacks when I heard a knock on the front door. I peeked through the front windows and Tim Cousins waved at me, defeating the purpose of what had come to serve as my security system. Some day soon, I'd have to have a peephole installed. Or even a camera. I was sure Aunt Tess never needed one, or expected to need one. What was happening to North Ashcot? I hated to think my coming back had anything to do with the ill winds.

"I thought she'd never leave," Tim said, scraping his

heavy work shoes on my welcome mat. "The chief," he added, as if I didn't know who he meant.

Why did it always feel like an ambush when Tim came around, at my job, at the market, at my home? I certainly didn't entertain romantic notions toward him. The age difference was too great, for one thing, and his behavior reflected that. I doubted he viewed me that way, either, but at times I felt I was fending off a high school sophomore who had a crush on me.

"Don't you ever call first, like a normal person?" I asked with a forced grin.

He gave me a coy look. "Would you be happy to hear from me? Would you invite me over? Would you let me cook dinner for you?"

Uh-oh. Did Tim know that Quinn had cooked for me, or was that his throwaway line? Either way, though I still considered him a possible envoy from Derek, I was no longer annoyed. I laughed and moved aside to let him in. "Probably not."

He took the chair recently vacated by Sunni. "Looks like some good snacks here," he said, reaching for a pretzel. "Do you mind?" With Tim's drawl slipping in, the request came out as one word. "D'yamahn?"

My better self said I should warn him that the pretzels were not fit for company, being well past their expiration date. My better self lost out. "Go right ahead," I said.

"Do you think I could get a drink? Water would be fine."

"Only if you tell me why you're really here."

"A guy can't make a neighborly call? I got a delivery of insulation for my basement today. Thought you might be interested in knowing about it."

As if I believed the purpose of his visit was to update me on his construction supplies. "Sure," I said, determined to find out what his relationship was to Derek's scheme, if there was a scheme. This morning, we'd both skirted around the topic. I'd give it fifteen minutes tonight, I decided; then if I hadn't made progress, I'd usher him out.

I was about to fill a glass from the system on the door of my fridge when I thought I should be more hospitable. I stuck my head around the corner and asked, "Ice or no ice?"

To my surprise, Tim wasn't at his place on the chair, but standing up, the seat cushion in his hand. He seemed to be digging for something where he'd been sitting.

"Something wrong?"

His face turned red. "Uh, no. I was just adjusting the seat. No ice, thanks." He shivered. "It's cold enough tonight, right?"

Strange. But I filled his glass and delivered it, and thought of a way to confront him more directly than I had this morning, and without implicating Wanda.

I remembered a conversation between Ben and me, and chided myself for not recalling it when Sunni was here. With all our tossing out of theories, I'd neglected to share a real, live story about an extra telephone line that had been installed in someone's home, an incident that had caused Wendell some distress. Might as well bring it up now.

"I've been meaning to ask you something, Tim. I heard about a situation, where Wendell Graham had trouble at work and you came to his rescue. It involved a complaint about a telephone bill, I think? A charge for a line that wasn't ordered? Sound familiar?"

"Hmm, I remember something like that. It was a while ago, though, and I don't recall the details."

"A customer didn't know that an extra phone line into his house had been connected. Does that ring a bell?"

Tim laughed and slapped his thigh. "'Phone line.' 'Ring a bell.' Cool."

"Tim," I growled, giving him a look, one that might have worked between a teacher and a student who was misbehaving.

"Okay, no, it doesn't ring a bell."

He had ten more minutes. "So, you never straightened out an issue like that for Wendell and one of his customers?"

He shifted in his chair. "You know, there was something. I think I brought my dad in on it, since he used to work for the phone company back in Texas. That must be it."

"Must be," I echoed. "You didn't have anything to do with it?"

"Nope."

"Okay. There's one other thing I've been wanting to ask you about, something we touched on this morning. There's an e-mail floating around—"

"In the cloud, right?" Tim said, beginning to fidget.

I was undeterred. "Derek sent it to Wendell. Your name was listed, along with others, as someone who was a 'new opportunity.'" I mimicked Sunni and drew quotes in the air around the phrase. "Does *that* sound familiar?"

Tim squirmed in earnest now, unnerved at the inquisition, I imagined, making me glad I'd undertaken it.

"I dunno," he said.

"This morning you referred to a deal Derek approached you with, something to do with the phone company."

"I did?" he said. "I probably should apologize if I rambled this morning. I was distracted by this load of insulation.

236

I thought they cheated me on the shipment, you know, and I was about to lose a lot of money if I couldn't prove it. You wouldn't believe the ways you can get cheated in the construction business."

I took a long breath. "In your rambling, you said you were hesitant about accepting an opportunity from Derek. I think your own words were that you wanted to avoid getting snared into one of Derek's schemes."

"Honestly? I must have had too much coffee." He ran his hands over his head. "Or not enough." Another forced laugh, and an expression that said he was ready to leap from the chair if I didn't quit.

"You asked if I'd been approached, in fact. I can't believe you don't remember, Tim. What schemes does Derek have? Is he holding something over you?"

He stood, bumping into the coffee table in his eagerness to leave. "Time I took off," he said. "Thanks for the snack."

"I'm glad you dropped by," I said, almost meaning it.

On one hand I was back to square one; on the other, I had confirmation that Derek Hathaway was a schemer who'd gone from the bullied high school boy to someone powerful enough to scare a construction worker.

Back in my rocker, with Tim gone, I tried again to relax. I'd never seen a man act as guilty as Tim had, though guilty of what I didn't know. A telephone scam? Murder? Both? What if Tim was Derek's hit man, and was facing an unhappy end of his own if he implicated Derek? Were there more such jobs lined up for the man in Albany? I gasped at the idea. It hadn't occurred to me until now that the list of people in the e-mail could be a hit list. That would make Wendell the hit man. And Quinn one of the victims.

I needed a spreadsheet to keep everyone straight. If only I hadn't nearly flunked that course in Software Refresher for Postmasters.

It didn't help my state that I was facing the chair Tim had sat in, the same chair that I'd thought was out of place a couple of days ago.

Why was Tim really fussing with the seat? What if he'd planted a bug and came back tonight to collect it? I shook my head, hoping to clear it. All this talk of wiretapping, hacking, phreaking, and various other refinements of scamming—I was seeing spies and fraudulent activity everywhere.

Tim might have been innocently looking for his keys or pocketknife. No, he would have said so, I told myself. Maybe he's low on cash and was searching for loose change, his or mine.

I went to the chair and lifted the cushion; there were not too many adjustments that could be made to the seat of an easy chair. It was old, granted, probably dating back to Aunt Tess's early years in this house, but it wasn't threadbare. The stuffing seemed even, not lumpy. I inspected the seat and both sides of the cushion, not sure what I expected to find. I found nothing.

I moved on to motive. Why would Tim bug my living room? To get the same kind of information that he'd been asking me for since the very beginning, since an unnamed body was found in the woods?

I had a flash of insight into Sunni's life. Was this what it was like for her, or even for Ross? Always questioning, doubting, inspecting, thinking the worst of everyone, of the simplest acts? I hoped not.

I could at least put an end to investigating for the night.

I turned to my sounding board, Linda Daniels in Boston. She always knew how to set me back on track and, as long as she didn't stray into the forbidden territory of coaxing me back to within shouting distance of Fenway Park, had good advice. The big question was whether Linda would be home on a Friday night waiting for a call from her wayward buddy.

I sent Linda a quick text.

Home 4 Skyping?

And received a reply right away.

Sadly, yes.

I figured we broke even. She was home: that was good for me, if too bad for her. A few minutes later we were connected. Linda sat across from her computer on a rich black couch. She wore her oldest sweats, which I remembered from our running days, when the royal blue top and bottom were brand-new. They were now too faded to be identified by the French designer whose name they bore, good only for Skyping with a best friend.

"I see you're not expecting company," I said.

"I was. But let's not go there right now. Too depressing." She held a candy bar up to the camera.

"Candy at night. It must be bad. Sorry."

"Let's hear about your day."

I told Linda about Quinn's sudden, unannounced (to me) absence. "I could use some candy," I added.

"He might be going home to straighten out that thing with his mother."

"You mean how she's in jail, waiting for her murder trial?"

"Okay, calling it a thing might be little bit of an understatement, but what if he decided to testify? It's the right thing to do and he'd have to accept the consequences. Wouldn't that be an indication of his character?"

"Not if he did it. Killed his stepfather."

Linda gasped. No wonder. I surprised even myself. I'd never voiced that suspicion before, and I hadn't considered it since the beginning of this drama, prior to coming to know Quinn and welcoming him into my home. All of four days ago, I realized.

"You said he'd been almost forty miles away, coaching a ball game in the suburbs with a million kids and their parents present."

"I'm flailing here. That was Derek's alibi for Wendell's murder."

"Yes, you are. Would you rather talk about the ins and outs of the new family medical policy we've had endless meetings about, writing and rewriting section fourteen-point-three, slash Roman numeral two?"

"You bet."

"I see you mounted the print I sent. It looks very nice in your bedroom."

"Yes, you know that's one of my favorites."

Before either of us could get sentimental about the famous Childe Hassam scene, I switched to Linda's sorry state of dating. I learned why was she was home on a Friday night, free to talk to a girlfriend. In short, "Paul, the new guy, was a bust."

We signed off, as usual, with a wave and a virtual hug.

I sat up in bed and propped the novel I was reading on an extra pillow on my lap. I had a hard time concentrating, and faced the reality that I couldn't stop my speeding mind. I replayed the day, ending with my unsolicited visit with Tim.

I looked over my notes. Sunni and I had gone over the Derek-to-Wendell e-mail more times than I could count, discussing all four of the people—Barry Chase, Margaret Phillips, Tim Cousins, Quinn Martindale—and came up with nothing that excited either one of us as a real lead. I couldn't shake the feeling that we were neglecting something, but a nagging feeling was no more of a clue or a lead than we already had.

Now and then my mind wandered back to the lately flown-away Quinn Martindale. I tried to figure which was worse in terms of being dumped—a four-year relationship that ended with texts, or one that had great promise, but had barely started?

I wondered if Sunni knew more than she'd let on about Quinn's trip or his reasoning or his future plans. In any case, I wasn't surprised that she didn't share the details.

It was less stressful to return to my pondering of the murder case. Maybe there was more to the misuse of telephone lines than we'd thought. I went to my trusty search engine—after resolving to stop taking my laptop to bed with me, and breaking my ten-minutes-ago vow to stop investigating—to see what other kinds of criminal activity could involve phone lines. I scrolled through little-known (to me) offenses, such as "cramming," the addition of hidden or unordered charges to a subscriber's telephone bill; which was different from "slamming," a fraudulent charge having to do with competition among Internet service providers. Another sneaky, illegal activity involved billing for a call as soon as the telephone began ringing, even if the call went unanswered.

Nothing clicked as the breakthrough we needed.

It was almost tomorrow, the weekend, and all I had to look forward to was a funeral service.

19

I never attended a commemorative service without thinking of my parents' final memorial. Since I was barely
sixteen at the time, and barely alive myself, though not from
any physical condition, Aunt Tess had taken charge of the
arrangements. I'd resisted any attempt on her part to include
me in the decisions and choices.

She'd prepared posters with photos of happy events in
our lives. Mom and Dad as Aunt Tess, Dad's sister, had
known them—on ski trips, fishing, hiking, on tree-to-tree
aerial tours in the Berkshires. All of us white-water rafting,
ballooning, in attendance at concerts at the Tanglewood
Music Center. I remembered staring at candids of birthday
parties, graduations, bon voyage cakes, landmarks of favorite places.

Even then, I understood that Aunt Tess had meant well,
trying to focus everyone's attention on the lives my parents

lived, beautiful memories. But I'd been in no mood to think of anything but my great loss, and deep guilt that I hadn't been with them. I wanted to tear the posters apart, burn them, stomp on the ashes, and scream for my parents to come back, to embrace me, to scold me, to smile at me, to send me to my room.

One of the photos showed me with Mom and Dad at my eighth-grade graduation. I stood between them, my dad's genes prominent as I was almost as tall as he was and already taller than my mom. I wore my hair down to my waist at the time. After I saw the photo in the mortuary on the day of their service, I cut my hair as short as I could get it and kept it that way until I was in college. The feelings I had during those years faded as I grew older, but it didn't take much to bring them back. Like today's service for Wendell Graham.

Wendell's service was at a different church in North Ashcot, a very small building closer to the edge of town, where he'd been killed, but they were all the same to me. This church was made of blond wood with off-white gauzy banners here and there and a choir dressed in off-white gauzy robes.

Sure enough, the table in the vestibule held standup posters with happy photographs. I caught a glimpse of the young Wendell in his quarterback uniform, cradling a football, and turned away. I could imagine the rest, whether I wanted to or not. I hoped the photograph-album trend would be over by the time someone had to plan my funeral.

I'd arrived late to this service on purpose, when most guests were already seated. I sat at the back. No one needed to see me fall apart, if that's what was going to happen.

Another advantage to my position was that I could see most of the mourners, seated in front of me, in case I decided to take notes. If there was any truth to the myth that killers always attended their victims' funerals, I was ready. Playing sleuth was a good alternative to breaking down.

I hadn't expected so many people to attend today. Perhaps Wendell's self-image, as reported by Wanda, was off-base, and he wasn't the loser he thought he was.

I spotted the town's elders, "Call-me-Moses" Crawford and Harvey Stone, who, I figured, were regular funeral go-ers. Coach was there, more formally dressed than he'd been at the impromptu meeting at the post office right after Wen-dell's murder. Under different circumstances, I might have taken my notebook and queried Coach, and everyone else as to why they were present.

I recognized many others from around town or as post office customers. Several people stopped on their way past my pew and greeted me in hushed tones. I smiled and nod-ded at all the "Hi, Cassie" whispers and the nudges. A few who knew we'd been friends those many years ago offered condolences.

"I know you were close," said one classmate I vaguely recognized. I didn't correct her.

"So sorry for your loss," said another, as if I, and not Wanda and the people in the front row, were Wendell's family.

I looked around for Barry Chase. I'd never met him, but I'd seen his photo and felt he must be here. Maybe represent-ing his client Derek Hathaway, who had pressing business this Saturday. I examined all the suits I could see, searching for the most expensive looking. I looked for Mr. Comm and

Jimmy, Wendell's replacement at the phone company, but didn't see either.

Gert was in a middle row. I wondered if she had a purse full of her flyers. What a great venue to spread the word about the evil betting establishment and what it could do to a town.

I shifted my position to see the Graham family in the front row, across the aisle from me. I picked out Mr. Graham, Wanda's father; her older brother, Walker, from Florida; and her sister, Whitney, who'd moved to Maine for college and stayed there. I wouldn't have recognized any of them, except in this context.

I wondered if they'd all agreed on using the joyful photo array. I had to remind myself that people were different, that everyone grieved in their own way, and that, for some, the photos were a source of comfort. Maybe someday I'd be ready to derive comfort from such memorabilia, but not today.

At the front end of the aisle was a table with candles and a large photo of Wendell, as if the ones in the entryway weren't enough to bring us to tears. The setting, the music, the smell of candle wax, the hushed tones made Wendell's death all too real for me.

"Dear family and friends," the preacher began.

Family and friends, I thought. And we're all sitting here, doing nothing useful.

I had a burst of awareness. It was time to find out who did this. No pussyfooting around, no following rules. What did it matter who investigated, who found a lead or searched out information, as long as the killer was caught? Someone murdered Wendell and almost a week later we still didn't know who. It didn't seem right. Was I having flashbacks of my parents' deaths? The challenge thrust upon me to accept what had happened? So what? It didn't matter.

If the preacher hadn't chosen that moment to tap the microphone, starting the formal service, I might have stepped to the front of the church and announced an official interrogation of everyone present. No holds barred. Never mind that I noticed one of the last people to arrive, in her dress blue-grays: Chief Sunni Smargon. I was afraid she was going to sit in my row, but she marched toward the front and joined a young couple she seemed to know.

I settled down, but things were different for me now. I wouldn't be able to live my normal life until the world was put right for Wanda, especially.

I slid to the end of my bench, stood, and quietly left the church. As I walked the few yards to the rear door, with my back to the preacher, the mourners, and the gauzy banners, I felt all eyes on me, but the eulogy had begun and I detected no change in the preacher's words or cadence, and felt no arm on my shoulder to stop me. I reached the vestibule. Two large men, formally dressed in black, stood at attention as I approached. Without questioning me, they each opened one of the double doors so that I could exit easily, into the sunlight.

Neither man asked where I was going or why; I guessed I looked like I knew what I was doing.

For lack of other ideas, I drove home. The day was crisp and bright, in direct contrast to my mood. I wished last night's thunderstorms were back. What right did anyone have to enjoy clear skies?

I knew Wanda would be looking for me at the reception, as would Sunni. But I couldn't imagine myself standing around with a cup of coffee and a paper plate of snacks, chatting, as if we were having a picnic. Eventually, I'd admit to both women that I just couldn't take it.

My plan, such as it was, was to brew my own coffee, then sit down and organize my thoughts and information, starting from the beginning, which I defined as last Monday morning, five days ago. I thought of using a storyboarding technique I'd learned as a project manager.

I could buy a big whiteboard, or simply use large pieces of paper, and diagram the time line—plotting Wendell's murder and other out-of-the-ordinary events and activities, the suspects, and whatever shreds of evidence I had that were pertinent to the case. Something might pop out. I hadn't been that bad at math, and this project was like one of the proofs we used to do in geometry, or the logic puzzles I used to love. *If Wendell sat next to Derek, and Wanda did not eat the same snack as Quinn* . . .

Maybe it wouldn't be as easy as I hoped to arrive at a solution, but I had to try.

I parked in my driveway, stomped up the steps, and opened my front door.

And surprised the man standing in my living room, his mouth and eyes wide open. Tim Cousins, in overalls, as startled as I was.

I knew he hadn't come for sugar.

"Cassie. I thought you were at the funeral service."

"What are you doing here?" If I'd looked more closely at the scene, I wouldn't have had to ask. Tim stood next to the easy chair he'd sat in last night, holding a thin black pen between his thumb and index finger.

"I was looking for this," he said. More of a question than a statement.

I was stopped in my tracks, but not for more than a few seconds. I'd read enough thrillers and seen enough movies and television crime dramas to guess that it was no ordinary pen. Besides, the look on Tim's face, decidedly not made for poker, showed all. It was looking as though I hadn't been paranoid, at least not about Tim bugging my house.

He hadn't come for a pen, or my jewelry, or my cash on hand, or any valuable antique handed down from Aunt Tess, any more than he'd come for a cup of sugar yesterday morning. Tim had put some kind of listening device in my chair, and maybe elsewhere in my home.

"I thought you were at the funeral service," he said again, clearly having a hard time believing he'd been caught.

"You said that. And I thought you were anywhere but in my house." I looked more closely at the pen, tempted to step up to him and grab it.

He followed my gaze to his hand, his expression turning sheepish. "Cassie, I thought—"

"Please don't tell me you thought I was at the funeral service. You're bugging me in more ways than one. Is this the first time? Or the tenth?" I asked.

I held out my hand and he placed the pen in my palm. I turned the pen over and over, feeling its surface. I was amazed to find ink on my palm. Could this be nothing but a real ballpoint after all? I ran my fingers around the surface again, pushing here and there, and found the "on" switch, so to speak, by sliding the clip down.

"I guess we'll be recording the rest of this conversation," I said.

He gestured to the chairs around my coffee table. "Can we talk?"

I couldn't believe I acquiesced. How did I catch someone red-handed like this, and two minutes later let him engage me in a conversation? I was determined at least to take charge of the talk.

"Before I call the police, I'm going to ask you once more what you're doing here. Why are you bugging my house?" For emphasis, I pulled my phone from my purse and maneuvered my thumb into position for action.

He took a breath, picked up the pen, and switched it off. "It's a really neat thing. A gig of memory. You can listen to the recording through any headset, and you can download the audio onto a computer."

"Tim!" I couldn't remember the last time I'd used my scolding voice, except in this room a few minutes ago.

I picked up the pen and switched it on. I hoped it wasn't more complicated than that.

He shrugged. "I'm sorry."

"That you got caught, you mean. I need to know why, Tim. What are you doing here?"

"I can't really say too much."

I tapped my phone. "Well, you'd better."

Tim hung his head between his knees. I could barely hear him. "You don't understand," he said.

He looked more frightened than anyone in my memory, the fear directed somewhere outside my living room. I almost felt sorry for him. But it took only a moment's recollection of Wendell's murder, its effect on his little sister, and the events of the week for me to move past any sympathetic feelings.

I waved the pen between us. "Is this for Derek?" I didn't say that I thought Tim himself was a little too dumb to be the mastermind of some big operation that required unlawful recording of personal conversations, but he probably got the idea. "Do you want to pay for this crime all by yourself?" No answer. "You know, maybe I'm wrong and this *is* all your idea." I moved the phone to my lap and flicked the screen on. I was one slide away from the chief of police, and Tim knew it.

"Okay, wait." He blew out a breath. "Yes, the recordings are for Derek. They're voice activated." He cleared his throat. "I've stopped in a few times to download the conversations and recharge the battery with my tablet."

"You've been in this house *a few times*? Without my permission?" Now my voice wasn't scolding so much as it was a high-pitched whine.

"Derek needed to know what you were talking about with other people, what you knew about his"—he squirmed and seemed to have felt a shiver—"his activities. I'm just the guy way down the ladder from everything."

I could believe that, but it didn't let him off the hook. I thought of my own desire to have Wendell's murder solved sooner rather than later, and how, in a way, Tim's intrusion into my home could help me fill in the many gaps in my knowledge. Was I saying the break-in was a good thing? Maybe, but he didn't have to know that. He just had to think that he had no other choice but to tell me everything he knew.

"It doesn't matter where you are on the ladder, Tim. Do you realize how quickly I can have a cop here, how easy it will be for me to press charges against you? Would you like to spend a night or two in jail while Sunni figures out what else you're guilty of, besides breaking and entering? And it might take a long time for me to inventory this whole house, to see what's missing. For all I know you've walked out with my property."

"I didn't steal anything, and I wasn't really breaking in."

"What?"

He reached into an enormous pocket in his overalls, which were colorful as usual from paint drippings. I felt a shiver of fear for the first time since coming upon him in my home. From the moment I saw him here, Tim looked almost innocent, more afraid of me than I was of him. Besides, the funeral service, or walking out on it, had imbued me with a new strength and resolve.

Until this minute, I'd never thought Tim might have a weapon. "Not breaking, just entering," he said, producing a flat silver object.

I gasped. In some ways, it was worse than a gun. He had a key to my house.

"How . . . where . . . ?" I couldn't frame the question.

"You probably don't want to know," Tim said.

"Wrong!" I said, close to screaming. "I want to know everything, and the sooner you start, the less likely I am to speed dial my best friend, the one with handcuffs, who's only minutes away at the funeral service you were counting on."

"What do you want to know?"

"I told you. Everything. But I'll play it your way for now, Tim. You'd better give me straight answers." He gave me a shaky nod. "First, was Wendell hooking and unhooking extra telephone lines in people's homes?"

He seemed surprised that I knew, or guessed, that much. He squeaked, "Yes."

"So that Derek could use those lines for his own purposes."

He raised his eyebrows and let out another weak "Yes."

So far, so good. Confirmation of wild guesses from Quinn, Wanda, Sunni, and me. "What was the purpose of those lines?"

Tim shrugged. "Don't know."

I wasn't buying it, but I was willing to move on for now. "Did the people know that extra lines to their phones were being used by Derek?"

"Some did; some didn't. Derek wanted to use lines already set up in customers' homes, without their knowledge. You know, most of us have four lines kind of automatically, though we may only use one. But as you mentioned last night, that one time he tried, the phony billing system he set up didn't work."

"How does Derek have so much power with the phone company? He's a developer, a construction guy."

Tim gave me a kind of *duh* look. He used his hands as if they were the pans of a scale. "Housing and construction"—he made a weighing motion with his right hand, then switched to his left hand—"telephone lines, cables, communication systems."

"Okay, I get it. He's got everything covered. Why did Wendell get into trouble that one time?"

"The customer's charge for the second line was supposed to be diverted, but instead he was billed for it and made a fuss, and Wendell got caught. It was cleared up without disclosing the scam, but it was close, and made Derek scrounge around for different ways of doing business."

I recalled how far the word of that incident had spread, such that even Ben knew about it. "So he brought people in on the operation, people who would agree to have their extra line used but not registered."

"Right. Ideally, people who had something to hide and wouldn't make a fuss if something went wrong."

"Is that why Derek was so interested in Scott James? He even sent his lawyer to get him out of police custody."

"Derek is always looking for potential recruits to his operation. When a new guy comes to town for no apparent reason, like Scott James—you know, with no family here, or even a job waiting, Derek figures he's a good candidate. He looks him up, and in Scott's case, when he finds he's living under a different name, he figures the guy's on the run. Perfect. So, if things get dicey, he has something to hold over the guy's head."

"And that's the reason Wendell might have had Scott's name in his pocket. To arrange for that extra line, or whatever."

Tim nodded. He seemed more comfortable talking to me now. Maybe he forgot what might be in store for him if Derek knew he'd been caught. I realized I'd forgotten to lock my front door, having been thrown off my routine by the sight of an intruder. I got up and locked it now, just in case.

"Good idea," Tim said.

I gave him an annoyed look. "Why is Margaret Phillips's name on a list of potential new lines?"

Tim looked surprised, then figured it out. "That e-mail you told me about."

"Yes."

"Wendell told Derek he was running out of ways to hide the installation. Also, he was afraid his boss was getting suspicious. And frankly, I think Wendell was getting tired of all the stress. Derek told him to keep it up, just find people less likely to figure it all out, and Margaret happened to be one he thought would be a good candidate. I don't know why, really. Maybe he met her somewhere and felt her out, you know. Or maybe she had a secret life. Who knows?"

"And someone like his lawyer, Barry Chase—he'd know and agree, of course."

"Of course," Tim said.

"Do you have an extra line hooked up in your house?"

"I do now."

"Since that e-mail went out and Wendell approached you."

"Yeah."

"Do I have an illegally used line?"

"No."

I picked up the offensive pen. "Are there any more bugs in my house?"

"No." Tim raised his hand, Boy Scout–style. "No, I swear."

I figured I could decide later what percent of Tim's responses were trustworthy, perhaps only the ones where he raised his hand and swore? Only the single word answers? It was time to try an early question again. I hoped to catch him off guard. "What was Derek doing with those extra lines?"

Tim simply shrugged higher and longer.

I thought about all the options Sunni and I had discussed and that I'd searched out online. It was a long list, from blackmail to phreaking to more varieties of fraud than our Hole in the Wall had donuts.

"It must be related to drugs, I bet, all that money . . ." I said.

Another shake of the head. "I don't know what he was using the lines for."

I didn't believe him, but I had a bigger question.

"Do you think Wendell was trying to get out of the job and Derek killed him because of it?"

Tim gasped. Either a genuine reaction, or good acting. "I don't know, okay. And now I'm really telling the truth."

"And all the rest of your answers up to now have not been really the truth?"

"That's not what I meant."

If I only knew what Tim meant, throughout this very strange conversation between a homeowner and an intruder.

20

Tim and I sat in silence for a couple of minutes, each in our own world, I imagined. We'd come to an impasse. Tim refused to, or honestly couldn't, answer the key questions: what Derek was using the unregistered telephone lines for, and whether he'd murdered Wendell.

As if to signal the end of the first round, my cell phone rang. The noise startled both of us. I picked up the device I'd used to threaten Tim, set to call the police. Curious that the police were calling me. The caller ID seemed larger than usual today and I was sure Tim noticed the letters NAPD staring at us.

I slid the phone on. I hoped Tim was impressed—my threats were justified; the chief of police was my friend, a phone call away, as I'd claimed. Derek Hathaway wasn't the only one who was reeking of power and connections.

Arrogant, I knew, but at least I stopped short of putting Sunni on speaker.

"Are you home?" Sunni asked.

"Yes, the service was a little too teary for me."

"Understandable. I'm glad you took some time for yourself."

I looked at Tim, now fidgeting in his chair.

"I'm relaxing," I told Sunni.

"Can I come over? Feel free to say no."

"I'd love for you to come by." Much easier than having to figure out when and how to break some news to you.

"I'll bring lunch. Wanda is putting together a plate for you."

"Great. I'll put the coffee on."

"Excellent idea. ETA: twenty or less."

Less time than I hoped to have before I'd have to decide exactly what I was going to say, but maybe that was for the best.

I tapped the phone off. "That was Sunni," I said to Tim, as if he didn't know. "You'd better go."

"Can I get a quick cup of coffee first?" I gave him a look that said, "Don't push your luck."

"Okay, okay. But what are you going to tell the chief?"

"She needs to know everything." All of a sudden, I'd adopted a full-disclosure posture.

"Does she need to know about"—he spread his hands over my living room furniture, making me question whether there were other hot spots—"this? About how you found out about the telephone lines?"

"I'll think about it," I said.

Tim blew out a breath and shuffled his feet, as if preparing to run. "It would be nice to know what you're planning. As far as Derek, you know?"

It dawned on me what would be foremost on Tim's mind. "You're worried about Derek finding out his field operative has been caught."

Another loud breath. "Wouldn't you be?"

"Are you also the one who exploited the Girl Scout who slashed my tires?" Might as well go for broke.

"I'm not proud of myself for any of this, Cassie."

"I'll take that as a yes. And I'll be sending you the bill."

"From your attitude, I suppose I should run for the hills."

"Whatever."

I was also surprised at my attitude. I was buoyed by having made some progress in my resolution to discover what had shaken my world. And even though today's breakthrough fell into my lap, as I'd walked in on Tim, I was determined to accept it anyway, and make the most of it. It almost made up for four slashed tires, an invasion of my privacy, and the mental debris from another guy who ditched me.

Tim stood and put on his jacket. I held out my hand, palm up.

"What?" he asked.

"My key."

"Oh, right," he said, and dug it out of his pocket where, for some insanely hopeful reason, he'd returned it. I couldn't help wondering if Tim wished he could have a few minutes in my house by himself, maybe to retrieve, or plant, other bugs.

It was going to take a while before I'd feel completely comfortable alone in my home.

* * *

The chief of police deposited two plates covered with foil on my kitchen counter.

"Nutritionally balanced," she said, pointing to the plates in turn. "This one has sandwiches and salad; this one is all sweets."

I didn't trust my stomach with food before I cleared my conscience and got everything off my chest. I poured coffee and ushered Sunni back to the living room, where she took the formerly bugged seat. I was itching to check it to be sure Tim hadn't rebugged it. I wasn't sure whether it was a good sign or a bad one that he'd left the recording pen on the table.

"You didn't miss much," she told me. "It was clear that the preacher didn't know Wendell very well. He used every platitude in the book. Wanda missed you, however. I encouraged her to give you some time before contacting you. I hope that was the right thing to do."

I nodded. "Definitely. Thanks. I'll catch up with her later."

"Sure I can't serve you lunch yet? It's very good. The Grahams provided catering from that deli in South Ashcot. Cold cuts and cheeses. And all kinds of sweets from our very own bakery. I picked up the mini pecan praline Bundts I thought you liked, and a couple of brownies."

Strange that Sunni knowing my dessert preference almost moved me to tears. "That was really thoughtful of you," I said, my voice choked. "But there's something I need to tell you first."

"I'm listening," she said, sitting back, crossing her ankles, since her legs weren't long enough to cross at the knees on the deep chair. She was still wearing her funeral service clothes, sharp dress blues.

I took a long swallow of coffee. With the virtually non-existent prep time for this talk, my only choice seemed to be to tell all. I started with how I'd walked in on Tim. I handed her the recording pen. "For backup," I said, then did my best to paint him as a guy who'd made some bad choices, now caught in Derek's web.

I filled in all the details about the extra phone lines and how Derek managed them with the help of Wendell and some of his customers.

"It's not much," I said, "but at least we have confirmation and a few specifics about the basic concept of unregistered lines."

"I'm proud of you," Sunni said when I finished.

"Because I was lucky enough to come home to a source of information?"

"Because you're telling me. I'm assuming that if I hadn't shown up, you'd have contacted me anyway."

I assured her that was correct, holding back only the suspicion that I might have edited the information if I'd had more time.

I did my best to show my appreciation for the plates of food Wanda and Sunni had put together. I was eager to talk to Wanda, to apologize in person for walking out of Wendell's service, but for now, I had to deal with only one person at a time, and Sunni was it. We agreed to suspend talk of business for a while, but not before she assured me she wouldn't leave until she'd had a look around my house with her cop eyes.

She made the transition by handing me her phone, queued up with photos of the quilt she was making for her daughter. I scrolled them and listened while she narrated.

"The top is done. I just have to quilt it," she said, something I always found curious in quilters' terminology. It wasn't a quilt, I learned, until the last stitches were laid down, holding all the layers, including the stuffing, together. The pretty part, all the colors and patterns, was only "the top."

Not having a hobby to share—yet—I confessed that I spent time tracking the sale of special stamps online. Many were auctioned for much more than the face value. A sheet of fifty six-cent stamps commemorating the Battle of Bunker Hill had recently sold for one hundred dollars.

"Wow, that's three dollars' worth of stamps," Sunni said. "Who would pay more than they needed to for stamps?"

"They're collectors; they don't plan on using them. The Bunker Hill stamps have the artist John Trumbull pictured on them. They're from nineteen sixty-eight."

"So, they're not even adhesive-backed, I'll bet."

"I'll bet you're right."

She struck a glamorous pose. "Can you put me on a stamp?" she asked.

I was fairly sure she didn't want the standard lecture on commemoratives, but I gave it to her anyway, explaining that the postal service doesn't decide what stamps look like. Styles and images are determined by the Citizens' Stamp Advisory Committee, made up of people from all fields: philatelists, educators, historians, writers, artists, scientists, and whoever else the postmaster general sees fit to appoint.

"Except for a U.S. president, a person has to be dead for at least ten years before they can be on a stamp."

"Never mind, then."

"You can always go online and buy those custom-made stamps."

"The ones that cost a fortune? No, thanks. I guess I'll have to wait."

We lapsed into a companionable banter while we watched local news and mustered up excitement over the junior high girls' basketball win and the repaving of the parking lot in front of the town hall. We shuddered appropriately at the thirty-second ad featuring Gert Corbin waxing ineloquently— something about not accepting the proposal to corrupt our citizens who shouldn't be asked to resist the temptation to squander their money.

"Too many negatives in that sentence," I said. "Is she for or against a gambling parlor?"

We laughed and switched off the set in the middle of her next thought.

"Refill?" I asked, standing up, ready to collect her empty mug.

"I'm good." Sunni looked at her watch. "It's after two. I need to be at the station for an interview pretty soon. Do you have a few minutes to strategize?" Sunni asked.

I thought I must have heard wrong. Maybe she'd said "eulogize," referring to the preacher at Wendell's memorial; or "synchronize," as we'd worked around each other to tidy up after lunch. Had something materialized while I wasn't looking?

"Do you?" she asked.

"Do I what?" I was taking no chances.

"I know you heard me." She gave me a playful nudge and pointed to the chair I'd been sitting on. "Sit," she said. "That's an order."

"Thanks," I said, not saying for what.

"We still have three big questions."

I could think of only two: Derek's machinations and Wendell's killer. I said so.

"You forgot 'Are they related?'"

It hadn't occurred to me that they weren't. "Whether they're connected or not, can you arrest Derek on the basis of what Tim told me?"

"It's not that simple. Right now it's hearsay. It's all about what he said Wendell and Derek did. I need to hear from Tim firsthand. Then we'll see where we are with respect to Derek."

"Are you going to question Tim?"

"He should be arriving at the station in a few minutes."

"You've already had him picked up?"

"As soon as your back was turned."

"He's the interview you're going to?"

"Uh-huh." She smiled, clearly pleased that she was a few steps ahead of me today. So was I.

It seemed a moment of truth had come. I had the sudden thought that Tim might deny everything. Novice that I was at spy technology, I wasn't sure how much of our talk had been recorded on the pen. How would Tim answer Sunni's questions? It was one thing to tell all to me, another to confess to the chief of police. Would he tell Sunni a different story? Refuse to answer questions at all? Have a lawyer present? Worse, Derek's lawyer? I had little doubt that Derek would know Tim Cousins was at the police station in an interrogation room. Another billable hour for Edmund Morrison, who'd liberated Quinn earlier in the week?

I closed my eyes and breathed deeply, trying to sort out my feelings. Worry, relief, and guilt for starters.

"Are you going to sweat Tim to see if he'll give up Derek?"

Sunni laughed. "You watch too much TV. You need to get out more."

I couldn't disagree.

She twirled the pen as if it were a cheerleader's baton. "I'll listen to this and see what I can use. I do need to know whether you're willing to file B&E charges against Tim. If it comes to that."

I pushed away the image of the boyish-looking architect with the slight Southern drawl, a charming manner at his beck and call. I focused instead on the latest picture I had of him, in my home, which he'd entered with a key that I didn't know about, doing fieldwork on his electronic listening device. All this, plus misleading and intimidating a young girl into committing a crime against my tires.

"I'm willing. Whatever you need," I said.

Sunni picked up her jacket, preparing to leave. I wished I could accompany her and listen in on the interview with Tim, but I thought better of pushing my luck. It had been a fruitful enough day.

I picked up the recording pen. "Do you have any way to tell if there are other bugs in my house?"

"As long as they're switched on, our guy can find them. I'll send him by. He's sort of on call, a semi-retired guy who likes these little projects."

"Like Ben," I said.

"Exactly like Ben. Sometimes annoying, but indispensable. Are you going to be around later if he's free to stop by?"

"I need to go to my office for a while."

"On a Saturday afternoon?"

"For a short time. I need to finish up some administrative things. I might just gather some files and take them home to work on. It's been a crazy week. I'd like to get off to a fresh start on Monday morning and I'm way behind on background stuff."

"You mean it's not just cops who have tons of paperwork?" she said.

"You mean cops have management memos and amendments to rules and regulations?"

"And new protocols and updated evaluation forms," she added, snapping on her gloves.

I knew we could both go on for a while about time-consuming office work. "I guess our jobs aren't that different," I said.

She faked a frown and pointed a black leather finger at me. "Yes, they are, and don't you forget it."

"Kidding. You can tell your guy I'll be home any time after about six."

I let Sunni out, locking the door behind her. Which reminded me. If there had been one unauthorized key in Tim's overalls pocket, there were probably more of them around town. I researched locksmiths and found one who offered emergency and weekend service. He could accommodate me around seven this evening. Perfect.

It was looking good for sleeping well tonight. My house

had already been checked out by the chief of police, and it would soon be debugged and outfitted with new locks.

I sent a quick e-mail to Wanda, apologizing for bailing out of the service and promising to see her soon, then changed my clothes and headed out to my well-protected office.

21

I parked in front of my building and entered through the front doors, the quickest way in. The first thing I did was pull the shades over the windows, to discourage anyone from thinking I was opening for business, fair game for mailing services on a Saturday afternoon.

I couldn't resist a few minutes of tidying up the lobby—tossing wrinkled forms and emptying the small wastebaskets into the larger receptacle in the back. I wanted Monday to be as pristine as possible.

On my laptop was a giant to-do list that I intended to check off before I left today. I took it out and started from the top. Number one was "Clear E-mails," which was no small task, given all the outside solicitations and inside memos that landed in my in-box every week.

Linda had forwarded me links to several bulletins that

usually wouldn't be disseminated to local offices until a bottom line decision had been reached. This week an old debate had resurfaced about whether to provide packaging tape and other supplies to customers who arrived with boxes inadequately wrapped. The hard line was that we should sell the tape to the customer, not offer it free of charge, and certainly not wrap the package ourselves. Pitted against that position was the goodwill that such a small service would garner. The best parts of these memos were Linda's side comments, always either very wise or very funny, like the time she noted on a memo about upgrading equipment: "We're pushing the envelope here." Post office humor; it wasn't for everyone.

Today I printed out memos on workplace harassment (inappropriate behavior from Ben? I chuckled), labor relations (between me and lovely, motherly Brenda, my part-time cleaning helper? Another chuckle), and the limited services of campus substations (useful when a college was established in North Ashcot. A soft "ha"). I set aside the memos for later insertion into a binder, and deleted the electronic versions.

Checking off tasks was so much easier without lines of customers in the lobby. I worked uninterrupted until almost five o'clock. I was deep in the utility closet, taking inventory of supplies, when my phone pinged. A text from an unknown caller. Why not? I slid my phone on and read:

Can u Skype? Quinn

Quinn? *The* Quinn? Had he decided to make his exit more formal? Might as well close that loop.

Sure.

OK. c u in a minute.

I arranged my laptop on my desk. Before I opened Skype, I fluffed my hair (embarrassing to admit), straightened my sweater on my shoulders (likewise), arranged the pad on my desk chair (might as well be comfy for a dismissal), and sat with my back to the side door, facing a set of three posters on the wall between the mail sorting area and the community room.

One poster warned of hazardous materials prohibited in the mail: explosives, poison gas, flammable liquid, infectious substances, and more. A second poster listed various restrictions regarding unacceptable activities on USPS property, including: no spitting, littering, gambling, or drinking of alcoholic beverages. I smiled as I remembered when Ben had circled one item on the third poster to make a point: DOGS AND OTHER ANIMALS, WITH THE EXCEPTION OF SERVICE ANIMALS, MUST NOT BE BROUGHT ONTO POSTAL SERVICE PROPERTY. As if he hadn't already made his position clear. As if I would stop weighing cute little coatimundi.

The posters, in patriotic colors, were meant to be visible to customers at or near the retail counter, but I'd always thought the printing was too small to be useful unless you were as close as I was now.

I opened a bottle of water and dropped the cap onto the floor when I heard the signal that Quinn was calling me on Skype.

Not that I was anxious about this chat. In fact, the events

of today had been so intense and, in some ways, satisfying that my issues with Quinn seemed to fade in importance. It was hard to match a home invasion that turned into a breakthrough in a murder case.

However, when Quinn's face popped into view, clear as it could be on a laptop, I felt a few twinges as my jaw tightened and my fingers itched to reach out and smooth the collar of his denim shirt.

"Cassie. Wow. It's so great to see you." Big smile that I remembered well.

"Same here," I said, neutral as possible.

"Looks like you're at work?"

"It was a busy week," I said, before giving it much thought.

His face turned serious. "I know." He hung his head, rubbed his forehead. "I can't tell you how sorry I am for running out like that. I'll make it up to you. Somehow." The smile returned. "But there's terrific news."

"About your mother's case?"

He nodded, in a jerky, digital way, as some bits were lost between North Ashcot and San Francisco, if that's where he was. He was sitting on a couch in what seemed to be a den. A dark drapery was closed over the window behind him. No glimpse of the Golden Gate Bridge or a cable car on a hill to reveal his location.

"Remember that letter you delivered to me by hand?"

I thought of saying, "Vaguely," but settled for a simple "Uh-huh."

"A witness was ready to come forward, if I'd come out here and talk to her, and make some promises, which weren't that hard since I'm only about four degrees of separation from someone who could get her what she needed, and . . .

well, the main thing is, my mom's home." He shook his head and took a breath. "She got home this morning."

"She's free? That's wonderful."

"It is wonderful, but I didn't mean to imply that it's completely over. The charge against her was dismissed, but without prejudice, so technically she can be charged again, if something comes up. But it's unlikely, and I feel like a huge weight is off my back."

"That's the best news, Quinn," I said. "Do they know who did kill your stepfather?"

"The witness pointed to someone he owed a lot of money to, someone connected, as they say, who she claims was her boyfriend. To call my mother's late husband a gambler, betting beyond his means, is an understatement. There might be a trial for the accused, might not, depending on the lawyers."

"You'd think they would have let your stepfather live to collect."

"I guess in some cases it's more important to set an example."

"Then why did they try to frame your mother for the murder?"

"I didn't say they were smart. Apparently that wasn't their intention, but as long as their other clients knew he'd been murdered, that's all they cared about. Then this girlfriend finally had enough and decided to come in."

"That's the best news in a long time," I said again, because I didn't dare ask any meaningful questions like, "Are you ever coming back here?"

"Here I am rambling and I don't even know what's going

on there. Did you go to the memorial for Wendell? I'm so sorry I wasn't there to support you. I felt I had no choice but to do whatever it took to get my mother out of that situation."

"Out of jail," he meant, but I could see why that would be hard to say.

"You did the right thing, Quinn. I'm really glad it worked out the way it did."

"And you?"

"I'm okay," I said, wondering whether this was a very sweet form of farewell forever, or . . .

"I can't wait to see you," he said, leaning in toward the camera.

I cleared my throat and gulped, not too loudly, I hoped. "Are you coming out this way?"

"I'm on a flight back the middle of next week. I want to take a couple more days to make sure Mom is settled. But she has a great group of friends here, and she's happy that I've found a new home."

A new home? I thought I heard right. Quinn had called North Ashcot a new home. Sometimes it was better not to see the person you were talking to. It was a lot easier to hide an emotion when you weren't face-to-face, technologically speaking. But it was too late for that. I knew my smile was as big as the distance between us. "I'm so glad to hear that, Quinn."

"Then you forgive me? For all the subterfuge and crappy communication I've offered so far?"

We both laughed and I marveled at how much we'd said without really saying it. I hoped I was right, forgiving him so quickly, trusting him with so little to go on. I knew I'd eventually have to let go of my bad experience with Adam. Maybe this was the time.

"Just don't let it happen again," I said.

"Can you give me an update so I won't be too far behind when I get there?" he asked.

I pushed my chair back and put my feet up on the so-called guest chair while I briefed Quinn on the events of today, including the fortuitous intrusion by Tim Cousins.

"All that in little more than a day?" he asked.

"Hard to believe, I know."

Moving around in my government-issue chair gave me a new perspective on the wall in front of me. I zeroed in on one of the red, white, and blue posters. One phrase seemed to stand out. NO SPITTING, LITTERING, GAMBLING . . .

"No gambling," I said. Quinn had mentioned that his stepfather was a gambler. The word kept coming up.

"What was that? I missed something."

"What if Derek is using those telephone lines to carry on an illegal gambling business?"

I thought of Derek's aggressive opposition to a betting parlor in North Ashcot. It made sense that he wouldn't want competition. Why would anyone participate in his shady deal if there were a safe, legal way to gamble right in town? Was I questioning Derek's motives as a citizen concerned for the morals of the community and its well-being? Yes, I was, and with a great deal of excitement.

Quinn came to it at the same time. "All he'd need is a secure way to talk to a crew of bookies."

"Dedicated telephone lines that no one would be able to trace."

"No problem if there was a telephone lineman in his pocket," Quinn noted.

"Until Wendell's conscience got the better of him," I suggested.

"Or he got greedy and wanted a bigger cut of the profits," Quinn countered. "Betting is big business."

I liked my theory better and would probably offer only mine to Wanda.

"It was right there in front of me all this time," I said. "All that talk about how North Ashcot absolutely, positively should not introduce a betting establishment. The flyers all over my coffee table."

"A place where people could gamble legally."

"Wow," we both said, more or less simultaneously.

"Do you want to hang up and contact Sunni?" Quinn asked.

I looked at the time on the laptop screen. Five-forty. "I need to be home by six for that electronics guy."

"To debug your house."

"Right; I can probably call Sunni on the way. I'd better think about moving along."

"I hate for you to leave."

"Me, too."

I made a move to end the Skype call.

"Wait," Quinn said.

"I don't want to go, but I really do have to—"

"No, something's moving behind you. Did someone come in through the side door?"

"No, it's always locked." I turned and saw nothing out of the ordinary.

"It looked like a person. I'm going to hang on here while you check."

"There's no one here, Quinn. The front door's locked, too. I came in that way and I'm sure."

"Just humor me and go and check, okay? I'm staying on the line."

I didn't want our call and happy reunion to end either, but apparently Quinn was even more determined to linger. I walked back toward the stuffing side of the post office boxes where there were a few cartons piled up, but no stack was tall enough to hide a person. The side door had a small window at the top, but not too high up for me. I stretched a bit and looked through it. No activity within the cone I could see.

The restroom door was closed as usual, but I thought I'd peek in anyway, to satisfy Quinn. How touching that he was concerned. Even more touching that he was coming back in a few days.

I waved to Quinn, across the room on my laptop screen, though I doubted he could see much detail. With the other hand, I turned the knob of the restroom door.

And was knocked off my feet. A strong arm dragged me partway into the lavatory, twisting my upper arm in the process. I yelped in pain.

I struggled to crawl back outside, hoping to be able to close the heavy door with me on the other side of whoever was fighting my efforts.

I let out another howl, maybe several of them. A cloth or scarf was wrapped around my head, covering my mouth, cutting off my breathing and any sound I might have been issuing. I tried to keep screaming, but it was useless and exhausting. Besides, I felt a hard object poking my back and heard a breathy whisper.

"Quiet, or you'll be sorry." A woman's voice. Familiar, but not too much. Had I surprised an intruder for the second time today? Not for a moment did I think she was a customer angry that there was no postal service on weekends. "Well, you'll be sorry anyway," she said. "But let's not make this any more unpleasant than we have to. You're a nuisance to this town. Nosy and stubborn. Not even the chief of police can control you. You should have stayed in Boston."

I was willing to agree with her, if she'd let me go. I could hear Quinn yelling in the background but the woman drowned him out. Not that I was in a position to follow any instructions he might have had, anyway. I was out of sight of the computer and so was my attacker. We were both just outside the restroom now, about halfway to my desk and my phone, both of us struggling to retain balance. If it weren't for my useless arm and that poke in my back I might have simply pushed myself off my knees and made a run for it.

My hands were more or less free and I thought of using them to feel around behind me, maybe to get some leverage to push away. If that really was a gun in my back, however, it wouldn't matter if I managed to run even a few feet.

I took my chances and twisted my arms around in a direction they were never meant to go. I ignored the pain that pulsed through them. What were my fingers feeling? Flesh, under silky fabric. Stockings? Was the woman wearing knee-highs? Pantyhose? What did it matter? I swallowed hard and tried to focus my energy.

I grabbed her ankle with my good arm and tugged as hard as I could at such a strange angle. The woman went down with a loud thud, toppling a stack of bins, the mail they held flying all over. I heard the gun clattering across the floor, though I couldn't tell which direction it traveled. I made my way to my desk, still crawling, and caught the woman in my peripheral vision, moving slowly, facedown, in the same direction as me. I saw the gun now; it had slid across the nicely waxed floor, to a spot under my desk.

I rolled away, on my side, ignoring the pain in my shoulder and arms, ahead of her by a few inches. Above me on the corner of my desk, I saw what I needed. I struggled to grab it as pain shot up my back. I wished I'd kept all my resolutions to exercise, to do yoga, to ride my bike to work, to buy a set of weights. All I'd done was invest in a pair of leggings and a cute matching tank top. I swiveled, sending another sharp pain up my spine.

I lifted myself on one arm and stretched the other as far as I could. Just far enough. Ben's antique green metal spindle from the nineteen forties, its point as sharp as ever, was sitting where I'd put it yesterday when I removed it from its hazardous position on the retail counter.

I still hadn't figured out who my attacker was, whether I knew her or not. She was moving with labored breaths, sounding even more out of shape than I was. It hardly made a difference. I swung around and let my stiffened arm fall, sending me to the floor while my other arm plunged the spindle in an arc, hardly aiming, hoping to do just enough damage for me to make an escape. She screamed, a much healthier sound than I'd been able to make, as the point of the spindle sunk into her leg. A fleshy leg, I noted. I closed my eyes against the spurt of blood.

The wounded woman kept screaming, drowning out all

other sounds. I was together enough to realize that Quinn would have called Sunni immediately. If my attacker would only stop howling, I might be able to hear the sirens on an NAPD cruiser.

I finally opened my eyes and looked across the small piece of floor that separated us.

Selectwoman Corbin stared back, the spindle stuck in her leg, blood pouring around it, an angry look on her face. "Gert?" I cried.

The one other item on my desk that proved useful was a roll of packing tape. The red-white-and-blue-trimmed tape wasn't the strongest on the market, but it would do to keep the selectwoman's hands and feet banded together until I heard the cruiser. For good measure, I ran the tape around her legs all the way to her chubby knees. I wondered if I could charge the city for the roll of tape. I'd have to reread that administrative memo.

Gert was too smart to say anything. For all she knew her last words as a free woman would be sound bites on tomorrow's nightly news. I tried to take up the slack, to tease her into responding.

"I know about Derek Hathaway's operation," I said. "Him and his bookies."

No comment from the woman whose name was on a pot holder.

"I guess you used your power as a low-level politician to keep things in order for him. No nasty inspections or audits, I'll bet. And no problem having people look the other way when he was in a pinch."

No comment from the woman who preached good, clean living, free of vices like legal gambling.

I tried another tack.

"Poor Wendell," I said. "He was an innocent victim in all this. He didn't want to be involved in something so slimy. He just wanted to live his simple life, with his sister and his friends. He had no interest—"

"A lot you know," Gert said. "Wendell couldn't keep his good fortune to himself. He was warned over and over not to overdo the spending. But he went out and bought everything he'd ever wanted, redoing his house, a look-at-me car. You can't do that when you're committed to a long-term operation. You have to stay under the radar." Her ample bosom rose and fell rapidly. "That last time we met, when I tried to talk some sense into him, he asked me what was the point of having all this money if you couldn't enjoy it?" She shook her head, then winced at the painful aftermath. "But you have to be smart. Spend a little at a time. Get a loan even if you don't need one. That's the way the game is played."

Gert finally stopped, before she gave away the store, but I felt she'd tied loose ends up nicely. Also, I was grateful to be learning how to handle newfound, dirty money. I'd remember it the next time I wanted to be part of a criminal enterprise.

At last I heard the sirens. Two cruisers and an ambulance pulled up, parking horizontally, thereby taking up all the spaces except the one occupied by my car.

With Gert neatly wrapped as priority mail, I limped toward the front door. And fell on my knees. The only way this was going to work was if I crawled.

Which I did, alarming Sunni and Ross, who checked for blood on me as soon as they were inside, then joined the EMTs taking care of Gert. I heard a chuckle from the ones who went back to my desk area, and assumed they appreciated the specially wrapped package I'd left for them.

"I guess a killer goes priority," I heard one of them say. That was before I blacked out.

22

Staying overnight in the hospital wasn't my idea, but I didn't have either the strength or the authority to over-rule the chief of police this time. I heard words like "frac-ture," "separated shoulder," and "possible concussion" bandied about.

"It's all over," Sunni said. "Except to get you on your feet."

"I'm fine," I said. "Thanks to you."

"And Quinn, and Ross, who knew enough to summon me immediately when he received Quinn's call."

"If you won't let me go home, at least tell me an interest-ing story."

"Once upon a time, there was a rich man who ran a gambling ring."

I smiled. The only muscle movement that didn't hurt. "It

was really old-fashioned when you think of it. There has to be a way he could have used the Internet."

"Do you want to look into it?" Sunni asked.

I shook my head. Bad idea. "More painkillers, please."

"Actually, the rich man had started to branch out and use lines in his own larger office buildings, where he could operate independently of the phone company, though he still would have needed a guy like Wendell Graham."

"Does this story have a happy ending?"

"It will soon enough. Tim is waffling a bit, trying to decide whether to take his chances with the same lawyer who'll be representing Derek Hathaway. Derek, of course, thinks he's in the clear. No one has proved anything yet, and at the time of Wendell's murder, he was forty miles away, in Albany having dinner with his current girlfriend, who swears up and down that Derek is a good man."

"Does that mean he'll get away with it? With everything?" I asked.

"Not a chance. His crime crossed state lines, so the feds will be coming in, and Tim will have no choice but to talk to them."

I gulped, concerned about my own victim. "How about Gert?"

"She's claiming no one will believe she went into the post office to attack you, even though the gun we found under your desk is registered to her father. She says she saw the light on and wanted to talk to you."

"Hardly."

"I know. And I'll be shocked if Ballistics doesn't come up with evidence that hers is the same gun used to kill

Wendell. I'm sure she'll eventually confess and tell her constituency that 'mistakes were made.'"

"Is her leg okay?" I asked, though I cared less every time I thought of her as a cold-blooded killer.

"Oh, yeah. She's down the hall with a state trooper outside her door. I wouldn't advise dropping in with a get-well card."

"I'm not happy about stabbing someone, even if she did murder Wendell."

"I'm sure you're not. But as for your method of containing her, I don't think anyone who was there will forget how she looked wrapped in that tape. I wouldn't be surprised if photos of her adorned body go viral. Of course, I have no knowledge of any professional emergency worker who would do such a thing."

I'd have joined Sunni in laughter, but it would have hurt too much.

I convinced Quinn that he didn't need to fly back immediately. I'd sustained only surface bruises and small fractures. I'd just as soon have them heal before I saw him, anyway. We talked and Skyped over the next couple of days as I recuperated at home, second-guessing what would have happened if Quinn hadn't seen the moving form in the background. I was sure Gert had been waiting in the restroom until I finished the Skype call, when she would have come out and done the deed before I knew what hit me. It unnerved me that I'd been working in the utility closet, next to the restroom, when Quinn's call came in.

We got regular updates from Sunni on the circle of

three—Tim Cousins, Derek Hathaway, and Gert Corbin— pointing fingers at each other. Tim had carried out his duties only because he thought Derek would kill him if he refused. Derek saw no reason why a simple sport like betting on a race should be illegal anyway, no matter how the operation was run. Gert Corbin had gone to the post office only to warn the postmaster that Derek might be coming after her.

The chief of police of North Ashcot had no doubt that they'd all fall down eventually and receive their fitting punishment.

Though it didn't bring her brother back, Wanda was smiling in the way that I remembered. She came by a couple of times with the most beautiful bouquets of yellow roses, claiming to have discovered a miracle powder that made them think it was summer.

My friends in my old/new hometown organized a party, timed for Quinn's return, a week after his hasty departure.

Sunni, who was in charge of food, ordered clam linguini for all. Wanda took care of baked goods. Ben, who could hardly contain himself (in a happy way) when he learned that his beloved antique spindle had been used in defense of his friend and his place of business, brought his niece, Natalie, and cardboard carriers with drinks of all kinds.

I gave only a fleeting thought to Adam, wondering briefly what he'd have thought of the first party I hosted in my new home. He would have been outraged that nothing matched. In fact, the glasses and platter were loans from Wanda, left over from her brief marriage—the only good thing about it, she said.

"Lending them for good causes makes me feel less guilty about not returning the gifts when the marriage collapsed."

Linda got a prize—a box of the Berkshires' best candy—for traveling the farthest, and looking the greatest, though I didn't embarrass her with a best-dressed trophy. She was wearing designer everything, claiming to have started with Kate Spade shoes and a bag and built the outfit from there.

"A little prim, but also a little preppy to take the edge off," she explained, indicating her accessories. "I had a hard time figuring out how much I wanted to blend in."

"Did you think everyone would be in cowboy boots?" I asked.

"No, those are back in fashion. I figured classic pumps for the girls, tassel loafers for the boys."

Though I had to sit down a lot during my own party, I took delight in watching my friends mingle and chat and laugh in my home. Quinn hardly left my side, which suited me fine.

North Ashcot was once again my hometown, where love and friendship took priority.

POST OFFICE STORIES

Cassie's connection to the U.S. Postal Service goes way back to when she was a kid and loved to see envelopes addressed to her. She admits to sending away for things just to receive letters or packages with her name on them. "Send for more information" was an invitation she never refused. As a result, she acquired such items as brochures from the army, surveys from drug companies, and pamphlets from universities far and wide.

Here's a small collection of her favorite postal stories, some funny, some strange, all very interesting.

HI, DWAYNE!

A friend of Cassie's was convinced that the postmaster, Dwayne, of her small town in West Virginia, read all postcards as they passed through on the way to delivery. She was so convinced that she added a note to every card she sent from her vacations: "Hi, Dwayne." (Dwayne swore he never saw or read them.)

THE BIRTHDAY BOY

When Cassie was a college student on one of her Christmas vacation shifts delivering mail, Nicky, a small boy on the route, greeted her nearly every day. From the number of swings in the backyard and toys strewn over the lawn, she suspected she was filling in for the missing companionship of his school-age siblings.

Nicky would be watching out the front window around ten every weekday morning, ready to pop out and wave from the top step of his front porch. Sometimes he engaged Cassie in examining a new toy, until his mother scooped him inside with a friendly smile for her.

On one of the last days of her working vacation, Cassie showed up as usual, to find both Nicky and his mother waiting on the steps with an envelope addressed to The Mail Lady.

"His birthday is next Monday," Nicky's mother explained, "and when I asked who he wanted to invite to his party, he said, 'The Mail Lady.'" The mother's tone was apologetic, but Cassie rushed to assure her she was flattered to be included.

Unfortunately, Cassie would have to leave for school next weekend, but on the Friday before, she brought Nicky a small package wrapped in birthday paper.

He opened it and pulled out a toy postal delivery truck. His wide eyes and happy dance were all Cassie needed by way of thanks.

RIDDLES

Q: What's sent all over the world, but is always on the corner?
A: A postage stamp!

Q: What starts with P, ends in E, and has a million letters in it?
A: POST OFFICE!

(Cassie can hear your groans.)

POSTMARK COLLECTING

There's a lot of action when postmark collectors get together! Ernie, one of Cassie's Boston colleagues, came into work with a big smile on his face and a Danish for everyone whenever he'd acquired a treasured postmark. She recalls one from Cool, California, which has a population slightly higher than that of North Ashcot; one from Whynot, Mississippi; and another from Quicksand, Kentucky, dating back to before their postal facility closed.

A first day of issue is a special postmark, along with the triangular stamps that accompany them.

CHANGE FOR A 20

The highlight of one of Cassie's first days at a new job: a customer with a package that cost $4.68 to ship handed her a twenty-dollar bill. "Can I have my change in stamps?" she asked.

"All of it?" Cassie asked.

"Yes, all of it. In stamps."

"Okay. What denomination would you like?" Cassie asked.

"Doesn't matter."

"Do you want different denominations? Commemoratives? Sheets?"

"Doesn't matter."

"Okay," Cassie said again, and handed the woman first one sheet of one-dollar stamps, then two sheets of ten-cent stamps. Then she tore off one more one-dollar stamp, careful not to compromise the adhesive backing. She added six five-cent stamps and two one-cent stamps and counted out the change: fifteen dollars and thirty-two cents—while the line grew longer.

The good news: Everyone except Cassie seemed to know the woman and stood patiently by.

FUN FACTS

- The U.S. Postal Service delivers to over one hundred fifty million addresses nationwide, and handles more than forty-three percent of the world's mail.

- Almost forty million changes of address are processed each year.

- The postal service has zero dependence on tax dollars, relying on the sale of products and services for its operating costs.

- There are nearly forty-two thousand zip codes in the country.

- As many as fifty thousand inquiries are received annually recommending stamp subjects and designs.

- The ZIP in ZIP codes stands for Zoning Improvement wwto Holtsville, New York, and the highest (99950) is in Ketchikan, Alaska.

CELEBRITY USPS EMPLOYEES

Many famous people have spent time in the postal service. A few examples:

- Presidents Abraham Lincoln and Harry S. Truman served as postmasters in New Salem, Illinois, and Grandview, Missouri, respectively.

- Rock Hudson and Walt Disney worked as mail carriers.

- Aviator Charles Lindbergh worked as an airmail pilot.

- Novelist William Faulkner served as postmaster in University, Mississippi.

POST OFFICE LINGO

Some phrases have a meaning all their own among postal employees:

- "Kill the lives" means "Cancel any stamps that aren't cancelled ('lives')."

- A Mailhawk hawkbill reacher is a reaching tool used when snow is blocking the mailbox.

- "Franked mail" is official mail sent without postage pre-payment, by members of Congress and other authorized individuals. The mail bears a written signature or other acceptable marking instead of a postage stamp.

M2G0610

WELL-CRAFTED MYSTERIES
FROM BERKLEY PRIME CRIME

- **Earlene Fowler** Don't miss these Agatha Award–winning quilting mysteries featuring Benni Harper.

- **Monica Ferris** These *USA Today* bestselling Needlecraft Mysteries include free knitting patterns.

- **Laura Childs** Her Scrapbooking Mysteries offer tips to satisfy the most die-hard crafters.

- **Maggie Sefton** These popular Knitting Mysteries come with knitting patterns and recipes.

- **Lucy Lawrence** These brilliant Decoupage Mysteries involve cutouts, glue, and varnish.

- **Elizabeth Lynn Casey** The Southern Sewing Circle Mysteries are filled with friends, southern charm—and murder.